THE MASQUERADE OF THE MARCHIONESS

CLAIRE DELACROIX

DEBORAH A. COOKE

THE LADIES' ESSENTIAL GUIDE
TO THE ART OF SEDUCTION

REGENCY ROMANCES

The Ladies' Essential Guide to the Art of Seduction is a series of Regency romances. In each story, a marriage in dire straits is rescued by the lady's consultation of Miss Esmeralda Ballantyne's incomparable volume of amorous advice. Over the course of the series, Esmeralda matches wits (and more) with the resolute Duke of Haynesdale, who is determined to stop her endeavor, no matter the price.

1. **The Christmas Conquest**

2. **The Masquerade of the Marchioness**

3. **The Widow's Wager**

...

PROLOGUE

November 1813—Arlingview Manor, Shropshire

"No one will believe it, Philomena." Penelope sat at her sister's bedside, striving to persuade her twin of good sense and not for the first time. She should have known that such an endeavor was an exercise in futility.

She had come to Arlingview Manor at her sister's behest, puzzled that Philomena would have chosen to retreat to her husband's country home when she was ill. Her sister might have remained in London and summoned any number of competent physicians, as well as saved Penelope an arduous journey of her own.

But Philomena had never been one to change her thinking once she had resolved upon a path.

Now she was resolute that Penelope must assume her place and pretend to be the marchioness. They had traded places often as children, as a jest, always at Philomena's insistence, but this was of too great an import to be considered a jest.

The sisters argued mightily, to no avail, yet never spoke of one old secret.

The manor was old and draughty, its furnishings

from an earlier era, and on this night, the weather was foul. Penelope had never seen such rain or heard a wind so determined to whistle in the cracks. Her sister's chamber remained chilly, no matter how the fire was fed on the hearth, for it had large windows that overlooked the gardens. On this night, the wind made the glass panes rattled and seemingly found every chink.

Though Penelope had been told her sister had a fever and an ague in her lungs, she had arrived to find the chamber filled with the scent of blood and the linens stained. No one in the household attended Philomena, at that lady's instruction, all fearful of the supposed infection. Only Philomena's lady's maid, Sara Underwood, tended to her, that woman's expression grim.

This illness, though, was not contagious. Philomena clearly intended that the truth of her circumstance should remain a secret.

"They will all believe it," Philomena insisted in response. "I have planned for every detail."

"Save that we are utterly different in nature," Penelope noted.

"Speak quietly," Philomena advised in a whisper. "I do not know the servants in this house well, but then, that is why we are here. Only Underwood can be trusted."

"Philomena, this is too much. You contrived this plan without speaking to me of it. You lied about the nature of your illness!"

"It is the best way," Philomena insisted. Penelope knew her sister would not listen to dissenting views, but still she tried.

"It is the worst way. What would possess you to suggest that your own husband be deceived, as well as your sons?"

Philomena waved a hand. "None of them will know the difference."

"Philomena!"

"The boys are interested only in their studies and Garrett seldom is at home."

"I will not do it."

"You must!" Philomena seized Penelope's hand. "What of the boys? Who will ensure their welfare in my absence?"

"Do not say such things. You will recover." Even as Penelope spoke, she doubted her own assurance.

"I am dying," her twin said with chilling conviction.

"Then let me summon a physician! I do not understand your unwillingness to see sense in this matter..."

"Do you not?" Philomena demanded with rare impatience. "Look at this chamber."

"There is a fearsome amount of blood," Penelope had to concede.

"And Underwood has told them all that I have a horrible ailment in my chest, possibly pneumonia. She, too, has coughed as if it is contagious." She coughed loudly, ensuring the sound was wretched. Penelope's lips tightened as coughing made the blood flow with greater vigor. "Not even a country physician would be fool enough to believe that once he stepped into this room."

"You should have told the truth."

Philomena laughed. "And then Garrett would have killed me for certain."

Penelope was horrified. "How can you say such a thing of the marquis? He is an elegant man, a true aristocrat."

"He is a demon with a handsome face," her sister insisted. Penelope was skeptical, for she knew that her sister was inclined to dismiss truths that did not suit her. "You have not seen his truth. His temper is fearsome, Penelope. Trust me, when you consent to this, you must never, ever provoke him."

"I will not consent to this scheme. It is madness and doomed to failure."

Again, Philomena seized her hand. "He will wed again. He has mistresses one after the other and will choose one."

"No!"

"Yes. You have no notion what I have endured in this marriage." Philomena blinked away tears and Penelope sensed that they were not entirely honest ones. "She will push aside the boys and there will be no one left to defend them."

"I cannot believe the marquis would treat his own sons so cruelly."

"That is because you believe him to be a man of honor. I know his truth." Philomena sank back against the pillows, clearly exhausted, and Penelope could not ignore the signs of her failing. Her sister closed her eyes. "Why do you fight me in this?" she whispered. "I know what is best for all of you. All you must do is accept my advice." Her eyes opened and she slanted a glance at Penelope, her tone turning sly. "Unless you want to return to father's house and the roving hands of Mr. Neilson?"

Penelope straightened at the distasteful reminder of her situation. "You know I do not."

Philomena did not abandon the point. "Unless you have another suitor willing to wed you at eight and twenty summers of age?"

"You know I do not," Penelope ceded tightly. She wanted more from marriage than financial security, though she knew she was unlikely to ever have it.

Her sister appealed again. "Then do this thing. Do it for me and the boys even if you will not do it for yourself. I could not bear to know that any of you suffered in my absence."

"They are not so young anymore, Philomena. James is seven…"

"They are children!"

Penelope shook her head. "They will be going away to school soon."

"They need a mother's love."

"Then do not die."

"It is too late for that." Philomena's voice rose. "He drove me to it, and it cannot be undone."

Penelope looked between her sister and Underwood, whose expression was wooden. Drove her to what? In that moment, she had a terrible suspicion. "What have you done, Philomena?" she asked in a whisper.

"It does not matter. What is of import is that you will do as I ask. Promise me!"

"I cannot lie, Philomena, even for you."

Her sister shook her head. "You have always had an unfortunate affection for the truth. It will be the essence of simplicity. Underwood will help you."

"You have arranged matters with your lady's maid already?"

Philomena fixed her with a look, as resolute as Penelope had ever seen her. "I have considered every detail. Why do you think I am at this wretched country house? It is because no one knows me here."

"But surely the marquis will wonder about the missing child."

"I have not yet told him of it. Indeed, I dared not!"

"Philomena!"

"I have one dying wish, Penelope. I beg you to take my place."

Penelope did not so promise, and the sisters continued to argue. But when Philomena was at her last, her grip slackening and her skin as pale as milk, Penelope made the pledge requested of her. She had never been able to deny any request made by her twin for long.

Even though she feared the ruse would not survive long.

TO ALL APPEARANCES, it was Philomena who returned to the London house a fortnight later, though the weight of the gold band on the left hand of the lady in question was unfamiliar. The tale was that it was her devoted twin, Penelope, who remained in the church-yard, a victim of her own kindness in tending her sister alone through an infectious illness.

But Penelope was not Philomena in truth, and she could not embrace life with her sister's abandon. She also hoped that the marquis, a man she found alluring beyond all others despite Philomena's assurance of his fearsome temper, remained away from home for the moment. Penelope knew that was unlikely. The moment the marquis returned home, the ruse would be revealed, if not before, but until then, she would do her best to use the position of the marchioness for good.

There had to be some merit to this deceit.

She would make every moment count.

And when he arrived, she would tell him the truth.

No matter what the consequences might be.

CHAPTER 1

January 1817 – London

If ever there had been a woman who could name a man's desire before he spoke of it, that woman would be Esmeralda Ballantyne. The infamous courtesan watched Garrett Wright, Marquis of Arlingview, swirl the brandy in his glass and did not disguise her appreciation of the view. Gauging his mood as pensive, she decided not to disrobe just yet. Her guest had arrived late, well after midnight, yet was utterly sober. He wore evening dress, as elegantly attired as was his custom, but seemed distracted.

Sadly, he was not distracted by her.

Esmeralda took the opportunity of studying his profile. The marquis was a dangerously handsome man with his dark hair and blue eyes, distinguished by a touch of silver at his temples. His jaw was square, giving him a resolute appearance, and he was taller than most men. He was his late thirties, a particularly fine age for men in Esmeralda's view. His height combined with the muscular breadth of his shoulders to give him an imposing presence.

It was impossible to guess his thoughts most time, for the man was as impassive as a statue, and perhaps that mystery contributed to the delight of his companionship. She looked forward to their encounters, for he always surprised her—in bed and out of it.

But such earthly pleasures might not be savored on this night. He had not even shed his jacket, but remained staring out the window at the street, brooding over some matter.

Esmeralda knew better than to pout. "Is the brandy a good one?" she asked as if unaware that he slighted her with his inattention. She lounged on a chair before the fire, twining a loose curl around her fingertip. She knew the pose and the light favored her, as did her sheer dress, but the marquis barely glanced her way. When he did, his gaze certainly did not linger.

It was another woman, to be sure.

"Yes. Why?"

"I thought to order more if it was of merit."

She earned a hard look for that. "Have you not tasted it?"

"I have no desire for brandy these days," she said lightly.

Arlingview smiled wickedly then, his eyes glittering. "Feeling the years, are we?"

Esmeralda looked daggers at him, which clearly amused him, then composed her expression. She was supposed to be the perceptive one. "I prefer wine these days, that is all."

He nodded once and swirled the glass again. "Curious thing, changing taste," he mused.

Esmeralda waited but he did not continue. She smiled and deliberately prompted him. "How so?"

"Who can anticipate it? Who can predict it? One is certain of what one wants until…one is no longer certain of any matter at all." Arlingview shrugged and took the barest sip of the brandy before setting down the glass. "I should leave." He reached for his hat, but Esmeralda rose smoothly to her feet, stepping into his path.

"There is no rush." She placed a hand upon his chest, and he looked down at it with a frown.

He should have covered it with his own, then led her to bed.

Instead, he lifted her hand away with a polite smile. "You may have other guests."

"Not on this night." He could not leave so soon! She had cleared her schedule for him! "Stay and talk a while." She gestured to the seat opposite the one she had chosen. There were two before the fire, facing each other, both upholstered in ruby velvet.

He met her gaze, as direct as ever. "I did not think you were interested in conversation."

It was Esmeralda's turn to shrug, then she sank into her chosen seat. "We are old friends, are we not? Who else should converse late at night in privacy?"

Truth be told, she hoped his confession would lead their interaction in the usual direction. He would soon realize that this other woman, whoever she might be, could not compare to Esmeralda's skills.

Arlingview considered the suggestion for a moment —rather too long of a moment for Esmeralda's satisfaction—then abruptly decisive, he set aside his hat and sat down opposite her. He braced his elbows on his knees, utterly earnest as he locked his gaze with hers. What a glorious man! "I do not want to do it any longer," he said, his manner blunt.

Esmeralda shrugged her lack of understanding.

"That is not true, exactly," he said, qualifying his claim. "There is much to be enjoyed in gambling, dancing and attending raucous parties. There is yet more satisfaction in seducing beautiful women and even in arriving home in the middle of the morning. But I can no longer summon much interest. The sense of discovery is gone, the thrill of forbidden pleasures is banished. I walk into a gaming hell, it is all the same as ever it was, and I am bored."

"You crave novelty." Esmeralda understood this urge. It often came upon her clients as they grew older. She had wigs. She had costumes. She could provide novelty, to be sure.

"Perhaps. I have been to Paris three times this year, to Brighton and even to Edinburgh. Nothing stirs my curiosity or captures my attention, and I cannot explain the change."

"Your sons?"

"Both excel in their studies and are fine marksmen."

"Your father, the duke?"

"May never die, God bless him, and I would not have it any other way."

"Your properties?"

"Are competently managed and as profitable as they can be expected to be."

Esmeralda took a cherry from a bowl on the table and bit it slowly off the stem. She chewed it elegantly, but her guest was not even interested in her action or any implication. "Your wife?" she asked finally, hearing the slight edge in her voice.

Arlingview threw up his hands. "Busy, practical and competent. I have never met a woman more driven to improve the world." He frowned. "Nor a man, come to think of it. She is not the woman I wed, to be sure, and her activity makes me feel my lack of industry."

And there it was. Esmeralda heard the marvel in his tone, even a tinge of envy. His wife had a purpose, one that drove her choices throughout every day, and the marquis did not.

"Perhaps another child?" she suggested.

He shook his head. "Philomena and I agreed before our marriage that two sons would suffice. We negotiated that detail before our marriage, and I will not press her beyond our agreed terms."

Esmeralda was intrigued. "She does not enjoy your moments of intimacy?"

The marquis laughed, the move making him look young and reckless. "Evidently, she endured them, for the sake of the future." There was a shadow in his expression, one that made her expect a confession, but he did not offer one. "I thought it uncharacteristic at the time that she was so determined to keep our agreement, but she has changed of late." He shrugged. "Perhaps we both tire of fleeting amusements."

Esmeralda sighed, fearing that she would not experience such intimacy again with the marquis. There was something final in his manner, and she recognized a man who had made a decision. There were only two decisions men made in Esmeralda's vicinity: to be seduced or to abandon any connection. Given that she had already seduced Arlingview, he could only have chosen the latter.

Pity.

That meant, of course, that she had little to lose in this discussion.

Esmeralda chose another cherry and studied it. She could not imagine any woman simply enduring the attentions of the marquis. He was a playful and considerate lover, irresistibly charming and energetic beyond expectations. Yet she knew he and his wife were estranged.

She recalled the few times she had seen his wife of late, a pretty woman, but definitely a practical one. It was strange, now that she considered the matter, for she had heard for years that the marchioness was a woman much enamored of parties and dancing. There were rumors of her scandalous affairs, and she was reputed to be the very mirror of her rakehell husband. The woman pointed out to her as the marchioness, at Carruthers & Carruthers' lending library just a month before, had been sober and serious.

"Your wife has a fondness for reading, does she not?"

"She has developed one in recent years. I hear that she usually has a book in hand."

"And that is a change in her habits?"

He nodded. "Indeed."

"Have you a notion what might be responsible for the change in her nature?"

"Her sister died, and she took the loss very hard." He frowned. "Evidently, she has reconsidered all of her former habits and found them lacking."

"It is no small thing to lose a sister."

"And worse, the sister had come to tend Philomena in her illness. Philomena recovered, but Penelope took the illness and died."

"She must feel some guilt then."

He nodded. "She insisted upon summoning her sister, for she wanted no one else in her company."

"Not even you?"

"I was abroad," he said tightly. "I received word of her illness but did not come." He flicked a glance at Esmeralda. "She did not send word to me herself and I understood the implication."

It seemed to Esmeralda that the marchioness was not the only one experiencing a measure of guilt. There was an undertone to his voice, a hint that his pride was bruised that his wife had not appealed to him in her moment of need.

That could only be because the lady did not know what she spurned. Once this pair had wed and conceived two sons. Then they had become estranged for some reason she did not know or care to know and both had embarked upon a bout of merrymaking. Now that both tired of such revels, they might find happiness together once again.

If Esmeralda helped. It had been enormously satisfying to encourage the wife of Baron Trevelaine in igniting the slumbering passions of their match over the previous Christmas, and Esmeralda knew she spied her next candidate for similar assistance. She liked Arlingview and if he was not to return to her, he should have satisfaction in his marriage.

Fortunately, Esmeralda had kept the costume for the meddling and fictitious Mrs. Oliver.

Her mood lightened immediately. She would send a message to Ophelia Pearl, the actress who had assisted her with the disguise, this very night.

"It sounds as if you need a new distraction," she said to her guest, who nodded.

"But I do not know what it is, much less where I might find it." He looked up as if recalling where he was and his manner became polite again. "But I bore you for no purpose. I do apologize that I am such poor company this night." The marquis reached again for his hat. "I thank you for your indulgence and will trouble you no longer."

In a heartbeat, he was gone, striding from her drawing room and the many pleasures she could offer. Esmeralda ate another cherry, planning her course.

Mrs. Oliver needed to encounter the marchioness and soon.

A call at the premises of Carruthers & Carruthers was in order.

~

SHOULD he have confided in Esmeralda?

Garrett's had not truly been a confidence, because he had kept back the more interesting details. Indeed, it had been more of a performance.

But a necessary one, to his thinking.

He reviewed the exchange as he rode home in his carriage through darkness and rain. Even the perceptive courtesan had not known of his role during the war working as a spy for the crown. To be sure, he missed the danger of those days, and its challenges. Was he the only loyal Briton who regretted the victory at Waterloo?

The end of the war meant he was left with his disguise as a reckless rake, which was highly unsatisfactory. He yearned to shed that whimsy, but a carefully constructed disguise could not be plausibly abandoned in a heartbeat. The supposed change would have to be made slowly, if it were to be credible at all, and even then, he knew many would have their doubts.

Beyond that, what Garrett needed was another challenge, a new quest, a task to employ all his facilities and give purpose to his days. Sadly, he had no notion where to find such a project and he frowned as the carriage halted before his London home.

And then there was Philomena. His wife had utterly changed her nature by all reports since the death of her sister. Indeed, the twins might have changed places, given Philomena's assumption of her sister's modest and dutiful habits. When first he had heard of the change, he had attributed it to grief, suspecting that Philomena could not endure such sobriety for long.

But it seems she mourned her sister more deeply than he had anticipated, for more than three years later, she was a different woman than the one he had wed.

Once before, he had been deceived about her nature and he would not make that error again.

But then, he was not the same man who had stood before the altar, either.

In truth, there was little to criticize about her new-found taste for responsibility. She ran his household efficiently, had the respect of his servants and the outright admiration of his father. There were no more parties, no more lavish bills from dressmakers and shoemakers, and perhaps no more lovers. He could not imagine she had the time for such indulgences, given the duties she had assumed after his mother's death at his father's charities. It would have been better if one of their many arguments had compelled his wife to change her spendthrift ways, but Garrett was prepared to welcome the result, no matter how it had come about.

If this change was as enduring as it seemed to be, the courtship of his wife's affections might offer the challenge he sought. The bitter words and accusations they had flung at each other after the birth of their second son could not be forgotten. They had been estranged when he had taken the role of a spy and had seen little of each other in the intervening years.

But the woman Philomena had become was infinitely more interesting than the one who had vexed him so mightily.

Perhaps they had grown into a couple who could live together with affection, as he had once hoped.

Perhaps it was time to rekindle their relationship.

Garrett stepped out of his carriage and looked up at the house. There was a light in his wife's chamber but as soon as he spoke to the driver, it was extinguished.

Perhaps he could use his experience as a spy to unveil the reason for his wife's altered manner. His success might also give an outward explanation for the abandonment of his own disguise.

All the world, after all, admired a man who repented of his wayward habits in pursuit of a lady's heart.

The very notion made Garrett smile in anticipation.

THE SITUATION WAS INTOLERABLE.

Three years before, Penelope had been skeptical of her sister's claims about her husband's character. She knew full well that Philomena had a casual relationship with the truth when it suited her, but it seemed that her twin's evaluation of the marquis had been overly kind. The man was never at home. He might as well have been the dead partner these past three years.

To be sure, he sent gifts to the boys on their birthdays, but seldom crossed the threshold himself. He had not even come home for Christmas this past season—though the boys had seen him at Montford when they had visited their grandfather, the duke. Penelope had gone to her own family at Clapham that day, wanting the duke to have some time alone with his grandsons. It turned out that the marquis had been there, as well, a joyous surprise to the boy's view.

Penelope might have concluded that he was avoiding her, but she suspected he was avoiding Philomena.

The question was why.

And the difficulty was that she had no opportunity to tell him the truth. Even now that he was in residence at Arlingview House, Penelope caught only hints of his presence. His gloves and hat might be in the foyer. Books were moved in the library and brandy glasses left on the dining room table. She caught the scent of his skin at unexpected intervals but never a glimpse of the man himself. He returned home routinely just before the dawn, often singing loudly, prompting Penelope to watch the light beneath the door that connected their rooms. Thus far, he had not come to her, but every night she watched, her heart in her throat. He slept late and evidently went to his club in the afternoon, when she was out herself. She knew he was in the house at intervals, yet she had never yet been in the same room as him.

It had been almost a week, and a more vexing six days could not be imagined. To put an end to this charade encouraged by her sister, Penelope had to find the man to make her confession.

The marquis' activities, though, did give credence to Philomena's claims and his reputation. His late hours, the rate that brandy now vanished, and his apparent indifference to his wife certainly indicated his renown as a rakehell was deserved. Had Philomena been right about his temper? Truth be told, Penelope's life suited her quite well, and had it not been for the deception at root, she might have been happy. She certainly had no desire to return to the house in Clapham and be beneath her mother's thumb again.

If only the man would allow himself to be found.

Was it not curious that he had not troubled to speak to his wife, much less to communicate his intentions? Penelope's parents had talked endlessly, bickering over every detail, to the point that anyone might have wished for a moment of silence. She had no notion what other married couples expected.

In truth, the marquis' silence would only have earned her sister's ire. Philomena had never suffered a situation when she was not the focus of attention. Penelope was content to be ignored, save when a discussion was inevitable—as one was currently.

Perhaps that was why he did it, to vex Philomena.

It had to come to an end.

When Penelope left her room for luncheon, she was so bold as to rap upon the door of her husband's chamber. Her heart was in her throat, but there was no cause for concern. There was no reply.

She reasoned that he might yet be in a drunken slumber. She listened but could not hear him snoring or the sound of his voice. The head housemaid appeared in that moment, bustling along the upstairs corridor. She curtsied, then opened the door to the marquis' chamber.

It was devoid of one particular gentleman.

He was awake, then.

Penelope continued down the stairs briskly and looked in the library. There she found only an empty brandy glass and the fire burned down to embers.

The man might have been dead.

Irked, she continued to the breakfast room. She had no confidence that the butler, Wrigley, would reveal his master's whereabouts, for he had been most annoyingly vague when asked of late. She carried a book from the lending library that she planned to finish at her solitary meal, then would visit Carruthers & Carruthers this very afternoon for the second volume of the novel she was reading. The heroine in question held the attention of her dashing beau with enviable ease and Penelope hoped to learn something from the volume. Sadly, many of the salient details occurred between chapters or were merely implied, causing Penelope some vexation with the author's creative choices.

She had already dressed for the afternoon in a dress of yellow and white. It was not a new dress, but the benefit of ordering garments of good quality and conservative style meant they were suitable for years. This one would be suitable for some time yet.

If only she could locate the marquis.

Routine would diminish her agitation. She had never liked surprises as much as Philomena. Penelope knew she would be served a soup made from the chicken that had been roasted for dinner the night before and smelled that Mrs. West had added a bit more thyme to the stock, doubtless the result of her gentle comment the night before. Wrigley swept open the door to the breakfast room at her approach with his usual flourish and she thanked the butler as always she did. She glanced down at the tray of newly arrived mail left by her place as her chair was drawn out for her by a footman.

Then she blinked, astonished to see that several of the letters had been opened. Worse, no attempt had been made to disguise that fact.

Who had dared to read her mail?

The footman who held her chair cleared his throat in a most impertinent manner. She bit back a comment and sat down, sparing the silver salver one last glare. She was about to summon Wrigley, but the audacious footman didn't move away. Indeed, a quick glance revealed that his hand was not gloved.

She glanced up, prepared to deliver a lecture upon proper deportment.

But her words died on her lips when her gaze collided with that of the marquis.

Her husband.

In name, at least.

She had found him in the most unlikely of places.

Why was he here? Penelope's mouth went dry. She stared but the man in question did not vanish. He was clearly no illusion.

Nor was he as cavalier as his reputation. His gaze was so steady and so piercing that she was certain he could read all of her secrets. She strove to recover from the surprise and seize the moment to begin her confession, but he smiled, and she could only blink in awe.

Goodness, he was a handsome man.

And as she stared into the marquis' impossibly blue eyes, Penelope could not recall the words to make the confession she knew was overdue.

The man's affect upon her had not diminished a whit in thirteen years.

CHAPTER 2

"Good day, my lady," the marquis said, four words making her tremble deep inside. Penelope swallowed and found herself unable to avert her gaze. His eyes were so vehemently blue that a woman could drown in them.

And that smile was dangerously confident. Knowing. Penelope's heart skipped a beat, stopped cold, then galloped like a colt that had broken its tether.

His was the expression of a man who knew a secret and meant to act upon it. No, it was the look of a cat that had cornered a mouse and meant to play with it before the kill.

Had he guessed?

Philomena's warnings of his fearsome temper filled Penelope with dread.

"What a welcome surprise, sir," she managed to say as her thoughts spun.

"Is it?" His voice was deliciously low, the words a bare murmur. She might have considered that a voice for the bedchamber, for wicked propositions and enticing whispers. She knew it was a good one for confidences exchanged in the shadows, which was a most untimely recollection.

It *was* warm in the breakfast room.

"It appears I have quite confounded you, my lady," the marquis said smoothly. "I do apologize. It was not my intention to do as much." He looked, in decided contrast to his claim, as if he had surprised her on purpose.

That could be no good portent.

Penelope's thoughts spun. She frowned again at the mail as her heart skipped. Had the marquis been the one to open the letters?

Why was he awake at this hour?

Why was he even *here*? The man never took luncheon at home.

"I did not expect you, sir," she said, which was true, even if her stiff words might make the man feel unwelcome.

"Clearly." He sauntered toward the other end of the table. He was dressed in dark breeches and boots, his white cravat tied with impeccable flair. She took the opportunity to study him, for it was a rare one. His hair was still as dark as ebony, though there was a touch of silver at his temples. He was as taut and trim as ever had been, though she thought his chest might be a bit broader than in his youth. Indeed, she found him more handsome than when he had first invited her sister to dance.

She had always been convinced that the dissolute lost their looks, but that was not true of the marquis.

Once she had watched him swim in the lake at his father's country house. It had been the summer before Matthew's birth, just before he had absented himself with such frequency. She had been there to comfort Philomena during a difficult pregnancy. Something quivered deep inside her at the recollection of his sleek power as he moved through the water with ease. He had been beautiful, like a Greek god come to life.

There was a memory unexpected and one that shook her composure a little more. Penelope took a breath and strove to control her errant thoughts.

Surveying the man in question might not have been the best means of doing as much, but she dared another glimpse all the same. He wore a brocade vest, one wrought of silk in a hundred hues of gold and blue, and she thought the color a fine choice for him. He was freshly shaved, and so completely at ease that they might have met daily under similar circumstance.

Even if he had not guessed the truth, there were other possible explanations for this change in his behavior. He might admit to having a paramour, for example. Such a confession could imperil her own situation, for it hinted at love that would not be constrained.

He might put her aside even without realizing she was not Philomena.

The rain increased its cold onslaught against the windows and Penelope wished she could think of a clever way to reveal the truth and be done with it.

I have deceived you these past three years seemed unlikely to be welcomed.

Perhaps after luncheon would be better.

She certainly could use those few moments to think.

The marquis' place at the opposite end of the table was always set even though he was seldom home. He shook out his napkin, eying her as if she was the unpredictable one.

He was waiting, though she could not imagine what he expected her to say.

"You are not customarily at luncheon, even when you are in town, sir," Penelope said finally, thinking hers an inordinately feeble comment. In this moment, she was keenly aware of her inability to flirt, to beguile or even to hold a conversation with a man. Her sister had laid claim to all those skills and more.

"I thought to indulge in the novelty," he said as the soup tureen was brought to the table. Steam rose from it, a welcome sign that it was hot. On a day such as this, only a very hot soup would do. "I typically begin the day with a brandy. Instead, it seemed a bowl of soup might be an intriguing alternative."

"You cannot have known…"

He interrupted her with a playful glance that prompted a flight of butterflies in her stomach. "You *always* have soup for lunch, Philomena." He shook his head, so clearly bored with her routines that she bristled. "Every midday, for several years, you have had soup."

"How could you know as much?"

"I have asked Wrigley."

What else had he asked the butler about her? "Soup is nourishing."

"Doubtless."

"I like soup," she said.

"But you are not obliged to eat soup, Philomena."

She did not reply until her bowl had been filled and the footman had retreated. "Nor are you, sir."

"But for me, it is a departure and for you, it is a choice. A habit, if you will."

"I fail to see the import of my choice of luncheon, since you never appear for the midday meal."

He raised his hands, indicating himself, then smiled.

Penelope could only stare.

Then she shook herself. "The first time means it is hardly an event that could be anticipated." As soon as the words were uttered, Penelope feared she had erred. Had he eaten luncheon with Philomena? It was yet another detail she did not know.

"No, no punctual habits for me," he replied easily

and fixed her with an intent look, one that banished every sane notion from her thoughts. "What of novelty, Philomena?"

"I have heard it well spoken of."

"Once you swore you could not survive without it." The marquis tasted the soup and nodded approval before considering her again. There was a laziness about his expression that was undermined by his sharp gaze. Many people underestimated this man, Penelope was certain. "Once, I suspected I would be berating you for the rest of my life, imploring you to dance less and spend less, but you might have become a different woman since your sister's death."

Opportunity approached.

She opened her mouth, but no sound emerged. Her imagination conjured an image of the marquis imploring her for some favor and could not move beyond it.

"Surely you recall your twin, Penelope?" he asked, his tone a little harder.

"Of course! I think of her every day." She did not have to contrive the catch in her voice, and she saw his expression soften.

"Since she came to tend you in the country and took your illness herself, you have been less merry," he said gently. "I am not the only one to have noticed it."

"I am surprised you took note of any such change at all, given your customary absences."

He smiled and his tone turned teasing again. "Have you *missed* me, Philomena? There is a marvel indeed." He shook his head. "How you infuriated me that day, but then, I have never been one to easily accept a betrayal of any magnitude."

He calmly ate his soup as she stared at her own. There was a warning, to be sure.

As well as an indication that Philomena had been

right. Did Penelope dare to admit her own betrayal after those words?

"I believed it was grief for the longest time," he mused finally. "For you were twins, and twins are said to be much closer than other siblings. It would be natural to mourn the loss."

"She was half of my soul," Penelope said fiercely, which was true.

Too late she realized that Philomena would never have made such a claim.

"And without her, you are less than yourself," he concluded, and she blinked back unexpected tears.

He watched her, as if puzzled.

"I knew it could not have been my own request," he said then, his tone resolute. "You never heeded a word that I said, so why would that change?" Penelope eyed him, mystified, but he turned his attention to his meal. He was utterly inscrutable, though Penelope sensed there was some detail of import she did not know.

What had he asked of Philomena?

When he spoke again, he abandoned that subject, to her relief.

"My point about luncheon is simply that you are a marchioness, Philomena." His voice was smooth, almost seductive. "You could dine upon whatever you desire. Roast quail. Hare with mushrooms. Fish with a cream sauce. The possibilities are nigh limitless and once I know you explored them with enthusiasm. We had the bills to show for it."

"I..."

"While I appreciate your newfound frugality, you need not display such a rigorous discipline forever."

"Soup is a suitable luncheon for a lady."

He lowered his spoon and considered her. "Are you not weary of it?"

Penelope bristled. It was an absurd choice to dispute. "I enjoy a variety of soups. Each day, there is a different one and they are all admirable." She realized then what had to be troubling him. "Although it may well be that you will not find soup to be a sufficiently substantial luncheon, sir." She paused, then could not resist temptation. "Perhaps in future, you should dine at your club when you have not given any indication that you will attend a meal."

To her surprise—for she felt very rude as soon as the words were uttered—her companion did not appear to take offense at her suggestion. "Did the boys find it sufficient?" the marquis asked instead. The soup seemed to find favor with him, for he was rapidly emptying his bowl.

It was very good and wonderfully hot. Mrs. West had a marvelous talent with soups.

"I always had more prepared for them. They simply began with the soup."

He nodded once, then gestured to the tray with the morning's post. "There is a letter from James." He *had* opened the mail then and she could not fault him for wanting to read a letter from his oldest son. That smile curved his lips again, a most beguiling sight. "Of course, there is not one from Matthew." His eyes twinkled in a way that invited her to smile. "At least one of them had to follow my example."

"Matthew wrote last week. He is not so irresponsible as that." Penelope sounded protective and she knew it, though there was justice in the marquis' claim. The elder boy, James, was the responsible one, while Matthew did seem to follow his father's rakehell example a little more. She, though, had survived years of comparisons between herself and Philomena, and knew how it stung to always be the one to fall short of the measure. She glanced toward the mail with yearning.

Had she been alone, she would have read the letter from James while she ate.

She did miss both of her nephews terribly, though she knew they had to go to school.

"Do you call me irresponsible, Philomena?" He clicked his tongue. "Surely you do not disapprove of me? You were once similarly ardent in your pursuit of pleasure."

And he fixed her with an intent look. Penelope was certain that her face was afire. She avoided his gaze and studied her soup, painfully aware that he was amused by her.

She should just say it.

But she could not.

"Matthew has a notion of a Grand Tour," she said instead.

The marquis laughed aloud, a wonderful merry sound. "Then that was the inspiration. James makes the same suggestion and I marveled at it. I now see the influence of our second-born."

"You need not be so proud of him," Penelope murmured, earning another chuckle from her companion. How curious that she had only observed him as playful or teasing once, and so long ago that she could readily believe her memory mistaken. Of course, she had absented herself when he visited the boys, or he had arrived when she was with her own family, as at Christmas. Now she wished she had seen them together, for she might have had a better idea what to expect of him.

"Have no fear of this notion's import." He continued easily, misinterpreting her silence. "You will not be required to stir yourself from England, much less to absent yourself from your charities and circuits. Now that you prefer a sedate life, I will not be the one to disrupt it. Your choices were always your own, after all."

Penelope glanced up at the sudden sharpness in his tone. Was he bitter? Did he miss her sister's gaiety? "Then you will dissuade them?" It made no difference for she would never go on this journey, but she was curious about his choices.

He shrugged, his eyes alight with a devilry that was enticing beyond all. Penelope did not wish to even blink. "Perhaps I will accompany them. We might all have an education of one sort or another." He shook his head. "It is a marvel, to be sure. Who might have guessed that the toast of London in her debut season would be content to remain at home forever?"

Again, his words were punctuated by a searching look.

Penelope put down her spoon. "I would speak to you about a serious matter, sir."

"Sir?" he echoed, his brows rising. "Have you forgotten my Christian name, my lady?"

Penelope felt her face heat. "Of course not!"

"Then address me by it," he said, his tone slightly cross. "I will not sit by while you pretend you are in the company of another."

Penelope gasped. "I do not, sir."

He impaled her with a glance.

She swallowed. "I do not, *Garrett*."

He smiled then. "I remember when you uttered it with slightly more affection, but beggars cannot be choosers, as they say."

"Perhaps I have had so few opportunities to use your name that I have forgotten the appropriate tone of an address," she said before she could stop herself.

He appeared to be startled, then he laughed aloud. "It seems you have missed me, my lady."

The fact that he did not address her by her Christian name, or even that of her sister, was a timely reminder. "I would speak with you, to be certain, and there has been little opportunity of late."

He raised a hand, inviting her to continue.

Penelope found herself keenly aware of the proximity of the servants. Hers was a tale that would travel quickly once confessed. "In private, if you please, sir."

"Then it cannot be today. My father expects me and you, I am certain, have an entire list of obligations to fulfill today."

"I do," she agreed, finding herself grateful for the opportunity to escape. She would compose a confession this afternoon, then present it to him. She could even write it out and leave it for him, then depart the house before he read it. The plan sounded cowardly, but this man's very presence cast her thoughts to the winds.

The marquis rose to his feet and strolled around the table, once again holding her chair. Penelope hesitated for a moment then stood, halting when his hand landed on the back of her waist. The weight of it and the way his fingers curved around her waist sent an unexpected surge of pleasure through her. Her knees weakened at this casual gesture of intimacy. She was keenly aware of his scent and his heat, so very close. She felt her throat work and wondered whether he had noticed that she had been struck to stone in his proximity.

"Philomena," he murmured, his lips almost against her ear and she closed her eyes. "Let us put aside the harsh words we once exchanged and begin anew," he urged, his words low with encouragement.

In truth, Penelope would have given him anything in this moment.

But what had he and Philomena argued about?

She looked up and found sympathy in his expression. Banished was his merry mood and the mischievous glint in his eyes. Indeed, he seemed like the man she had originally thought him to be, all those years before. Which marquis was the true one? The notorious rake, the one with the furious temper who Philomena had feared, or the man who appealed to her now, seemingly the very soul of sincerity and integrity?

Penelope knew what she wished the answer to be.

"I know you mourn your sister, but it is time to put your grief aside," he added, lifting a fingertip to her cheek. That casual caress made everything within her melt. "For the boys, if you cannot countenance it for me."

Penelope's heart clenched and she uttered a truth she never meant to surrender.

"I should have been the one to die," she confessed in a whisper.

The marquis' eyes darkened and he drew her into his embrace, a dizzying and entirely wondrous experience. Penelope blinked as her heart raced. "No, never say as much," he insisted with heat. His lips touched her temple with a reverence that shook her to her marrow. "You did not choose for her to die. Neither of you did. It dishonors her kindness to say as much."

Penelope felt faint then. If ever she had made a wish, she made one then, that this moment should last just a little longer. She was fairly aching for him to kiss her but knew that was too much to expect. The tightness of her throat meant she struggled to summon a word, and she raised her hand to him as if to deflect his piercing gaze. She was overwhelmed and did not care.

The marquis caught her hand in his and pressed a sweet kiss into her palm as she stared at the top of his head. It was not the salute she had hoped for, but it was a marvel all the same. A glorious heat emanated through her from that point of contact. He looked up at her, so close, so enticing, and smiled crookedly even as he closed her fingertips, as if to hold the kiss captive forever.

"Come to me again," he urged, and she did not immediately understand his meaning.

His gaze was so piercing that Penelope suddenly understood.

At night. He wished for her to come to him at night.

She stared at him in mingled horror and delight, but he only smiled.

"Soon," he murmured, touching his lips to her knuckles all too briefly. "I vow to make the interval worthwhile." That devilry lit his eyes again and she strove to confess the truth.

But he pivoted and strode to the door, evidently oblivious—or indifferent—to the turmoil he created within her. Penelope seized the back of the chair in order to remain upright, feeling that she quivered from head to toe.

The marquis gestured to the mail as he passed the tray and spoke so lightly that he might have been discussing the weather. "There is also an invitation from Lady Augusta Rutherford, who means to open the season with her masquerade ball. I have already declined, for I know that you no longer partake of such frivolous amusements."

Penelope found herself repeating him. "You have already done as much?"

His smile flashed. "I wished to surprise you with my uncharacteristic efficiency." He lifted a brow as he pivoted to face her. "Are you impressed with me, my lady? Or did I err in my estimation?" Once again, he was the charming rogue, the man she could not truly respect.

She could only regret the loss of his other more serious side.

"Surely you will not forgo such a gathering?"

"Of course not. But I prefer to scandalize my hostess

by arriving late and unexpected, and truly, I believe Lady Rutherford is enamored of that choice, as well." The marquis glanced back from the doorway, his thoughts hidden once more. "I wish you success with your errands, my lady, and once again apologize for the intrusion. The soup, however, was very good."

And then he was gone, leaving her staring after him like a hound abandoned in the kennel when the hunting party rode out. Penelope felt like a fool. Her sister would not have been trembling like a maiden just because the man joined her for lunch.

She should not have been so witless as to have surrendered the opportunity to tell him the truth.

Then she recalled his own admission that betrayal infuriated him.

Penelope frowned as she fanned through the mail, deferring James' enthusiasm for the Continent in this moment. She opened the invitation from Lady Rutherford and read it slowly. She had not attended any balls since her debut season with Philomena. Even then, she had not enjoyed them as much as her sister.

That kiss, the one that still made her palm hum, tempted Penelope to believe in possibilities. What if she attended the masquerade herself? Might she, like Cinderella, find a prince of her own? Wedding any man had to be better than returning to Clapham.

But fairy tales did not come true in real life. She knew that well enough.

"The carriage is ready, my lady," Wrigley said from the doorway.

Penelope glanced at the clock. It was just after one, precisely as she had instructed. She should not be dreaming of a ball but composing that confession.

CHAPTER 3

arrett found himself intrigued.

He had been certain he understood the reason for the change in Philomena. It was only today, with the unexpected confession that she should have been the one to die, that Garrett considered an outrageous possibility.

What if the woman living as his wife was not Philomena?

Could the twin sisters have traded places?

The fact was that Philomena would never have regretted the loss of another to the point of wishing herself dead instead. If their places had been reversed and an ill Penelope had summoned Philomena, Garrett doubted that his wife would have even undertaken the journey. To tend another one in sickbed was not an entertaining pastime—when the illness was infectious, it could even be dangerous. Philomena had never been one to sacrifice her own comfort for another.

To be sure, she had been a delightful companion at a party, always prepared to dance or indulge, always quick with a jest, always charming every soul in attendance. When he had proposed, she had insisted that she would conceive only once, to provide his required son.

Garrett had negotiated for a second son, thinking that by that time, there would be sufficient intimacy between them to consider further progeny. But after Matthew's birth, Philomena had been adamant that she would not conceive again.

Such an opinion was one matter: catching his wife with her lover had been quite another. They had not spent much time together since that argument and he had not journeyed to the country house when he had word that she was ill. The sisters could have changed places readily there, for Philomena had never spent time at that house. She was always in London, where there were more parties and shops.

The notion might explain so much. It might explain the sudden frugality in his wife's spending, her diminished affection for parties, her newfound concern with fulfilling her responsibilities. It might explain her undertaking more obligations by choice, like his mother's roles in his father's charities. It might even explain soup, for goodness' sake!

If Garrett was right, the fact was that his current wife was an infinitely better choice of partner for him than the one he had married. He had used Philomena as inspiration for his disguise as a rogue and a rake, for it was not his nature to be so indulgent.

Nor had it ever been Penelope's.

And the lady with whom he had dined had been wary of his attentions. It was as if she had never been touched by a man before. Perhaps he should have surrendered to impulse and kissed her, right in the breakfast room. That would have proven the truth of her identity—and if not, it might have satisfied his own curiosity.

Sadly, it was too late to regret that choice.

What did she wish to speak to him about? He would not learn that truth soon.

There had been another letter in the mail and Garrett's hope of its arrival had been the true reason for his early appearance. Fortified by a superior soup and a newfound interest in the lady who shared his home, he retired to the library to read the missive again. He heard the lady's measured tones carrying from the foyer as she spoke to Wrigley, but he resisted the urge to emerge and bid her farewell.

He could not forgo the pleasure of watching her from the window. He told himself that he sought a difference between wife and twin, but the truth was that this woman already fascinated him. Her step was as light as Philomena's had been when they wed, her figure trim and her spine straight. She was just as tall as Philomena, yet for all the resemblance, there was something different about her. He felt different in her presence, and it was not just the result of seeing her so little of late.

Garrett studied her from behind the drapes, admiring the grace of her steps, recalling the feel of her in his arms just moments before, and desire stirred. She had been so uncertain, so close to tears, just moments before, missing her sister. He had felt a primal need to console and defend her.

That was different.

Were his instincts wrong in this? Garrett wanted very much to know.

Only when the carriage pulled away did he read again the letter he had secreted beneath his vest. It was a summons from his father, purportedly to discuss some business matter of the duchy. He could only help but hope that the duke had some new assignment for him, one that would provide a suitable distraction.

The last time his father had summoned him with this particular excuse, the marquis had become a spy.

~

THERE WAS A COMMOTION AT CARRUTHERS & Carruthers that threatened to imperil Penelope's busy afternoon schedule. As soon as she alighted from the carriage, she could hear the strident tones of an older woman, interspersed with the soothing lower tones of Baroness Trevelaine. The well-married daughter of the proprietor, Lady Catherine Bettencourt née Carruthers, was only occasionally in her father's establishment and Penelope hastened her steps. She was delighted to have the opportunity to take the baroness' counsel, for their reading tastes were almost perfectly aligned.

Once within the shop, she found a discontent older lady before the counter, leaning heavily upon her cane and loudly demanding satisfaction. "I requested that specific title," she complained. "I spoke to Mr. Carruthers myself, and now you tell me it is not only lent but for the entirety of the week. This is intolerable!"

"The volume is due to be returned on Friday, Mrs. Oliver," Lady Trevelaine said soothingly. A shopgirl stood behind her, eyes wide, and Penelope guessed that the baroness had intervened. "If you recall, you did not collect the book on Monday as anticipated, so it was lent to another patron."

"Outrageous!" Mrs. Oliver declared.

"Perhaps another tale would suit you? I know you favor stories of the occult, and we have a new title…"

"I desire the title I requested!" Mrs. Oliver insisted, rapping her cane on the floor for an emphasis that was utterly unnecessary. Her voice carried through the shop and out to the street. Even the men working the printing presses in the workshop at the rear of the building craned their necks for a glimpse of her.

The lady in question was short and plump, dressed in a ghastly gown of greyed blue, a hue that hinted the garment was either dirty or faded. The style of it was decidedly dated and the hem was worn to a frayed edge. Her grey hair was elaborately dressed in a coiffure popular in an earlier era, one that hinted she wore a wig. Her hat was swathed in so many veils that it was difficult to discern her features. She did not seem to be as affluent as the other patrons of Carruthers & Carruthers, though Philomena knew that some people became deeply frugal in their later years. Her garb might not give an accurate indication of her finances.

This lady poked a gloved and evidently misshapen finger at the book that had been placed before her. "I do not wish this story," she said, giving it a little shove. "I desire the other." Her tone turned acidic. "That was why I requested it."

"Then you should have collected it as planned."

"Impertinence! Your manner is most unbecoming for a clerk…"

"I am no clerk and you know it well, Mrs. Oliver." Lady Trevelaine eyed the lady, her own gaze steely. "I have no reply to better suit you. The book is regrettably no longer here. I will ensure that it is set aside for you again when it is returned."

"Whenever it *is* returned," replied Mrs. Oliver grumpily. "You cannot even know that its return will be timely!"

"If it is late, there will only be a small delay."

"Look upon me!" Mrs. Oliver roared with astonishing volume. She raised a hand, inviting everyone to do as she suggested. "I could be dead by the time the book is made available and that is a wholly unsatisfactory possibility, Miss Carruthers. I must know the resolution of the tale."

Lady Trevelaine's polite smile did not waver, nor did she correct the older woman as to her title. Her gaze grew a little cooler, though. "While I empathize with your situation, Mrs. Oliver, there is nothing else I can do. Unless, of course, you would like to buy the volume in question."

"Buy? *Buy*?! Do I look as if I am an heiress?"

"We do have one new copy–"

"Then lend it to me!" bellowed the older woman.

Lady Trevelaine hesitated, apparently prepared to consider that option.

"Go!" Mrs. Oliver commanded her. "Ask your father or your uncle. Tell them that I will be most displeased if I am compelled to leave this establishment without my reading material of choice on this day." She lowered her voice to a threat. "I have many friends, Miss Carruthers. You might not think a woman of my stature or age to be influential, but you may soon find the price of that error."

Lady Trevelaine's smile was polite but thin. "If you will excuse me?" She went into the back where the printing presses echoed.

The shopgirl bowed her head to Penelope and Mrs. Oliver grudgingly stepped aside. "Lady Arlingview. May I be of assistance?" Her relief in dealing with another patron was tangible.

"I would like the third volume of this novel, if it is available," Penelope said, setting down the book on the counter. She felt the weight of Mrs. Oliver's perusal and noted that it continued far too long. Such rudeness only deserved to be ignored. "If not, perhaps Lady Trevelaine could make a suggestion." She smiled. "I do admire her taste."

"Of course, my lady." The girl pivoted to check the shelves, leaving the two customers alone together. Penelope looked straight ahead, willing the moments to pass without conversation.

She feared she was to be disappointed, and she was right in that.

To her surprise, Mrs. Oliver reached out to finger the lace on her cuff, rubbing it between gloved finger and thumb like a merchant intending to buy. "Very fine," she rasped, and Penelope caught the barest glimpse of her sly expression through her many veils. "French?"

"Yes," Penelope replied because she did not know what else to do. She retreated a step, placing her cuff beyond the other woman's reach. She could not completely restrain herself from giving it a little brush.

Mrs. Oliver peered at her face. "Would you be the Marchioness of Arlingview?"

"I am indeed." She flushed slightly at the claim and saw the woman's eyes glitter. Did everyone suspect the truth?

"Wife of that enchanting rogue, Garrett Wright, the Marquis of Arlingview," the other woman said with an entirely inappropriate tone of approval. "Now, there is a man to welcome to one's chamber each and every night." Penelope glanced at the other woman, horrified as she fairly smacked her lips. "Robust, that man. *Vital.* Doubtless possessed of a boundless enthusiasm abed. Aye, I could appreciate a man of such vigor." She dropped her voice when Philomena had no notion how to reply. "A cold bed is the one detail of widowhood that troubles me. I sincerely hope that there is as lusty a romance in my book of choice as I have been given to understand."

Penelope gripped her hands together atop her umbrella and could not think of a single thing to say.

That did not influence Mrs. Oliver. "Of course, you cannot know me, for we have not been introduced."

"We have not," Penelope said, thinking that sufficiently safe of a comment.

"And you are unlikely to know of me, for I have no

title to my name and am only recently returned to England."

"Indeed." There was no discouraging the creature.

"Like your husband. Is he not recently returned? I will wager that you are glad to have him back in your chamber at night again." She cackled as Penelope stared at the far corner of the shop ceiling, wishing the floor would open and swallow her whole. Several other patrons were clearly listening. Mrs. Oliver moved a little closer, granting Penelope a whiff of truly loathsome cologne. "Aye, there is nothing like a man of *appetites*. I was swept away from these shores by the passion of a glorious scoundrel, and I never regretted a moment of our union," the older woman confided in a whisper that might have carried to Portsmouth. "I buried him and two more marvelous men, and now I am returned to England, at the behest of my seven children."

"Seven?" Penelope could not silence her query.

"And ten grandchildren." Mrs. Oliver nodded. "Three more on the way, with God's blessing. Reading is an entertainment for old women, my lady, not for those sufficiently vigorous to indulge in more active pursuits at night." She paused then, as if just realizing her own words. "Do you no longer welcome the marquis to your bed?" she asked. "I understand that he is a man who partakes lustily of the world's pleasures." She chortled then in a most salacious manner.

Penelope felt her lips part in indignation. That a stranger should dare to comment upon her intimate relations with her husband—or lack thereof—was utterly beyond expectation and she found herself unable to summon a word to her lips.

Mrs. Oliver cackled with satisfaction at the reaction she had provoked, no doubt by choice. "Aye, you do not look like one to appreciate a vigorous man, to be sure," she murmured, and Penelope caught her breath even as her cheeks burned.

What an audacious woman!

She spun to confront her. "Madame, I would ask you to refrain from such inappropriate commentary upon the situations of strangers," she said crisply. The amusement in the older woman's expression was most vexing and made Penelope wish she had more a talent for putting people in their place. Her own words were proving to be no deterrent at all.

In that moment, Lady Trevelaine returned with a brisk step and the older woman returned to her earlier dispute, seemingly forgetting Penelope. Lady Trevelaine declined to lend the new volume to Mrs. Oliver, quite firmly instructing the older woman to return on Friday for it. To Penelope's surprise, this decision was accepted, although not without several threats to influence friends against the establishment.

Clerk, daughter and patron all breathed a sigh of relief when the door closed behind Mrs. Oliver. "I have that volume for you, my lady," the clerk said, placing Penelope's requested book upon the counter.

Lady Trevelaine smiled as she glanced down at the book title. "I hope you are enjoying this story. It is one of my recent favorites." They spoke briefly about books, then Lady Trevelaine brought out another from beneath the counter. "I confess I thought of you when I finished this one the other evening. It seemed a story you would enjoy. The characters are quite charming, and the author's voice is delightful. There is a very fine description of a Christmas gathering at a country house. Would you like to borrow the first volume of it as well?"

With such a recommendation from a trusted fellow reader, Penelope could not decline.

~

GARRETT ARRIVED AT MONTFORD HOUSE, his father's residence, precisely on time. He was ushered into the library by Miller, the butler he had known from childhood, only to find that his father already had a guest. Three chairs were drawn up before the crackling fire in the large fireplace. His father, stroking the luxuriant silver moustache that was his pride and joy, sat in one and Damien DeVries, the Duke of Haynesdale, in the other.

Haynesdale was scowling, as was typically his expression in Garrett's experience. Though only a few years older than Garrett, he had considerable military experience and had been badly wounded in Spain. They had crossed paths during the war, but by mutual agreement, neither acknowledged as much. He had his cane on this day and rubbed one thigh absently. Garrett was surprised to see him abroad at all.

The youngest of three sons of the former Duke of Haynesdale, Damien DeVries had been a notorious scoundrel when his father bought him a commission in a desperate attempt at reform. The strategy had worked, and it was said the older man had been fiendishly proud of his son's service. Once injured, DeVries had returned to England but not in time to exchange a final word with his ailing father. Within months, his two older brothers had also died—one of pneumonia and one in a duel—and he had found himself in possession of a duchy, against every expectation, with a much younger sister to see married.

In these times, Haynesdale was reputed to be a recluse. If he was to be in anyone's company, though, it made sense that he would visit Garrett's father: his own father had been a great friend of the duke.

Greetings were exchanged, for all knew each other,

and Garrett took the remaining seat, the other man's presence convincing him that he had been summoned for his father's entertainment. The older man was often lonely, he knew, since the marriage of Garrett's youngest brother, though the duke would neither surrender the large house nor invite any others to live with him.

Brandies were poured and Miller absented himself, closing the doors to the library. Garrett's father nodded approval, even as the duke sipped his brandy with appreciation. "I was telling Haynesdale how you were at loose ends," his father said with a twinkle in his eye.

"Not that I or anyone regret the end of hostilities on the Continent," Garrett said, uncertain of Haynesdale's opinions on war after his injury.

The duke fixed him with a look. "I will speak only once of your contribution and here in privacy," he said quietly. "You should know that your valor and effectiveness was much remarked upon in influential circles."

"I thank you." Garrett inclined his head, aware that his father was beaming with pride. The three sipped of their brandies.

"Which is why I would ask for your assistance," Haynesdale continued, his voice a low rumble that would not carry. "It has come to my attention that there were two thefts over the holiday season, both from house parties."

"What manner of thefts?"

"Jewels," Haynesdale bit off the word. His brows rose. "Highly valuable ones."

"A pearl brooch with sapphires and a ruby necklace," Garrett's father said. "Quite distinctive as well. The rubies were carved to resemble berries."

"Bold ventures, both of them," Haynesdale supplied. "They were stolen in the midst of the festivities."

"The thief took advantage of the merriment to make the theft. Both occurred during dances with large numbers of guests. Both homes were hot on the night in question and guests moved about the houses in search of relief."

"Making it impossible to account for the whereabouts of all of them at any given time," Garrett guessed.

"There is even some doubt as to who was in attendance," his father contributed.

"How can that be?"

"Both balls were masquerades," Haynesdale said grimly.

"How clever," Garrett said.

"Fiendishly so," his father contributed. "And the villain evidently knew precisely what he sought and where to find it."

"How can you tell?"

"The thefts had been speedily done and nothing else was disturbed. The gem in question was simply missing. In both cases, the gems had been delivered to the house for the festivities." Haynesdale sipped of his brandy. "At the first party, the hostess had set aside her stole for the dance and the pin had been removed from it before her retrieval of the garment."

"Did no one have custody of it?"

"A masked woman who she mistook for an acquaintance had offered to hold it for her. Later, the lady in question vowed she had been dancing at the time, and other witnesses corroborated as much."

"The villain must have known of her disguise as well as the presence of the gem," Garrett mused.

De Vries nodded. "At the second, a guest's room had been boldly entered and the ruby necklace taken from the lady's luggage."

"It was left unguarded?"

"The lady's maid was to watch over it. She was found deeply asleep."

"Drugged with some potion," Garrett's father provided grimly.

"The lady had chosen at the last moment to wear only the earrings," Haynesdale said.

"It seems this villain knows a great deal about his prey," Garrett said.

Haynesdale nodded. "I believe it is one of the *ton*, not just because of the surety of the thief's movement though these events, but because such well-known jewels would have to be sold outside of England. The aristocracy travels with greater ease and less inspection, particularly now that the war is over." He stared into the fire and rubbed his leg, his manner thoughtful. "There also are many who have seen a change in their fortunes of late. Someone may have been driven to desperate measures."

A silence reigned then, Garrett's father watching Haynesdale with obvious expectation.

"And why are you telling me of these thefts?" Garrett asked.

"Because we have need of a spy, one with your cunning and experience. Your father has convinced Lady Augusta Rutherford to host a masquerade ball on Friday, by reminding her of her visit to Venice last spring for Carnevale."

"As a woman much enamored of spectacle, she seized upon the idea and claimed it for her own," Garrett's father said with satisfaction. "I suspect she has even forgotten that it was my suggestion at all."

"You would set a trap," Garrett said, understanding their scheme.

"Christopher and his wife will be among Lady Augusta's house guests for the weekend, as they are coming up from the country. She will wear her family pearls," his father said, referring to Garrett's younger brother and his wife. "Again, at my provocation, for I chided Christopher that she seldom showed them to advantage."

"I thought Caroline did not like them," Garrett said.

"She does not. She thinks the hue does not favor her and finds them weighty. I am wagering that she will remove them, as is characteristic of her, once she begins to dance."

"And Caroline is always quick to join the dance," Garrett noted.

His father nodded. "They will be entrusted, no doubt, to her maid, who will retire to their chamber, thereby setting the trap."

"Does Christopher know of your plan?"

"Of course. I had him order a copy to substitute it for the genuine pearls. I would ensure that there is no risk to his wife's legacy."

Haynesdale nodded approval. "And the maid will be warned."

"If she still employs Royce, she will enjoy a feint," Garrett agreed. "Christopher has told me that she is always first to insist upon a pantomime in the kitchens over the holidays and missed a calling to the stage."

"And you will attend to watch over the gems, if you deign to join us," Haynesdale said. "I deem it best if your father and brother act as if nothing is amiss, the better to feed the villain's confidence."

"Your pose as a wastrel will ensure that you are overlooked as a threat," his father said and Garrett nodded agreement, excited by the challenge.

"What can you tell me of the house?" he asked. "I know it is new and large."

Haynesdale smiled and reached for a satchel in the shadow of his chair. "I have persuaded the architect to share the plans, purportedly due to my own interest in constructing a new abode."

"Excellent," Garrett said, setting aside his glass.

"We will agree upon costumes, the better that we can identify each other," Haynesdale said.

"I suggest we add a sign of some sort," Garrett said. "In case we are anticipated by this fiend."

"An excellent notion," his father said heartily, and they all moved to the great desk to pore over the plans that Haynesdale unfurled there.

Garrett exchanged a smile with his father, knowing the older man had perfectly anticipated the challenge he needed. Even in peacetime, there was justice to be served and he was more than glad to do his part.

CHAPTER 4

*P*enelope was on her way to the meeting at the foundation for widows when she realized there was a sheet of paper in the book that had been recommended to her. She removed it, frowning at the elegant script. She did not recognize the hand.

She read it all the same.

Upon the boon and bane of habit...

Although familiarity does not always breed contempt in matters of romance, it certainly can lead to ennui. The difficulty is the contrast, of course: when affection is new and barely explored, the pulse leaps at even the prospect of a glimpse of one's beloved—at a distance, or across a crowded ballroom. The early exhilaration inevitably must fade, but that does not mean that a couple happily wed are consigned to find each other dull, predictable and unworthy of attention.

Penelope turned the sheet of paper over. There was nothing on the back and no hint of the message's origin. It appeared that someone was giving advice. Was it part of a letter? Had someone used it to mark their place in the book and forgotten it there?

She continued to read, feeling as if she explored a forbidden matter.

Routine is a blessing, in that each party learns what to expect from the other. Over time, we refine what is possible into a suite of expectations as to what is probable, and if we are among a fortunate few, those likelihoods suffice. Routine can also become a curse, however, allowing us to take our partner for granted and even to fail to offer our full attention to the cultivation of pleasure and harmony. Most couples must nurture opportunities for romance and actively pursue sensual satisfaction with each other. This is no burden, but an opportunity, and should be welcomed as such.

Penelope read on, intrigued by such advice. She found it hard to believe that she would become immune to the marquis' presence, but then, their ways would soon part.

A departure from routine—new positions or new initiative in one partner—can revive the most regimented of habitual unions. Even a change in the timing of an encounter or of location can provide the flavor of novelty. An unexpected seduction can be most alluring and go far to restore a mutual fascination.

Disguise, for example, especially an imperfect disguise, can create the illusion of seducing a new lover. This combined with the surety of meeting a familiar partner anew often results in a most successful and satisfying encounter, rekindling the thrill of a new amour.

Disguise.

Penelope's gaze clung to that single word. She was in disguise already, having taken Philomena's place.

The marquis already wondered how she might have changed so much. That path could only lead him to the truth and result in her return to the house in Clapham.

Unless she could find a suitor of her own.

Her notion of attending the masquerade might not be such an absurd one.

As much as the marquis' attentions made her heart flutter, Penelope suspected it was because no man had ever courted her before. She could imagine the whimsy of a future with him, but that could be no more than a fancy. A man who had chosen to wed her sister would never feel affection for Penelope.

The fact was that she was unlikely to find a suitor in Clapham. Her debut season was long behind her, and the festivities of London would be utterly inaccessible once she left Arlingview House. Penelope did not imagine that she could win the ardor of a suitor in an evening, like Cinderella, but what of one last indulgence?

What if she, like the marquis, attended Lady Rutherford's masquerade? It might be her last taste of such a fête ever.

In disguise, no one would even realize she was there.

Penelope read on.

Such investment in awakening desire need not be a burdensome responsibility: in fact, the certainty of what one's mate has appreciated in the past can present choices for the future. All that is required when the fire dims to a glowing coal is a breath of air from one party or the other to kindle the spark anew. When a couple share an abiding affection, the initiative of one will be met with enthusiasm of the other. In a couple devoted to the health of their union, such efforts would be equally shared, with each surprising the other at intervals.

It was a marvel to consider that routine and ennui might take the place of admiration in a marriage over time. Penelope found the notion rather sad, but then, she knew that Philomena had not been happy in her match after the birth of her sons.

Penelope turned the letter over, wondering again at its inclusion in her book. Lady Trevelaine had kept this specific volume aside just for her. But this note could not have been left for her eyes. A previous borrower had forgotten part of a letter, no more than that.

Still, the notion of a disguise was appealing. A masquerade ball was an enticing opportunity, especially with no one to govern her choices or behavior. The reward might well be worth any risk.

It would be easily done with little expense. She could wear one of Philomena's many dresses, with some augmentation to conceal her identity.

Before she could doubt her decision, Penelope reached up and rapped her umbrella on the roof of the carriage. "Would it be possible to make a brief detour to my dressmaker, Watkins?" she said to the driver. "I would have a quick word with her today if it can be managed."

"Of course, my lady."

That stop might even make her late for the meeting, but Penelope told herself she did not care. She would confound expectation, beginning this very afternoon, without fear of the consequences.

Indeed, this choice gave her several more days to compose her confession to the marquis.

~

GARRETT DESCENDED from his chamber the next morning with a high level of anticipation, even though he was likely to dine upon soup.

The previous afternoon, he and the two dukes had been so deep in discussion that the hour had become late. Garrett had accepted an invitation to dine with his father along with Haynesdale.

By the time he left Montford House, their plan was complete.

His sole regret was the sacrifice of any opportunity to speak to his wife again on the day before, but he would put that matter to rights at luncheon.

He nodded to Wrigley at the base of the stairs then halted at the sound of women's voices. His gaze flew to that of the butler who smiled.

"Lady Elizabeth and Mrs. Neilson, sir. It is their day to visit."

His mother-in-law and sister-in-law had a day to visit? These were unwelcome tidings to Garrett. It was not that he particularly disliked Philomena's mother and sister, or even cared that their origins were in trade, but simply that he had hoped to find his wife alone. Undeterred, he strode toward the breakfast room and Wrigley opened the door with his usual flourish.

"We will tell," a woman threatened softly just then.

Garrett frowned as the conversation in the morning room abruptly fell silent. He ignored the butler and entered the room as if he had heard nothing at all, inclining his head to his wife. She was pale, her eyes dark, and he knew he had heard correctly.

His urge to defend her was staggeringly powerful and utterly unexpected. He had never felt the need to protect Philomena, and that impulse in itself was a hint that his suspicions were correct. How dare these women threaten her? And in his house? Garrett concealed his reaction with an effort. What were they inclined to tell? To whom?

"What a delight," he said, bowing to the two women seated at the table.

His mother-in-law and sister-in-law stared at him, visibly astonished. They had not changed much since the last time he had seen them a year or so before, save that Lady Elizabeth was a little plumper and Mrs. Neilson was definitely with child.

Again.

He risked another glance toward his wife and almost smiled at the relief in her gaze. She wore the dark green dress he had always thought a fine choice for her. The hue made her eyes appear to be vividly green. Her coloring was so striking, with her dark hair and thick lashes, and he simply savored the sight of her for a long moment.

Once he had been beguiled by Philomena, but her nature had made him blind to her beauty. This woman, though, held his gaze steadily.

"Sir!" she said with what seemed to be genuine pleasure. "I had hoped you might be able to join us." Indeed, her apparent delight made him smile.

"It was my sole ambition on this day, my lady," he said gallantly. He held her gaze for a long moment, waiting for the color to rise in her cheeks and her lips to part. If only they had been alone, he might have kissed her. "Lady Elizabeth. Mrs. Neilson," he said, turning his attention to their guests with an effort. "I trust you and all your family are well." He took his seat, and his soup was served promptly.

If Garrett's theory was right, he would have expected his wife's own family to have noticed the truth early. His ire rose as he wondered whether the conversation he had interrupted had occurred previously. Did they routinely make demands of his wife in return for their silence?

His opinion of his in-laws definitely soured with

those three overheard words—and the threatening tone in which they had been uttered.

His wife's mother simply began to talk, as was her wont, perhaps to hide any sign of dissent.

"Oh, my lord, you flatter us overmuch," that lady said. "It is such a delight to see you, as generally you are out when we visit, undoubtedly at some important business or other. Why, I believe you have even been abroad, while Philomena remains ever at home." She laughed lightly before continuing. "But just this very moment, Arabella and I were endeavoring to persuade Philomena to visit us instead of our always coming to Arlingview House."

"You find displeasure in the house?" Garrett asked. "Or perhaps in the luncheon?" He nodded to his wife, who sat stiffly. "The soup is most excellent today, my lady. The beef stock is most fortifying."

"I thought it might suit you, sir." She smiled a little and he felt like a champion for improving her mood even that increment. "I shall tell Mrs. West of your favor." Their gazes clung over the table, which Garrett realized was set for more than soup.

Lady Elizabeth cleared her throat. "Your hospitality is most generous, my lord, and I would not have you doubt it. But it is not elegant, you know, to always be in the debt of another, and though we have often come for luncheon, Philomena has little time in recent years to accept our own invitations." She nodded in her daughter's direction and continued. "I must insist that you make fewer demands upon Philomena's schedule, if she is going to be obliged to neglect her own family. Why, we have not seen our dear girl since the last time we visited Arlingview House, a fortnight ago."

Their day, evidently, was every second Thursday. Garrett made a mental note of that.

Lady Elizabeth shook her head, the move making

her array of little curls dance, then sighed. "And so it goes, year to year, never any time to visit the shops with us, never a day to come to luncheon, never an opportunity to admire dear little Arnold, Anna, Albert and Audrey."

Garrett knew that these were Arabella's children. Philomena had attended their christenings and he had been glad to be abroad.

"I tell you, sir, our Philomena has her burdens to bear as your wife, and they are not all about scandal and gossip." She giggled then and Garrett thought she would have rapped his wrist with a fan if she had been holding one. He wondered how he had forgotten her apparent inability to be silent. How would she eat her soup? "You, sir, are most demanding of your wife. Even in your absence, she has such an array of responsibilities that she must scarce have time to take a breath!"

"I enjoy being of assistance to the duke," Philomena said mildly.

Her mother ignored her.

Mrs. Neilson ate her soup with impressive speed, as if she had not eaten in several days. She kept one hand on her rounded belly.

Lady Elizabeth turned to Garrett again. "With the boys at school, I cannot fathom how her schedule is so full. Such details aside, though, I miss my Philomena, and since my entreaties to her fall upon deaf ears thanks to her responsibilities, I must appeal to you to intervene." She smiled and finally fell silent, her manner expectant.

Garrett caught his wife's potent glance and understood. She was not burdened by overseeing his father's charities: she simply did not wish to go to her former home. If her family were demanding favors from her, he could imagine why that might be.

"I confess myself astonished, Lady Elizabeth," he

said. "I had no notion that my family's charities were so burdensome. I had understood that they appreciated Philomena's diplomacy and organizational skills, and truth be told, I thought she enjoyed making her contribution."

"Well, naturally, she would say as much…" Lady Elizabeth began.

"I say as much because it is true, *Maman*."

"Of course, dear." Lady Elizabeth smiled sweetly at Garrett's wife, who seemed to brace herself for whatever the older woman might say. "I would not suggest that you had *deceived* your husband and his family, but it is easy for a woman so generous as yourself to undertake too much obligation."

His wife's cheeks flamed then paled and Garrett did not miss the way her eyes widened slightly.

He turned upon her mother and continued as if she had not said more. "My father, the duke, relies utterly upon Philomena, of course, since he is himself less agile than was once the case." He spoke firmly, determined to give as good as others had been forced to endure. "But if you insist upon it, I could demand that she abandon the positions she has undertaken. He will not be pleased, to be sure, and there may be financial repercussions, as he has become a little impulsive in his later years. But as you say, a woman cannot be severed from her family. There are more important matters at stake than mere fortune." He nodded to the lady at the other end of the table and was beguiled by the glow of gratitude that lit her eyes. He turned his attention to his soup with an effort.

Her mother sputtered. "Well, we could not think to disappoint the duke!" she managed to say finally. "Especially if he is *failing*." A predictable gleam lit her eyes and Garrett regretted his part in putting it there. He said a silent prayer that his father might outlive his wife's mother. "I can well imagine that he is content with Philomena's efforts, for who could find a criticism with her skills?" She laughed lightly. "I taught her all she knows, to be certain."

Garrett highly doubted that and the claim passed without comment.

Lady Elizabeth cleared her throat pointedly and her spoon rattled slightly as she replaced it in her empty bowl. Arabella looked yearningly at the tureen, clearly in hope of another serving. Their hostess ignored this so completely that Garrett knew she had noticed her sister's expression.

Fortunately, the soup plates were removed in that interval and a soufflé was served, along with sliced ham. This luncheon was more like a light dinner, but he appreciated that his wife wished to be a good hostess to her mother and sister, regardless of whether they were good guests. A bottle of gooseberry wine from his brother's country estate was opened, much to Garrett's satisfaction as well of that of Lady Elizabeth.

"Are these new draperies, dear?" Lady Elizabeth asked after she had sipped mightily. She peered around the room with an avidity that made Garrett bristle.

"They are the same as they have ever been, *Maman*," his wife said calmly. "They are so pretty and suit the room so well. I see no reason to change them."

"But one must redecorate at intervals, to refresh one's home. Oh, I do not recall that commode. Is it a recent acquisition?"

"It has been in the house since before my arrival," the marchioness said, her tone resolute. "It did change places with the one on the opposite wall last year at Wrigley's suggestion, but they are very similar. You must recall that you have commented upon them before."

"Such fine pieces," Lady Elizabeth said with approval. "Are you entirely certain that you have need of both?"

Garrett looked up at that. His wife, though, was unperturbed. "They are a set, *Maman*, and specifically chosen to house the china for this room. They perform that task most admirably and it would simply be wrong to separate them."

"And you have flowers, as well. So lovely at this time of year to have hothouse blooms to cheer one. We, of course, could never indulge in their ilk."

At this, Philomena straightened slightly, and her smile seemed taut to Garrett. "It certainly would be, *Maman*, but if you look more closely, you will see that these flowers are dried. The arrangements were given to us by Lady Caroline, who dried the blooms at their home in the country. She has a most artful touch with their arrangement."

"How fortunate you are in your connections, my dear."

"Indeed." That lady contented herself with saying.

They ate in silence for some moments.

Lady Elizabeth then turned to Garrett. "You have the finest victuals, sir. I have said as much often to Philomena. Why, this gooseberry wine is a marvel and ever since we have first tasted it, I have yearned for another sip."

"It is made on my brother's estate in Shropshire. I find great favor with it myself."

"It is perfect at luncheon! We should welcome a bottle or two whenever you find an excess in your cellars."

Garrett met her gaze steadily. "Alas, it is always in short supply. We are indebted to my brother for whatever he manages to share with us."

"And this soufflé!" That lady continued, undeterred. "Why, sir, it is divine. I have often told Philomena that I should love for her cook to visit our humble abode. Though she might not find every ingredient at her fingertips—"

"—or every copper pot on our shelves—" Mrs. Neilson contributed with a smile.

"She would find a most enthusiastic company of admirers in my four darling grand-children. Why, those children have the best appetites and the most delightfully precocious manners." She laughed lightly.

"And I thought you had six grand-children," Garrett said, savoring the combination of chives and asparagus in the soufflé. His wife had accepted a small serving herself, while her mother and sister had not only made generous servings disappear but were taking a second. Their wine, similarly, seemed to have evaporated. He looked toward his wife, and she shrugged slightly, a hint that this was commonplace.

He supposed one could not choose one's family and he had been uncommonly fortunate.

"Oh, my goodness, sir! I did not mean to offend. I simply see James and Matthew so seldom that it is the easiest matter in the world to forget about them."

"And yet I see them scarcely more often and never forget about them," Garrett said, watching Philomena's smile light her eyes. It was a quiet smile of pride, one that made his own heart glow, for it revealed her own affection for the boys—whoever she was.

"You must bring them to visit!" Lady Elizabeth insisted. "We are only in Clapham. It is not that far for so fine a coach as you possess. You should come, all of you, for luncheon one day when the boys are home from school. Perhaps near Easter?"

"*Maman*," Mrs. Neilson said in an undertone that all were certainly intended to hear. "That is *five* more people."

"Tish," her mother said. "Philomena is always most

generous. You know she will bring gifts aplenty, for she is the heart and soul of kindness. It is not in her nature to fail to share her bounty with her blood family."

Garrett bit his tongue to keep from commenting upon that.

Lady Elizabeth turned to him. "And perhaps, his lordship might take an interest in Arnold's riding lessons. You must recall, sir, when your sons learned to ride and how challenging it was to find a suitable horse for a boy of fine birth."

Garrett was so surprised that he looked up from his excellent lunch. Lady Elizabeth held his gaze boldly, her expectations clear. "A suitable *horse?*" he echoed.

"Well, we have old Polly, of course, and there are the bays for the carriage, but their gait is different, is it not? I think a boy with a future needs a gelding of good lineage, a horse he can ride for decades with pride. I have no doubt, sir, that you are acquainted with many good breeders."

She thought he would buy her grandson a horse? Doubtless the creature would have need of stabling and a groomsman, which would be an additional cost difficult to deny once the venture was embarked upon. Subsequently, they might require a new carriage for their growing family, or even more horses. There could be no end to the requests, which Garrett suspected had been encouraged by a fine lunch every fortnight.

He did not possess a fortune because he spent money indiscriminately.

"I do," he said easily. "As a matter of fact, there is a baron at my club who is a most skillful breeder. I could introduce your son-in-law to him, to be sure, but you should be warned that his horses are expensive because they are so fine. Your son-in-law cannot expect to pay less than £50 for one of his colts, even a gelding."

Lady Elizabeth gasped. Mrs. Neilson's fork clattered

to the table in her shock. Garrett watched the utensil, which was sterling, to ensure it did not end up in her purse.

"But Philomena is Arnold's godmother," Lady Elizabeth protested. "I had thought she might be inclined to grant a gift to him for his next birthday."

"I have found a very fine history book for him," Philomena said smoothly. "I told you as much already, *Maman*. It will suit Arnold admirably with his interest in military exploits."

Garrett doubted she had paid more than fifty shillings for that volume, which was not cheap but a far cry from fifty pounds. "An admirable solution, my lady," he said, ensuring that his approval was audible. "You are always so adroit in encouraging the interests of our sons, as well." He smiled at her, suspecting that even this choice revealed the truth of her identity, then turned to her mother. "Philomena possesses the most remarkable talent in always finding the perfect gift. Is that a trait she learned from you, as well?"

But Lady Elizabeth was not to be cajoled. She flicked a dark glance at him and a darker one yet at her hostess.

Her youngest continued to make food vanish at an alarming rate. "Do you have a fruit tart today, Philomena?" Mrs. Neilson asked, her favored reply most clear. "The plum one last time was a marvel."

"Of course," Philomena said. "It is apple today."

"Apple? How pedestrian, my dear," her mother said, then winced at a thud from beneath the table. Had Mrs. Neilson kicked her mother? Garrett could not believe it, yet Lady Elizabeth's expression was startled. She managed a tight smile. "Of course, Arabella adores an apple tart. Why, only today she was saying that she yearned for one above all other things. It put poor Philip quite out of sorts. The man works day and night, but cannot keep his wife and family content." She shook her head, then finished her wine and another glass besides before the tart was served. The two guests devoured over half of the tart between them—Garrett seldom ate sweets and Philomena was evidently content with her tea.

"There is so small a piece remaining, Philomena," Mrs. Neilson said, her tone cajoling. "I do not suppose you would surrender it as a gift for the children? They have not had a tart such as this in many months now and with neither of you enjoying dessert, it will only go to waste."

Garrett knew the servants in the kitchen would have enjoyed it, but he sipped his wine and held his tongue.

"They had the rest of the plum tart a fortnight ago," his wife said sweetly. Her sister flushed but Philomena was already rising to her feet. "But of course, they shall have this, as well. I am sorry to bring our visit to a hasty conclusion, but I know that Garrett has errands this afternoon and I must attend a meeting at his father's charity for orphans." She smiled, but her expression was unyielding and her family evidently recognized as much.

"We can visit Brisbane's Emporium," Lady Elizabeth said. "And still be home in time for tea." The two took their farewells, gathering their shawls, purses and the remaining tart, then finally departed.

Garrett supposed it was churlish of him to be glad to see them leave.

CHAPTER 5

Garrett poured the last of the wine into his glass and drank it slowly in solitude. He heard the lady's footfalls as she returned and found himself smiling in anticipation of her arrival. He welcomed the prospect of even a few moments in her company.

Which was novel, indeed.

The lady paused in the doorway, her relief evident, and he chuckled.

"I could have warned you, if you had told me of your intentions," she said with a wry smile. She spoke softly, sparing a glance over her shoulder for the servants.

He had a lovely sense of being in league with her, one that he did not wish to be dispelled.

"Are they always thus?"

She nodded, her expression rueful.

"How much do you give them?"

"As little as I can manage. As you can see, they are easily encouraged to request more, and they do not show a care with their own finances. That has not changed."

"How so?"

"You could give them a fortune today, even every

penny you possess, and I guarantee it would be gone within a week." She frowned. "Once I was able to keep their spending curtailed, but my mother's finances are no longer my concern. Certainly, those of the Neilsons cannot be."

The twins had been the eldest children of a goldsmith who had gained a knighthood for his skill. The younger daughter had wed the goldsmith's apprentice, that man taking over the business and the house upon the father's passing. Mr. Neilson had also inherited his mother-in-law, for Lady Elizabeth continued to live with them.

Garrett could scarcely imagine a worse fate. He turned to look at the table, littered with crumbs, and could not keep himself from counting the silverware. It was all present and accounted for.

Then he realized that Neilson must have lived with the family from a young age, given that he had been an apprentice. He would have known Penelope for years.

He would have been able to tell the sisters apart.

In that moment, Garrett resolved to make a visit to Clapham this very day.

The lady spoke quickly, as if just realizing that her words might have prompted his recollections. "Thank you for declining to buy Arnold a horse. I fear such a gift would open the gates to endless requests."

"Thank you for arranging for the book."

"Fifty pounds, though? Is that not a lot for a young horse?"

"I could argue him down to forty," Garrett said with a shrug. "If he knows the horses are going to a good stable and owner. I bought the horses for the boys from them."

"They are magnificent creatures," she agreed. "But the stable in Clapham cannot compare to your stables here, let alone at Arlingview Manor."

"I suspected as much." He finished his wine and set the glass aside, fixing her with a look. "You have a fortitude, my lady, which is impressive." She flushed modestly and could not have looked less like Philomena.

"They are my family." She said this with resignation.

"And you are kinder to them than they are to you." He took her hand and kissed her fingertips, feeling her tremble a little at his touch. He did not release her hand when he met her gaze. "What did your mother threaten to tell and to whom?"

All the color left his wife's face. Her mouth worked for a moment and he was certain she would confide in him.

Then she blushed more deeply. "I could not say," she stammered and Garrett did not wish to press her.

He wanted her to confide in him.

He wanted her to trust him.

He wanted to protect her from whatever she feared.

Shaken by the vigor of his urges, he smiled. "Know that if ever you feel compelled to go to Clapham for luncheon, I will escort you."

She laughed lightly. "I thank you for your gallantry, sir, but I will forgo that pleasure for the foreseeable future."

Garrett lifted a brow and did not relinquish his grip upon her hand.

"Garrett," she said, correcting herself, his name a marvel on her lips.

He found himself staring at them, thinking of the kiss he had not claimed the day before, and it seemed she did not take a breath. Her eyes were wide, her attention fixed upon him. "Do you truly have an appointment this afternoon?" he asked softly.

"I do, but I am not late, as yet. I have my monthly review with Mr. Blakewell."

"My estate manager? Does he chide you for your spending?"

She shook her head and he wanted to see her smile again before they parted.

"Dare I hope that you do not find my own siblings so burdensome?"

"Of course not," she said with obvious relief. "Both of your brothers are most gracious."

"My father tells me that Christopher and Caroline are to be in town shortly. Might we invite them to dine?"

Her eyes lit with a pleasure that could not be feigned. "Of course! Have you a preferred date? I will make the arrangements."

And there Garrett saw his error. Instead of giving her an excuse to linger in his company, he unwittingly granted her another task. Before he could blink, she was confirming dates, summoning Mrs. West to review a menu and instructing Wrigley as to her plans. Though she was a paragon of efficiency, he felt the loss of her company most keenly.

Or perhaps the unaccustomed indulgence in gooseberry wine at luncheon was to blame.

Garrett knew it was the lady, to be sure.

~

TRUST HER MOTHER TO exploit a weakness.

Could the woman not have held her tongue for two more days?

Penelope departed from the house with just enough time to reach the offices of Mr. Blakewell, her husband's estate manager, for their monthly meeting. The marquis' unexpected and welcome suggestion of a dinner party for his brother and wife added a welcome burden to her list of duties for this day, but she did not mind. Both were charming and radiantly content in their marriage—it was sufficient to convince the greatest skeptic of the power of a happy match. She liked Caroline's sunny nature and admired that she always saw the best in everyone.

She would likely not be in residence when they came to dinner, but she could ensure that all was arranged before her departure.

Her mother should have had the wits to realize that telling the marquis that his wife was a fraud could offer no good repercussions. Penelope would undoubtedly be cast out, not only compelled to return to Clapham but there would be no more generosity from Arlingview for any of them. Telling was the most efficient way of ensuring they were all bereft.

Her husband's fortune was much in Penelope's thoughts as she met with the dour little Mr. Blackwell, a man who took his accounts most seriously. She liked the older man's passion for his trade and his satisfaction with the neat tallying of the accounts. While she did not exactly look forward to their monthly review of her spending, it was not so burdensome either. He always offered her a cup of the most wonderful China tea.

And on this day, she intended to ask him a question. She might not be destined to live with the marquis much longer, but she would see her curiosity satisfied about his nature.

The tea was gone, the finances for the month reviewed, and a small increase requested by the boys' school had been approved when Penelope mustered her resolve.

"I wonder, Mr. Blakewell, if I might make an enquiry of you over a matter which concerns me."

He beamed at her from the other side of the desk,

his brown eyes owlish behind his spectacles. "Of course, my lady. I am, as ever, at your service."

"The marquis' spending habits are not truly my concern," she began and Mr. Blakewell sobered.

He raised a hand. "You need not say it, my lady. You are concerned about the capital of his fortune, given his reputation for reckless indulgence." He said these last two words with gusto, as if he lived vicariously through the marquis' revelry.

She lowered her gaze. "I would not comment upon his choices."

"But it is only practical to be concerned about the repercussions of such wild living, not just for yourself but for your sons."

She cleared her throat. "My father was much inclined to invest in ventures that did not succeed, then to gamble in an attempt to regain his losses." She met Mr. Blakewell's sympathetic gaze. "This despite the fact that he was cursedly unlucky in those endeavors as well."

Mr. Blakewell cleared his throat delicately. "I had understood that your father's fortunes were…erratic."

Erratic was a perfect description. Penelope nodded approval of the choice of word.

Mr. Blakewell tented his hands together atop the desk. "And it seems to me to be only natural to be concerned at even the possibility of a similar situation recurring."

"Not just for myself, Mr. Blakewell. My father was severely abused by his creditors on several occasions." Even the memory of finding him on the doorstep, bloodied and beaten, made her innards chill.

"My lady, you have my condolences for what you have witnessed," Mr. Blakewell said solemnly, then leaned closer. "But you need hold no similar fears for your husband's finances. When the marquis embarked on this disreputable path, I felt I had to warn him of its possible destination. I could only do as much, you understand, because I have known him since he was a youth. He gave me his most solemn vow that his fortune would remain untouched by his merriment and any associated expenses. He assured me that he considered his fortune to be in trust for James and Matthew, and that he would never imperil the capital." Mr. Blakewell fixed a twinkling look upon her. "He swore upon it, my lady, giving his most solemn word."

Penelope frowned, for this made no sense. The expenses had to be paid somehow—unless the rumors of his indulgences were untrue. "But how does he fund his choices?"

Mr. Blakewell raised a finger. "I shared your skepticism, my lady, but it has been nine years and he has never once taken so much as a single penny from his fortune to fund his excesses. His expenses have been most temperate." He opened a ledger. "In the past six months, for example, he has retired the matched pair of bays for the carriage, sending those horses to Arlingview Manor while he acquired a new pair." Penelope nodded, for she knew of that. "He has ordered a new jacket from his tailor and a new pair of riding boots as well as three new shirts and cravats and one embroidered silk vest." Mr. Blakewell raised a hand. "That is the sum of it. These are quite modest expenses for a man in his position. The horses were expensive, but the last pair drew the carriage for fifteen years. I would anticipate at least so many years from this team."

Penelope clenched her hands together in her lap. "Then the stories of his wild behavior must be untrue."

Mr. Blakewell shook his head sadly. "That would be a futile hope, my lady. There are those who come to me to complain of his excesses, assuming that I must pay the bills, so I hear of many of them and can vouch for their existence. I would not offend you with the repeating of such rumors."

"But they are rumors."

"Rumors with basis in fact, I assure you, my lady. The details may be exaggerated, but there can be no doubt of the marquis' outrageous exploits."

"How is this possible? You said he had not spent much money this year. How could he fund such excesses?"

"Perhaps he wins sufficient in the gaming hells to cover those expenses." Mr. Blakewell shrugged. "The marquis always was uncommonly fortunate in games of chance." He smiled reassuringly. "I urge you, my lady, to spare no further concern to these matters. The marquis' fortune is untouched and I believe it will remain so."

But Penelope was not reassured. She recalled her father's beatings and feared the worst. There were those who would lend money to a man in dire straits but they were not principled in collecting their due in any possible way.

Just because the marquis had been fortunate thus far did not guarantee his future safety.

In her absence and that of the marquis, what would happen to the boys?

That was no excuse to continue her charade, but it gave Penelope a new concern.

Perhaps she could discuss the matter with the marquis. Perhaps she could convince him to abandon his wastrel ways. It seemed improbable that he would heed her advice, but perhaps he did not realize the risk.

She resolved to try, but in the end, it did not matter. She did not catch so much as a glimpse of the man before she left for the masquerade on Saturday night.

~

THE HIGH STREET of Clapham was bustling with activity when Garrett arrived. There was a considerable array of goods available, given the bounty in the shop windows, but he was interested solely in the goldsmith's establishment, Grosvenor & Son. In truth, there was neither a Grosvenor or his son surviving any longer but the name of the established business had not been changed. It was Garrett's hope that Lady Elizabeth and Mrs. Neilson might not be home as yet and he did not mean to waste a moment of opportunity.

He had only the most vague recollection of the blond man who greeted him, though that man bowed deeply before him. "My lord," Mr. Neilson said. "This is an honor."

"Mr. Neilson," Garrett replied, removing his hat and inclining his head. "Your wife was at luncheon today and her presence put me in mind of my need for a little gift for my wife."

"Lady Philomena," the goldsmith said with a nod. He surveyed the display cases in his shop and his brow knotted. "I am uncertain that I have any trinket sufficiently fine to merit her approval."

"Truly? I had no notion that she frequented your establishment."

Mr. Neilson laughed easily. "She has not set foot within it since her marriage, sir. I was apprenticed to her father at the age of eight and knew the family then."

Garrett guessed the man to be of an age with his wife. "Of course. You would have lived with the family."

Mr. Neilson nodded. "I remember Miss Philomena's taste very well. It was...extravagant. She always chose the most flamboyant piece, the largest stone regardless of quality, the most lavish setting."

That comment revealed that the goldsmith had known the lady well. "You are an observant man, then."

"It suits in my trade to recall such details."

Garrett strove to direct the conversation to any recollection of Penelope. "I can only assume yours was a happy apprenticeship."

"There was much to learn in those days, to be sure, and it was not all about the trade itself. I had never experienced such high and low tides of fortune."

"Indeed?"

"Indeed. Sir William could not save a penny to save his life, while his wife, Lady Elizabeth, would spend it three times over before he ever earned it. She always yearned for more for her daughters."

"Surely that is a laudable impulse."

"But one that should be tempered. She almost condemned them to the poorhouse at least twice in my recollection." He shook his head even as Garrett marvelled at this detail. "Then Miss Penelope, bless her soul, took them all in hand. Stern but fair, she soon had all set to rights. I am sorry to say that Miss Grosvenor mocked her for her prudence, insisting that no one of merit lived within their means."

Garrett did, to be sure.

"She did not like to be denied in those days, sir."

"I can well imagine."

"But Miss Penelope." Mr. Neilson sighed. "There was a woman of both beauty and practicality, though few appreciated her merit as I did." He visibly saddened. "I suppose it is no crime to admit now that I had hopes, for she was a fine young woman and would have suited me well."

"Did you ask for her hand?" Garrett asked when the man fell silent.

Mr. Neilson nodded, his expression woeful. "I did and made a most ardent appeal on my own behalf, but she declined me." He frowned. "It seemed…prudent to wed one of my master's daughters, you understand, so when Arabella smiled at me, I pursued the sole option remaining."

It was clear that the man was not entirely satisfied with his fate, but Garrett smiled politely. "And here you are, proprietor of your own shop."

"Here I am." Mr. Neilson's smile was just as polite. "Do you seek something specific, my lord?"

"I thought a pin perhaps, a brooch for my wife's birthday."

"In a fortnight," the goldsmith said, nodding at Garrett's evident surprise. "I still light a candle for Miss Penelope each year," he admitted and averted his gaze.

Garrett had the definite sense that the man's heart had been broken.

Mr. Neilson indicated a pin set with pearls, a circle of matched gems that would have been entirely too modest for Philomena. "Much as I appreciate the possibility of your patronage, I doubt that I can be of aid. This is the finest piece I have, you see, and I fear the marchioness would not admire it."

"It is lovely, but you are right, more subtle than her taste." Garrett frowned at the realization that he might learn more of use than a lady's nature. He stood, after all, in a goldsmith's shop. Someone might have tried to sell the stolen gems to Mr. Neilson. "I have a very definite idea, to be sure, and I wonder whether you might know where I could find such a piece."

"Describe it, my lord, and I will try."

"I thought a necklace of rubies, with the stones shaped like berries or fruit."

Mr. Neilson turned ashen.

Garrett continued, watching the other man. "Or perhaps a wide bracelet of pearls set with sapphires."

"Either, um, either piece would be quite a splendid gift, my lord," Mr. Neilson said, stammering mightily in his discomfiture. "But I have never seen the like."

"Never?"

The other man fairly twitched. "Never, sir," he vowed and even he must have heard that the claim was clearly a lie.

"What a shame," Garrett said smoothly. He indicated the pin with pearls. "That is a lovely little pin. If my mother were still alive, she would appreciate it beyond all."

"I thank you, my lord."

Garrett had a definite sense of the goldsmith's relief when he took his leave, and glanced back through the window to see the other man wiping his brow. He had recognized the description of the stolen pieces and Garrett wagered he knew precisely where they were.

The question was how much Mr. Neilson knew of their theft.

He gave his club's address to the hackney driver, for there was little over a day before the masquerade. His guise as an impetuous spendthrift might serve him well in seeking information about the missing jewels and the thief.

There was unlikely to be much sleep for him in the next few days and, even more sadly, little chance of learning more about the lady posing as his wife.

That pleasure would have to wait.

THERE CERTAINLY WERE those who whispered that Lady Augusta Rutherford was intent upon gaining the respect of good society at any cost. According to some reports, her husband, the Viscount of Bellingham, was among their number, particularly when presented with the bills for her entertaining. Their home was both newly constructed and generously proportioned, with so many rooms that there were jests of the Rutherfords not catching so much as a glimpse of each other for days on end.

Penelope could have told them that was not so much of a feat.

Rutherford House was situated well outside the fashionable neighborhood of Mayfair. Though a carriage ride to the recently laid-out square took less than twenty minutes on passably smooth roads, many of the ladies had responded to early invitations from Lady Augusta as if they must pack for a weekend in the country. Lady Augusta, not readily defeated by naysayers, had begun to host enormously lavish parties, to which everyone of import was invited. Given the generosity of the hostess and the splendor of the setting, in no time at all, it became unthinkable to decline one of her invitations.

Penelope thought that all those still seeking a glimpse of the splendors of Rutherford House were on their way to that abode on Saturday evening. The ride seemed to endure an eternity, partly because there had developed a line of carriages depositing guests at the door. The delay of waiting in line gave her sufficient time to doubt her choice.

In the shadows, she felt her costume was ridiculous. She was certain that anyone who knew her would pierce it with a glance. Her choice to appear as Artemis, goddess of the hunt, had seemed like a good jest since she intended to hunt a husband. Now, it also felt foolish. She had chosen a black silk evening dress with silver embroidery that had been Philomena's, one that she had never worn herself, but now feared that it might be recognized. Her red-headed wig felt like an inadequate disguise.

There was also the question of manners. Even in disguise, it was unpardonably rude for her to attend after the marquis had declined for them both. She eyed the line of carriages and had to admit it unlikely that one more guest would cast any budgetary considerations into disarray. She wondered how she would introduce herself and could not conceive of a reasonable reply. She might have ordered the carriage to turn around in the last moment, but they halted and the door was abruptly swept open.

There were liveried footmen lining the broad steps to the house, each holding a torch. The flames fairly licked the night sky, which was as dark and filled with stars as if they were in the country. It was a magical sight, the front of the house lit up with the golden torch light like an ancient temple. Penelope checked that her silver domino mask was in place one last time, then descended from the carriage, heart in her throat.

The air was crisp as she climbed the steps alone.

Was every gaze locked upon her? She felt utterly scandalous, not just because she was unescorted, but because her gown was cut much lower than was her custom. The black silk flowed behind her into a small train. She gripped her silver bow with one hand and her reticule in the other. She recalled Philomena's poise and squared her shoulders, summoning a smile. It was easier in disguise to find her confidence.

"Artemis!" a woman declared with delight and fell into step beside Penelope. She smiled brightly at Penelope's evident surprise. "May I arrive with you, my lady goddess?"

The woman was evidently also alone. The bodice of her gown dipped almost to her nipples, revealing an astonishing and flawless expanse of creamy skin. Her dress was black and white, embellished with many long white feathers, and her mask formed the shape of a swan's beak. Indeed, it seemed the swan was wrapped around her bodice and waist, its neck extending across her nape to her head and its wings covering her shoulders. Tall white feathers adorned her hair. Her green eyes glittered behind her mask and her ruddy lips curved in a confident smile.

"You are Leda with the swan," Penelope guessed and the woman laughed.

"Desired by all but claimed by few," she said, her voice low with amusement.

"Mother of Helen of Troy," Penelope said. "Whose beauty launched a thousand ships."

"Perhaps not," her companion said softly, then slipped her arm into Penelope's elbow. "Come, my goddess. Let us render mortal men silent in awe."

Penelope laughed despite herself, and they climbed the stairs together. She appreciated the other woman's company, though she could not guess her identity. She assumed her to be a widow, given that she was alone, for such a bold lady could be no maiden. It was her nature to solve every riddle before proceeding, but in this instance, she would simply welcome whatever opportunity came her way.

That change of attitude might be as good a disguise as the mask she wore.

CHAPTER 6

*P*enelope was nearly overwhelmed by the splendor of the house, the multitude of guests and the dizzying array of costumes. Her companion had vanished into the crowd of dancers as soon as they had entered the ballroom. When had she ever seen so many people gathered in one place, or so many candles set alight at once? The house was already hot and the sound was raucous, between the loud laughter of the guests and the volume of the music.

She accepted a glass of wine and surveyed the guests in her vicinity. At this fête, it was impossible to move toward a known acquaintance. She was surrounded by a glittering swirl of Roman gods and goddesses, no less than three Napoleans, a multitude of kings and queens, and several Norse deities. She spotted Cleopatra and members of the *Commedia dell'Arte*, any number of wolves, bears and rabbits, a fairy queen, a prince carrying a single glass slipper on a cushion, a butterfly and even Mephistopheles himself.

"Ah, the Cyprians have arrived," a man said in her proximity, his voice filled with anticipation. To Penelope's dismay, he touched her elbow, his gaze dark behind his red mask. He was dressed in red and white, with hearts embroidered upon his waistcoat, and carried a small bow, much like her own. His costume did not hide his paunch of a belly or the hungry gleam in his eyes. Penelope immediately disliked him.

"What prey do you seek this night, my lady?" He placed a red arrow in the bow, one with a heart as its point, and playfully aimed at her heart when he drew back the bow.

Penelope guessed him to be dressed as Cupid, but one seeking only physical affection. "I suppose you will tell me, sir, that you seek love." She tugged her elbow out of his grasp and stepped away, but he quickly pursued her.

"A lover, my lady, to be sure." He leered as he lowered the point of the arrow, aiming elsewhere.

Penelope bristled. "Then you seek satisfaction but not an abiding affection?" She clicked her tongue, enjoying the chance to speak her mind.

"Surely in your trade, you cannot hold satisfaction in disdain," he asked and reached for her with one hand.

Her trade?

"Only a cur seeks pleasure without affection, sir." Penelope stepped back and surveyed him, letting her mouth show that he failed to meet her measure. "I seek a gentleman with a true heart, for no less a man will do."

His astonishment was clear by his apparent inability to reply and Penelope seized the opportunity to escape him. A simmer of indignation lent speed to her steps, not only that he should assume her to be a courtesan, but that he would declare as much outright. She sipped her wine, regretted her wig for it was both heavy and hot, and surveyed the crowded ballroom. Even being tall offered little advantage, for many women wore tall ostrich feathers in their head-dresses.

Her hope of finding a suitor at this event was clearly a foolish one, but she would not leave almost as soon as she arrived. That was too soon to admit defeat.

A jig was called and the lively music began, some dancers thronging to the floor as others absented themselves from it. As she was jostled one way and the other, Penelope wondered whether Garrett had arrived. It was after ten.

Cupid still trailed behind her, making it clear that she was not the sole hunter in this gathering.

There was a mezzanine on the next floor that overlooked the dance floor. It must be accessed by either of the sweeping staircases in the foyer, for it was crowded with costumed guests. It would likely be cooler there.

Also from that vantage point, Penelope would have a much better view of the dancing guests. She might spot her prince yet.

∼

THE TRAP WAS SET.

Garrett was dressed as Harlequin for the Rutherford ball, his coat and breeches patterned in diamonds of alternating black and white. He wore a wide ruffled white collar and white gloves; his face was powdered white while his lips were red. His mask was a black domino and he wore a black tricorn hat embellished with a white ostrich feather.

In his lapel was a perfect red rose.

He was dancing with Lady Banbury with exaggerated gestures, as if he was drunk beyond belief. Dressed as a nymph, she appeared to be amused by his antics. She was also studying the other dancers so avidly that she was unaware she did not hold her partner's complete attention. Garrett had chosen her deliberately, for he knew she would be watching for the arrival of Lord

Standish. Truly, they two were the only ones in London who believed that no one else knew of their affair.

Though Garrett had anticipated a large gathering, the number of guests was astonishing for the time of year. He would never have thought so many of the *ton* would be back in London so early. If the thief took the bait this night, the sheer size of the gathering would facilitate his escape. Even now, well past ten o'clock, more guests streamed through the doors. Given the *melée* that covered a good third of the ballroom floor, it was impossible to know which guests had just arrived. The costumes made it challenging to be certain who was in attendance.

But they could not fail. The thief had to be stopped.

The sound of applause at the end of the dance was deafening. Garrett bowed to his partner, sweeping off his hat and kissing his fingertips, to Lady Banbury's great delight. She disappeared in a whirl of flowing gauze and Garrett surveyed the room again. He still had hope of noticing some important detail.

What he noticed was a lady in black and silver, dressed as Artemis, goddess of the hunt. She wore a silver domino mask and her vivid red hair was studded with silver pins shaped like stars. She carried a silver bow in the shape of a crescent moon as well as a small reticule. Her black gloves showed her fair skin to advantage. Her costume was striking, all the more so because he remembered it.

It was one of Philomena's gowns, albeit with different accessories.

The lady in question stood on the mezzanine, surveying the crowd. She might have been a ghost, a vision of the Philomena he had courted so many years before, and for a moment, he could only stare.

She laughed lightly at the comment of a man dressed as a wolf who leaned close to her, then retreated from him with ease. She vanished from view, doubtless heading for the staircase to descend to the ballroom, and Garrett found himself moving toward the base of the stairs. He stood there, watching her graceful descent, an undeniable yearning stirring deep within him.

He was not missing Philomena.

He was thinking of the lady with whom he had shared luncheon twice this week, the one who blushed so readily and trembled when he touched her.

The one he wanted to defend at all costs.

His heart stopped when she appeared at the top of the stairs and he did not even want to blink as he watched her descend. She wore a jet choker that seemed faintly familiar, but the dress he knew beyond doubt.

All the same, this was not Philomena and the difference was clear to one who truly looked. There was more caution in this woman's gestures and less of a desire to command every gaze. She moved away from men who approached her instead of cultivating their attention. Her laugh was rare and low, not pitched to be noticed by all, and her smile was more demure.

Garrett thought her utterly lovely.

The lady glanced up in that moment, as if feeling the weight of his gaze upon her and smiled, the sight sending a thrill through him. She recognized him, it was clear.

What was she doing at the ball? She turned away from him as a gentleman dressed as Cupid touched her arm with a boldness that was utterly unwarranted. His desire to defend her at the fore, Garrett smoothly intervened, nudging aside the Duke of Queensbury and his unwelcome attentions.

"Madame, I have awaited you most impatiently," he

said, claiming her hand. Her expression was filled with relief.

"Sir, I thought I might never locate you," she said. The merriment in her tone caught him unawares. She leaned closer, smiling most provocatively, and he was intrigued. "I must assume you have planned a merry seduction this night."

"I would change my plan to suit your desires, my lady," he said, watching her flush.

"But you did not attend with such a scheme in mind?"

"What mortal man would dare to hunt of a goddess, much less to plan it in advance?"

"Only one of uncommon valor and merit," she replied, then regarded him. "Would that be you, sir? Or is your playful reputation the sum of your truth?"

Garrett was surprised by her query, but strove to hide as much. Had she guessed that he only pretended to be a rogue? "Can you believe that you discern all of a man's truth with a glimpse?" he asked, his manner flirtatious.

"I am a goddess, sir," she replied in kind, then smiled.

He stepped back to survey her with undisguised approval. "I would certainly warrant that you are divine, my lady."

"Oh!" She flushed, then took a step back to echo his survey. "While you, sir, are a man well accustomed to triumph in amorous pursuits. You expect to win your way and often succeed, by dint of your charm and good looks."

"I could make the same assessment of many in this room, perhaps even of yourself."

"Indeed," she agreed lightly, then surveyed the dancers. "It seems we are surrounded by a merry company of scoundrels."

"Do you find that troubling?"

"I do not hunt their kind."

"Does that mean we are all unworthy of your attention?"

"I might hope that appearances were deceiving, in more than one instance." Her voice softened as she averted her gaze. "Or that perhaps there is one man who is more than he appears to be, one man whose heart is true."

"But if there is not?"

"Then I shall rue my attendance at this fête, to be sure."

"Is it not your custom to attend such events?"

"Not of late." Her gaze slid to his and her voice dropped low. "I have recently, however, been advised upon the merit of the pursuit of novelty."

Garrett smiled that she did recognize him. "And do you find that good counsel?"

"That depends, sir, upon what happens this night. I thought it advice worthy of further investigation."

He bowed over her hand. "Then you must dance with me, my lady, that I might defend the cause of new adventures."

"I will." She accepted his hand with a smile that made his heart pound, then let him guide her to the ballroom floor.

THERE WAS no costume that could disguise Garrett's identity when he stood before Penelope. From the line of his mouth to the timber of his voice, she knew this man to be the marquis, without doubt. The way her pulse jumped with his proximity and the flutter within her at the touch of his hand was only more assurance.

She felt the weight of his gaze upon her as they

danced, even when they were parted, and understood then why Philomena had so loved to claim a man's attention. It was thrilling to know that she was the sole object of his interest, to glance up and find him watching her, to know that he found her alluring and attractive. Penelope felt alive as she had not in years and welcomed the sensation, knowing that he was the reason. Even when he bantered with her, there was a seriousness in his tone and his protectiveness pleased her greatly.

Could this be his truth, disguised behind the illusion of another weary rake? Penelope hoped that it might be so and told herself it was for the sake of the boys and their future happiness.

Even she recognized that was not quite true. What a dream it would be to have a man such as this court her attention in all seriousness. Penelope could not imagine a better fate, though she knew this night's illusion would not last.

When the dance drew to a finale, she suspected that the marquis would abandon her to another partner. But he spun her from the floor, his every gesture commanding. Penelope's heart pounded to be so claimed. He led her toward the terrace and she wanted only to be alone with him in the night, perhaps to feel his kiss upon more than her cheek or her hand.

It seemed a small token before her life changed completely, before she left Arlingview House forever.

It was such a crush that they were jostled repeatedly before they reached the doors to the terrace. She even felt a tug on her reticule just before they reached the doors to the terrace. She gripped it more tightly as he swept open a door and a delightful chill touched her ankles.

It was glorious outside. Quiet, dark and chilly. The night sky was full of stars and the air was wonderfully clear. Penelope was reminded of one glorious evening in her debut season, when she had visited Vauxhall Gardens. That night had been one filled with the promise of romance, too, and a charming courtier who had made her heart race. She remembered it keenly on this night, and treasured the feeling of anticipation far more than she had that first time.

The terrace was blessedly empty, save for a couple in the far corner exchanging endearments. Could there have been a finer night for romance? The marquis guided her toward the steps to the garden in silence, his hand resting on the back of her waist. Her entire being thrummed in hope of whatever he would do. Once she had been cautious, but now she understood the rarity of such a magical night. She might never know one again, and that made her bold.

The music soared behind them, muted by the doors, and she could also hear the laughter of the guests. The patio was bordered by a cedar hedge save for the broad stairs that led down to the gardens. The white stones of the paths glowed in the light of the lanterns hung along the path. He escorted her down the stairs with singular purpose, striking a course for the darkened shadows around the perimeter of the garden.

"Am I accompanied by a rogue or a man of honor?" she asked.

"Would you prefer a man in pursuit of your shielded heart?" he said, his tone a confident low murmur that made her shiver.

"I would indeed." She glanced back toward the ballroom in time to see Cupid emerge. He clearly sought someone and she backed up a step, moving into the shadows. The marquis slid his arm around her waist, his hand flattening against her stomach as he drew her more closely against him. The hardness of his body felt so heavenly that Penelope closed her eyes.

"Are his attentions so unwelcome as that, my lady?" he murmured into her ear.

"They are," she said, wanting no doubt between them. "A man of merit should heed a lady's request, while he does not."

"Ah."

"And he is a most abominable dancer."

Her companion chuckled. "Is the ability to dance well a merit you seek above all others?"

She turned then and looked up at him, feeling his hands close around her waist. Such an exquisite sensation that she did not want him to move away. She did not even care if he thought she was Philomena—she simply wanted to know what it was like to be caressed by a man.

No, by this man.

"No. I appreciate a man who savors all of life's pleasures," she said. "And truly, such a man must enjoy the exhilaration of a fine dance, the sweetness of a good wine, the perfume of a perfect blossom." She bent deliberately to inhale of the red rose on his lapel. She could smell the clean scent of his skin and it made her toes curl in her slippers. She could feel the heat of his body and her breath caught at the unfamiliarity of her circumstance.

But she could not step away, not now, not when temptation was so near.

She sighed, wishing there was truth between them yet uncertain where to begin.

"Surely the bloom does not disappoint?" he murmured. His gloved fingertips slid beneath her elbows, lifting her slightly so her breasts collided with his chest. Her pulse skipped as she looked up at him.

"The flower is perfection itself. I sigh only because the cold air will destroy it."

"Is there no satisfaction in the fact that it lived, for

however short a while? Perhaps, given its merit, it lived well."

"You speak the truth, sir. Such a marvel can only be celebrated for every moment it endures."

"Indeed, I have often said as much of beauty," he said softly, leaning closer. He raised his hand to her cheek and Penelope could not take a breath. She stared up at him, wishing she could see his eyes clearly, but finding the gleam of them behind his mask oddly exciting.

"And how would you appreciate beauty, sir?"

"In the only reasonable way possible," he confided, his voice dropping to a confidential murmur. "By worshipping it."

Before Penelope could consider how to reply, he bent to capture her mouth beneath his own.

It might have been the moonlight and the mysterious shadows. It might have been the romance of the slumbering garden or the fact that this was her very first kiss. Penelope invented a hundred reasons for the wild thundering of her heart, but she knew the power of the kiss lay in the giver. In that moment, she did not care who he believed her to be. She wanted only more of what he chose to give, and she wanted it immediately.

Indeed, she might have been waiting all her life for this one heady kiss. She was not going to let it end too soon. Penelope slid her arms around his neck and surrendered to his potent embrace with uncharacteristic abandon.

IT HAD OFTEN BEEN SAID that no good deed went unpunished and Esmeralda recalled as much once she had entered the Rutherford's new house. She had only intended to help the Marchioness of Arlingview and had been gratified to see that lady had taken the advice under consideration. The marchioness hesitated outside the house, though, as if reconsidering her choice, and Esmeralda had only thought of getting her over the threshold.

In her desire to be helpful, she had not considered the assumptions men would make of the two women arriving together, especially as many recognized her. She had parted from the marchioness as quickly as possible, but the taint clung to the other woman. Lord Queensbury, that unpardonable lecher, was shadowing her in his guise as Cupid, doubtless making lewd and tasteless jests. Esmeralda was relieved beyond all to see the marquis come to the defense of his wife. She could not help but wonder whether either or both had penetrated the other's disguise, but dared to hope for the best.

The soirée was more drunken than she might have expected at such a comparatively early hour. Perhaps it was the hope that their identities were obscured, but a great many ladies and gentlemen were behaving quite badly. Several men snatched quite shamelessly at her and she heard the chortle of guilty giggles from more than one direction.

In truth, she tired of such indulgence without a regard for consequences. The *repartée* and the sparkle had once held an allure for her, but now she saw behind its mask, so to speak, to the discontent it often hid from view.

The last thing she desired on this night was to have anyone accompany her home.

Mercifully, the Duke of Haynesdale stood on the perimeter of the ballroom, glowering at the dancers as if he would insist upon an end to all merriment in his presence. He clearly had judged the attendees and found their moral integrity to be lacking, and Esmeralda was surprised to find that they shared that view.

He had taken little trouble with a disguise, she noted, for he was dressed in a dark jacket and buff breeches, tall dark boots and a white shirt with an impeccably tied cravat. His sole concession to the hostess's dictate was a black domino mask which did precisely nothing to mask his identity. He leaned hard on his cane and she wondered whether his injury was giving him pain, then dismissed her concern.

Why had he attended at all? He might have remained home in comfort. Had he simply attended to judge and find everyone lacking? She, at least, had attended in case the marchioness had been in need of a little assistance but had been surprised by the level of depravity she found.

Others might have found the duke's formidable presence and his obviously poor mood daunting, but Esmeralda could not resist the opportunity to speak with him. She could rely upon him, after all, to make no advances toward her and that was a welcome prospect. She accepted a glass of wine from a passing footman then strolled directly toward the duke.

Of course, he noticed her immediately. His gaze locked upon her and if anything, his expression became more forbidding. Esmeralda smiled and did not allow her steps to falter.

She did not fear this powerful and alluring man.

Although Mrs. Oliver perhaps should.

"Good evening, your grace," she said when she reached him, saluting him with her glass.

The disapproving line of his mouth did not change. "I thought your kind would not be welcome here," he said, taking no trouble to hide his disdain.

Esmeralda laughed as she took a place beside him, giving every indication of sharing his desire to watch the dance. "Then you have retreated from society too long, sir."

"How so?"

"My kind, as you so charmingly phrase it, are welcome wherever there are men in search of entertainment."

"They will not find that manner of entertainment at this event."

"Will they not?" Esmeralda mused. "It appears that many find it already." She watched a couple slip from the ballroom hand in hand, doubtless believing their departure to be furtive, and knew the duke watched their progress as well. She took a sip. "I would wager that Lady Augusta will find considerable disarray in other rooms of the house on the morrow."

"I will take no wager with you," he said stiffly.

Goodness, he had become dour. What had happened to so embitter him? It had to be more than the leg injury that all knew about. Now he snarled like a lion with a thorn in his paw when once he had been the very embodiment of merriment. What had been denied to the Duke of Haynesdale?

Esmeralda found herself wanting to know.

Then she wondered whether she might contrive to provide whatever he lacked.

CHAPTER 7

"Nor I with you," Esmeralda countered, earning a quick sidelong glance from the duke that was tinged with surprise. She smiled at him. "You might vanish to your country manor again, as you have in recent years, and never surrender your due. I so dislike when gentlemen do not honor their debts."

"I always pay mine."

"I would hope so, but it is of no import, since we make no wager, by your own choice."

"You assume you will win."

"I always win, your grace, one way or the other. It is my philosophy of life to triumph."

"Regardless of the odds?"

"Often despite them." The resolve in her tone seemed to attract his interest for he studied her for a long moment. Esmeralda feared she had revealed too much, for his gaze was searching, but she watched the dancers and sipped her wine. Generally, she did not imbibe much at such events but this glass's contents were vanishing with remarkable speed. She deliberately lowered the glass and resolved to sip no more until their ways parted.

"Not sufficiently fine for your palate?" the duke

asked in an undertone. The cursed man missed no detail. With another companion, she might have thought him fascinated with her, but she knew the duke sought only a basis for criticism. He studied her to find fault.

"It is lovely," she said sweetly. "I simply must keep my wits about me if I am to spar with the likes of your grace."

He almost smiled then but the expression did not last. "Spar? Do you mean to provoke me, then, Miss Ballantyne?"

"You were the one who chose to be provocative moments ago, as I recall."

"I was, perhaps, a little churlish."

"I warrant that is your favored mood, sir."

"You would not be wrong in that, Miss Ballantyne." He glanced at her again, a frown between his brows. "Why, precisely, is it *Miss* Ballantyne? Most of your… occupation call themselves Mrs."

"Because I will be owned by no man, sir."

"Are you not so owned when you are a kept mistress?"

"One could argue the delicacies of the matter, but I will never be a kept mistress again."

"I thought that was the objective of such women as yourself."

"Then it seems you know less of my kind than you believe." She smiled brightly as she met his gaze.

"You prefer to welcome many companions?" His view of that was clear.

"I prefer to choose, both companion and time," she replied, for it was true. "I find I tire of being at the disposal of another's whim."

"I can understand that well enough," he ceded, to her surprise. He frowned anew, turning his attention back to the dancers, and they watched the *allemande* begin in silence. "I remember when you first arrived in town," he said finally.

Esmeralda's mood soured. "As do I," she said with more than a measure of bitterness. It might have been said that she had leapt from the fat into the fire, though there was no changing the past.

The duke glanced at her, not having missed the change in her tone, and she appreciated that he was observant.

She smiled and spoke to deflect his curiosity. "But then, I remember when you would have thrown yourself into the whimsy of an evening like this, instead of arriving disguised as your own self, an embittered veteran."

He indicated the cane. "There are limitations to how much I might hide my identity."

"And there are ways in which you might have participated all the same. Was Hephaestus not the lamed smith?"

A reluctant smile lifted the corner of his mouth. He was still a beguiling man, and she counted herself fortunate that he smiled so seldom. "He was indeed."

"Or Poseidon with his trident might have been a choice. Your cane could have been disguised as well." She did not dare to consider the duke nude and bearded, bearing a trident. Even the notion gave her palpitations. With his powerful physique, he would be a sight indeed.

"I had not considered such possibilities."

"Perhaps you gave the matter little consideration at all." She eyed him and dared to give him a nudge. "Perhaps you did not even *try*, sir."

"And why should I?"

"As a courtesy to your hostess, if nothing else. But then, like many recluses, you believe that your own presence is sufficient to bring joy to those around you, given how infrequently you emerge from your haven."

He chuckled, a dark sound that gave Esmeralda chills of the best kind. "*Touché*, Miss Ballantyne. I see that if I am to frequent events where you are present, I will have to put more effort into my appearance and participation." He flicked a glance her way and sobered. "At least if I wish to gain your approval."

"My approval is much harder to win than that, your grace."

He barely refrained from scoffing, but Esmeralda could guess his thoughts. His words proved her right. "I thought all men with coin in their pockets had your approval."

"And you would be wrong in that, sir. I have only once found a man whose character urged me to admiration, a sure indication of how rare my approval is, given the number of men of my acquaintance."

"Yet, you are the companion of no man at this time, by all reports."

"Should I be flattered that you have enquired into my situation?"

"Of course not," he said gruffly, averting his gaze. "I have little interest in gossip, but I have been reminded it cannot be avoided."

Esmeralda considered him, sensing that he hid some detail. There was little gossip about her, particularly in such circles as frowned upon her occupation. He must have been seeking out such tales, though she could not imagine why he would be interested. She also could not imagine why he would frequent such unsavory locales as gaming hells, for he was said to have abandoned their so-called charms.

Why would he even speak of this?

"I suppose this man of merit found fault with your

choices," he said after some moments had passed in silence.

"You suppose incorrectly. He fell in love and wed that fortunate lady. They seem to be quite happy together."

The duke turned his piercing gaze upon her. "You speak like a woman with a broken heart, who seeks the good in her own misfortune."

"Love, sir, is a noble objective, perhaps the most noble one of all, and love in a marriage is a situation devoutly to be wished." He waited in silence and she found herself continuing. "I should like to believe that if a man of any merit loved a woman, he would find a way to wed her regardless of any obstacles between them."

He smiled a little. "Love will conquer all?"

"You need not be sarcastic, sir. My conviction is hardly original. The poets have written of it for centuries."

He studied her. "Did he break your heart?"

"I allowed it to be broken."

"How so?"

"By foolishly hoping he might act against his inclination. He would never have wed me, because he never loved me. I was sufficiently witless to ignore that truth."

"Or perhaps sufficiently smitten," he suggested, not unkindly.

Esmeralda did not reply.

"Who has done you injury, Miss Ballantyne?" he asked softly.

She laughed lightly. "Because you mean to defend me, your grace? I will not be cajoled into surrendering my secrets for such an unlikely prospect."

"How many secrets do you have?"

"No more than any other woman. No fewer than you, to be sure. But I guard mine diligently."

"Which precludes the enthusiastic consumption of wine." He nodded thoughtfully and she realized that he held no glass himself. His gaze slid away from her once more but she was not deceived that he was inattentive. "Would you do me the honor of a favor, Miss Ballantyne?"

"That depends upon your request."

"You pierced my own admittedly feeble disguise so readily." He turned and smiled at her, a sight that stole her breath away. The man could have charmed the sun from the sky, should he have so desired. Esmeralda could only stare at him in wonder as his tone turned cajoling. "Might you be inclined to identify some of the other guests for me?"

"Why do you care for their names?"

"I like to know who is in my company. Call it a souvenir of war."

There was more than that to his request, Esmeralda would have wagered, but she pretended his reply was sufficient. "Do you seek anyone in particular?"

He hesitated long enough that she wondered whether a lady had claimed his heart. "Are you acquainted with a woman known as Mrs. Oliver?" he asked and Esmeralda barely hid her dismay.

There could be no good import to this query.

"Mrs. Oliver?" Esmeralda echoed then frowned as if pondering the matter. In truth, her heart was leaping and she was aware of the duke's keen perusal. "I am not certain. Can you name any of her acquaintances?"

"She was a guest at the country residence of the Earl of Rockmorton over Christmas, pretending to be his elderly aunt. Even he was fooled. While there, she caused somewhat of a *furore*."

"A *furore* kindled by an elderly aunt?" Esmeralda laughed. "How remarkable."

The duke scowled again. "It seemed she took it upon herself to instruct a lady guest in the arts of seduction."

Esmeralda deliberately misunderstood him. "An elderly aunt seduced a lady guest? That would be most uncommon."

"She instructed the lady in ways to seduce her husband," the duke corrected with impatience.

"And how did that cause a disruption? Surely man and wife should seduce each other with some regularity."

"It was inappropriate," her companion replied with heat. "It was vulgar and wrong. A lady should never know of such details!"

"I should think that any lady who has born a child most know of such details."

"Of intimacy, perhaps, but not of *seduction*. It is unseemly..."

Esmeralda could only interrupt him. "And does the husband in question find fault with his situation?"

The duke fell abruptly silent, his manner hinting that he was seldom interrupted. "I would not deign to ask," he said stiffly.

She turned to confront him, unable to put aside her own opinion in this matter. "So, you would prefer that a wife know little of amorous matters and that a husband should seek out a woman like me for his satisfaction?"

"Of course not!"

"But then by your own edict, it is unseemly for a married lady to know of seduction that she might merrily meet her husband abed. You cannot have it both ways, your grace. Either men find satisfaction in their marital beds and *my kind* cease to exist, or wives remain ignorant of what their husbands could teach them and my trade flourishes."

She felt his perusal as surely as a touch. "You feel strongly in this matter."

"I tire of men and their edicts," she said, speaking more bluntly than was her wont. "I tire of their demands and their judgements and their refusal to see that the place of women in our society is of their own making. I tire of being blamed for what I cannot influence, much less control." She emptied her glass of wine with a flourish, then turned a hot look upon her avid companion. "If you will excuse me, your grace, you will have to find another, perhaps a more suitable, volunteer to identify guests for you. I have bills to pay this month." It was a crude and uncharacteristic reminder of her source of income, but Esmeralda was too vexed to care. She did not wait for his response but walked away, simmering at the injustice of her situation and that of other women, and resenting the duke's lofty assumption that he could judge them simply because he had been born a man and an aristocrat.

It just showed that a man of such promise could change with time and experience.

It just showed that men were never to be relied upon.

Esmeralda watched the progress of Harlequin and Artemis, glad that she had encouraged the marchioness to attend. The lady in question might have been a little less compliant though. Esmeralda knew that a man's attention was more securely captured if he did not taste victory too quickly. She should ensure that the marchioness received another message granting that advice. She wanted the marquis to have more than a brief affair with his wife, after all.

Someone jostled the marchioness then, a tall woman in black dressed as a queen. She had rather broad shoulders for a lady. Who could it be? The queen turned and dread uncoiled in Esmeralda's gut.

Jacques could not be here!

But he could. Even as she had the thought, she realized the truth. The war was over, the borders were more open again. She had tried to avoid even thinking of the possibility in the past year, and even now, she feared that her mind played tricks upon her. The ugly queen ducked toward the foyer.

Esmeralda had to be certain. She had no inclination to dance, much less to drink more wine or be in the vicinity of a certain duke, so she strove to follow her suspect.

She should not have been surprised that he eluded her. She found the black robe discarded in the hall to the kitchens, with only half a dozen scurrying footmen in livery in view.

She pursued the tallest footman, only to have a stranger turn to survey her at her touch upon his arm.

Jacques had vanished, as was his wont. Why had he been in attendance?

There could be no good explanation, to be sure.

THE LADY KISSED like she had never been kissed before, like she was thirsty for a sensation she had never known but recognized as right and true as soon as she felt it. That buttressed Garrett's growing conviction that she was Penelope. He was beguiled and overwhelmed by her sweet surrender, and wanted only to escort her to a private haven and finish what they had begun.

But Penelope had to be innocent, and she was not his to savor.

Even knowing as much, Garrett could not resist the temptation she offered. When she opened her mouth and leaned against him, he gathered her closer, wanting all that she had to give. His arms were full of her softness and sweet ardor. Her ripe curves pressed against him, making him forget every other concern of this night. She welcomed his embrace so passionately that he knew their thoughts were as one.

Philomena had never kissed with such abandon. Philomena had always measured out her favors, allowing only a sufficient increment for a passing satisfaction. This woman trusted him so completely that he could not imagine how glorious it would be to make love to her.

But why had Penelope attended the masquerade? What was her intention? The choice was so utterly unlike her practical self, never mind her costume, that Garrett could only break their kiss to study her anew. It was a balm to his pride to think that she had come in search of him, but she could have simply awaited him in his bedchamber.

He smiled at even the prospect.

She smiled up at him. "I would ask you to resume your kiss, sir," she whispered, her eyes sparkling. "It was most enticing."

Garrett smiled. "It was indeed," he murmured and bent over her once again, unable to resist.

But his lips did not touch hers before the air was rent by a scream. It was a most untimely interruption.

"My pearls!" a woman shrieked. The music stopped and the guests began to chatter in consternation. Garrett stepped out of the shadows, listening intently even as he sheltered Penelope behind himself. "My pearls have been stolen!"

It was Caroline, dressed as Anne Boleyn, Christopher fast behind her as King Henry.

"What has happened?" Penelope whispered.

The theft had occurred at the worst possible moment.

Garrett scanned the garden, knowing what would happen next. The plan would be put into action to ensure that the thief did not escape. Already, the butler was ushering the guests back into the ballroom, so they could all be searched. He heard solid footsteps on the gravel and knew that the garden would be searched as well. He seized his companion's hand, wanting only to spare her the ordeal that would follow. He led her away from the house with purpose, knowing time was of the essence. He knew every inch of this property, thanks to their earlier recognizance, and he wanted her away from this situation.

"But where are you leading me, sir?"

"There is a gate in the wall, just there, which leads to the drive where the carriages await the guests," Garrett said, his voice filled with purpose. He caught her shoulders in his hands and looked down at her, willing her to follow his instruction. "Go through it, find your carriage, and get home with all haste. You need not be embroiled in this matter."

"But I would like to be of assistance. What has happened?" She glanced back toward the terrace. "Whose pearls are missing?"

"You will be unveiled if you remain," he said, watching her doubts dawn. "Go, madame, I entreat you. I will ensure that you are not impeded."

"But..."

"Now," he commanded, his tone steely. She looked back, but then stepped toward the breach in the hedge. He opened the gate and she spared him a final questioning glance before stepping through it. Garrett lingered in the shadows to watch, relieved to see that his carriage was nearby. He whistled to Watkins, who looked around at the sound, then spotted the lady. The driver leapt down to open the carriage door for his mistress, his gaze roving over the shrubbery as he sought his master.

Garrett listened and waiting, knowing he would be needed inside but wanting to ensure Penelope's safety first. The horses nickered, the carriage door closed and his carriage creaked as it always did when first urged into motion.

Once he knew she was safely away from the fray, Garrett quickly returned to the chaos that had overtaken the party. There was work to be done this night, and he only hoped the villain was yet at the fête.

He would go through every chamber and storeroom himself, just to be sure.

~

IT WAS after midnight when Penelope reached the house, but she knew she would not sleep. Her thoughts spun with questions. Whose pearls were missing? Had they been found? And what had compelled the marquis to kiss her so sweetly? Even if he had thought her to be his wife, she could not regret the experience.

To think that married couples could share such pleasures at any time.

She truly had to find a suitor.

She kept her cloak closed until she reached the safety of her room, hiding her costume from the staff. Williams jumped up from where she dozed beside the fire, then began to pepper her with questions. Penelope described the house and the ball as well as she could, then listed many of the costumes. All the while, Williams was helping her out of her clothes and packing away both the wig and the silver accessories so they would not be spotted. It seemed an eternity before Penelope was in her nightgown and Williams was brushing her hair. She watched the girl yawn and took the brush from her hand.

"Go to bed, Williams," she said softly. "I will brush it myself."

"But my lady…"

"You have done so much this day in keeping my secret. Now, go."

The girl's eyes lit. "Was it worth it, my lady?"

"It was." Penelope smiled, thinking of that glorious kiss. "I had a lovely time."

It would be a memory to sustain her in the months ahead, to be sure.

The girl curtseyed, then left the chamber. Penelope finished brushing her hair, then noticed her reticule discarded on the bed. Williams had not put it away before being dismissed. She picked it up, intending to place it in the trunk, then frowned that it was so heavy. Penelope opened it then caught her breath at the pearl necklace that spilled into her hand.

There were five strands, each one strung from smallest to largest and back again, each pearl perfectly matched in hue to its neighbor. There was a gold clasp also, a starburst of square cut citrons set in the rays around a central star sapphire. Penelope sank down onto a stool and stared at the fortune that she could not even cup in a single hand.

The necklace looked familiar and she realized she had seen Lady Caroline, the wife of the marquis' brother, wearing the gems before. They were inherited from Caroline's family, if she recalled correctly, and of remarkable value. They gleamed in the light of the lantern, looking like a king's treasure in Penelope's hands.

How had they come to be in her reticule?

How could she ever return them without being suspected of theft herself?

Had the marquis put the necklace in her reticule? She recalled the tug upon her purse as they walked toward the terrace and a terrible dread filled her stomach. Surely, her husband could not be a thief? Why would he steal gems from someone in the family?

Was that how he financed his extravagant habits?

And why else would he have hastened her departure? If he had seized the gems and put them in her reticule, his insistence upon her departure had ensured that the pearls were away from the house before any search was begun.

Penelope could not believe him capable of such a deed.

And yet, she had no other explanation.

But she was not even certain of his true nature. Rake or demon or honorable gentleman?

That realization provided the sole impetus Penelope needed. It was time to resolve matters between them. She would confess her secret to him, then ask him outright for the truth about the pearls. There would be honesty between them from this moment forth, whatever the consequences.

She stood up with purpose, determined to speak with him immediately upon his return. She put the necklace back into the reticule, then listened at the door, gripping the reticule tightly. The house was silent. She left her chamber in haste, slipping silently down the stairs to the library. If the marquis was home, he would likely be there, savoring a brandy.

But Garrett was not there. The fire crackled on the grate in obvious anticipation of his arrival, but the library was empty.

Surely he would leave the masquerade shortly after she had done so.

Surely the fire was lit because he was expected.

Penelope settled into one of the chairs before the fire, prepared to await his return.

~

ESMERALDA ARRIVED HOME MUCH EARLIER than anticipated.

She was also alone, which suited her well.

Latimer opened the door to her, concern furrowing his brow.

"A wretched party," she said as she swept past him. "It is likely a drunken orgy by now." She abandoned her cloak and headed for the library, wanting only a restorative brandy.

"Mademoiselle," he said. "There is something you must know."

"It will wait until the morning, Latimer." Esmeralda cast her gloves on the table in the foyer as she passed.

"Mademoiselle," he persisted, but she opened the library door herself, wanting only the solace of privacy.

But she was not to have that, not this night or not anytime soon.

She halted to stare at the man seated in her parlor, lounging with a glass of her best brandy. "I see by your expression that you thought I would never find you," he said with that wretched confidence she remembered so well. "Tsk tsk, Esmé. I told you I would hunt you down and I have." He raised his glass. "You should congratulate me on my success."

Jacques.

Not only had the man come to London but he had the audacity to enter her home uninvited.

"Get out," she said from the doorway, speaking through her teeth. "You are not welcome here."

"But it is a fine residence. It will suit me well, Esmé. The location is quite excellent." He drained the glass, his calculating gaze locked upon her as he set it upon the table. "Do not be too hasty, Esmé," he warned, his voice so low that a chill settled in her gut. "I have found Sylvie, too."

"No!" That chill spread through Esmeralda with lightning speed as her worst nightmare came true. "Impossible!"

Jacques shook his head with cursed confidence. "Not impossible at all. I brought a letter from her to you, an entreaty, for she knows she will only be well so long as you do as I ask." He pulled a letter from inside his jacket and held it out to her.

Esmeralda stared at it as a wave of impotence swept over her. How she remembered this feeling and how she despised it. This man prompted no other emotion.

Save perhaps hatred.

"You are not asking for anything," she replied. "You are demanding it. This is blackmail."

"It is negotiation," he replied coldly. "Now tell your butler that all is well, close the door and sit down. I have instructions for you." He smiled. "As well as the missive, of course."

She did as he ordered then claimed the letter from his outstretched hand. The handwriting was Sylvie's, much to her dismay.

"And I will have another brandy, Esmé." Jacques held up the glass and snapped his fingers with impatience. His voice hardened. "Be quick about it. There's a good girl."

The words cast Esmeralda into a dark past, one she strove always to forget. But there was no forgetting the past now, not when it had once again become her future.

What was she to do?

CHAPTER 8

The clock in the foyer chimed thrice as Garrett crossed the threshold. He was tired and disgruntled. Somehow the genuine pearls and the false ones had been mixed up, the maid had fallen asleep despite the plan that she would not do so, and the thief had escaped with another prize. All they had gleaned from their many interviews was that the thief had been a tall woman in a black dress, which was hardly conclusive. There had been any number of women in black at the ball, including both Penelope and Esmeralda. Every facet of the plan had fallen apart and Garrett was mightily vexed.

He had changed at his father's house, where he had returned to confer with his father and Haynesdale. They had arrived at no conclusions and when their conversation began to circle, his father had sent them all home.

If it had not been for Penelope's kiss, the evening would have been a complete disaster.

Wrigley was waiting, as usual, and there was a fire in the library. Knowing he would not sleep soon, Garrett cast off his coat and hat and headed for the brandy decanter in the library. He poured a healthy measure then turned toward the fire.

To his surprise, Penelope was sleeping in the great leather chair there. She wore her nightgown, her bare feet tucked up beneath herself, and her dark hair loose over her shoulder. She looked soft and vulnerable, as well as cold. Her sweet beauty made his chest clench and his blood heat in recollection of that kiss.

Why was she waiting for him?

Garrett set down the glass beside her, then removed his jacket. He scooped her up in his arms and wrapped her in his jacket as she stirred to wakefulness, then took her place in the chair with the lady nestled in his lap.

"You are home," she said, her voice sleepy, then nestled a little closer to him.

"And you are cold," he replied, offering the brandy.

She shook her head and hesitated only a moment before leaning her cheek against his chest. He took a sip, feeling his body tighten at the sweet press of her against him, then set the glass aside again. He lifted her closer, sliding one hand along her cheek and into her hair. He ran his fingers through its length, watching the dark silken strands slide between his fingers, and felt the evening's tensions slip away. She was watching him, eyes wide, but she did not move away.

"I would have you wear it loose," he murmured. "Like a goddess at her bath." He smiled down at her. "Or a huntress in pursuit of her prey."

Her gaze flicked. "It would not be practical," she said softly.

"Beauty is seldom practical," he acknowledged. "But then, there is you." He felt her surprise, but before she could protest, he leaned down and captured her lips beneath his own. His fingers were tangled in the hair at her nape and he cupped her head, holding her close as he tempted her to join his embrace. He felt her caution and uncertainty, then savored the way she surrendered to him. She opened her mouth to him, trembling as his tongue flicked against her, then responding in kind so that his very blood was fired. His kiss deepened and became more hungry, but she met him touch for touch, following his example and driving him wild with her sweet passion.

He had to be gentle and proceed slowly, but her responsiveness made him yearn for satisfaction. He had no right to teach her about lovemaking, but her willingness diminished his concerns. He would give her whatever she desired of him and no more, and he would not regret a whit of it.

Neither of them would. Garrett would ensure as much.

She gasped and he swallowed the sound of her pleasure, his hand cupping her breast. He pinched the nipple through her chemise and she ground her hips against him, instinctively desiring more. He broke his kiss and pushed open the neckline of her chemise, bending to capture that taut nipple in his mouth and loving how tightly she gripped his hair. He teased and tormented it, grazing it with his teeth so that she caught her breath and fairly squirmed against him. His hand slid beneath the hem of her chemise, up the smooth length of her thigh. When his fingertips encountered the slick heat of her arousal, he knew they could not remain where they were. He lifted her in his arms and stood, cradling her against his chest as he kissed her possessively once again. She curled against him, kissing him with a hunger that echoed his own.

He took a step toward the door but she wriggled again. "You cannot carry me upstairs," she said in a whisper.

"I most certainly can."

"But what will the servants think?"

"That I am a fortunate man," he growled, stealing another kiss.

She eased free of him and he set her on her feet reluctantly, still holding her close. "You will become cold."

"Perhaps you should promise to warm me again," she replied with a welcome boldness.

"I will."

She kissed his cheek. "I will go to your chamber. Do not make me wait, sir."

"Have you forgotten my name again?" he asked, wanting to hear her say it aloud.

"Garrett," she whispered, her gaze clinging to his.

Indeed, the room heated well beyond the temperature coaxed by the fire. He could only stare at her, watching her lips part and her eyes start to sparkle.

She dropped his jacket and hastened from the library, walking with purpose to the stairs. She said goodnight to Wrigley with admirable dignity. Garrett had no doubt that the butler knew precisely what they were doing, but if the pretense pleased the lady, he would comply.

He turned back to take another sip of the brandy and noticed her reticule. The black and silver purse she had carried at the ball was on the chair where she had been sleeping. It had almost disappeared between the cushion and the chair itself, which explained why he had not noticed it earlier. He retrieved it, intending to return it to her upstairs, and was startled by the weight of it. Garrett opened the bag and spilled its contents into his palm.

He stared. He held Caroline's pearls.

How had they come to be in Penelope's purse?

Was she a thief? He could not believe it.

No, he did not want to believe it. He already knew she was a liar.

But either way, it was due to his efforts that the

pearls had been removed from Rutherford House without detection.

He thought of two masquerades at house parties over the holidays. He thought of the lady who had tempted his kiss this very night, the woman who was both Philomena and Penelope. A bold theft of jewels would have been completely in character with the Philomena he had known but he could not have named her sister's inclinations. Was this lady Philomena, bent on a ruse and determined to deceive him? Was his wife a thief? Was her daily manner the disguise? He recalled Mr. Neilson's guilty reaction and felt only dismay.

Perhaps *this* was the secret Lady Elizabeth threatened to reveal.

Was she as trustworthy and innocent as his instincts insisted, or was he beguiled?

Garrett frowned and went to his desk. He put the reticle in the bottom drawer, the only one that locked, and placed the key in its usual hiding place in a decorative vessel on the mantle. Still pondering the situation, he finished his brandy and left the library. He climbed the stairs thoughtfully, then entered his chamber and stared.

She was in his bed.

And she was nude.

Penelope smiled at him, her dark hair unfurled over her shoulders and her uncertainty clear, and in that instant, the pearls were utterly forgotten.

PENELOPE WAS both fearful and excited as she awaited Garrett. Only that could explain why she had forgotten to tell him about the pearls. To be awakened with such a kiss, to find herself in his arms and worshipped by his touch had eliminated every sensible thought from her head.

His chamber was the mirror of her own, but the furniture was larger and darker. The décor was in shades of blue and black, with touches of gold, and the lights were few. A fire had been set here as well and the bed was a great pillared haven, loaded with pillows and covers, much broader than her own. Penelope had wished for a stool when she climbed into it, then she had felt like a queen upon it.

When Garrett opened the door, his gaze hot, she was glad that she had removed her chemise. She wanted him to have no doubt of her willingness and she watched as he stared, then secured the door behind himself. He moved toward her with such purpose, his gaze locked upon her, that she felt beautiful as she never had before.

Her ruse would be discovered this night, to be sure, but she would not lose this opportunity to know this man's touch. She took a risk, quite unusual for her, and dared to hope for the best.

Garrett took off his vest slowly, his gaze unswerving, then cast aside his shirt. He watched her avidly, as if he feared she might vanish. Penelope studied him, endeavoring to look unsurprised by his powerful physique. He sat on the side of the bed to remove his boots and she wanted to run her hands over him.

Then she realized that she should surrender to temptation. She reached for him, touching his back and his shoulders, caressing him with growing confidence. He was warm and hard, and he cast a knowing smile at her over his shoulder. His boots hit the floor, then he rolled over, catching her with one arm and carrying her toward the head of the bed. He captured her mouth with his own, his weight crushing her into the mattress as he kissed her so thoroughly that she thought she might never manage to take a breath again.

It was heavenly.

His hand slid to the indent of her waist when he looked down at her. "It has been a while," he murmured, his lashes dropping to hide his thoughts. "Are you sure?"

"Yes," she said immediately and they smiled at each other that her ardor was so evident. "You still wear your breeches."

"For the moment," he said, then flicked his tongue across her nipple. "Tell me how you have imagined this encounter," he invited in a low growl, then closed his mouth over that taut peak. He suckled and teased it as before, the sensation so potent that Penelope was nearly overwhelmed. She liked the weight of his hand upon her waist and that he braced himself over her on his other elbow.

"Like this," she said and he chuckled, his breath fanning her skin and tickling her.

"You used to like to be blindfolded," he said, trailing a line of kisses back to her chin. He caught her head in his hand and kissed her slowly, his possessiveness making her heart race.

"Of course," she said, wondering about this.

"You said it made you feel more," he whispered in her ear, laving it then with his tongue.

Penelope could not imagine how she would feel more and live to tell about it.

"Or would you rather have your wrists tied to the bed?" he murmured, pulling back to survey her as she blinked at the very wickedness of the suggestion. "You used to like knowing that you only had to enjoy yourself." His gaze was piercing and Penelope caught her breath, certain he knew. She swallowed and saw his gaze drop, then watched his mouth curve in a seductive smile. His hand rose to her breast and he teased that nipple again, watching her closely.

"The blindfold," she said on impulse, not wanting him to turn away from her now.

Garrett rolled from the bed in a decisive move and fetched a silk cravat from his wardrobe. He pulled it taut between his hands, then instructed her to sit up. He sat behind her, moving her hair aside with his fingertips before he bound the cravat over her eyes. It was a wide smooth band, covering her from the top of her forehead and to the tip of her nose, and he wrapped it twice more around her head before knotting it securely. Penelope felt her breath catch, but immediately realized that he had been right. Her other sensations were heightened and when he drew her into his arms to kiss her again, she melted against him in surrender.

He eased her back to lie on the bed, his hands running over her unceasingly, his lips tormenting her, his kisses exciting her beyond all expectation. He kissed her nipples again, his hand sliding down the length of her, then his strong fingers eased between her thighs. In a way, it was easier to enjoy such intimacy without seeing his eyes and when he touched her, she parted her thighs instinctively to grant him access. She heard his chuckle of satisfaction, then he moved lower, trailing kisses over her belly. He captured her hands in his own as he eased his weight between her thighs and when she might have protested, his mouth closed over her in an intimate kiss that thrilled her very soul.

She shuddered in capitulation as he caressed her with his tongue, his bold touch coaxing her response with a surety that she could not deny. Penelope found her pulse racing even as a hot tide rose within her. She squirmed beneath his potent touch, uncertain what she sought but knowing her body rose toward some intoxicating goal. He drove her onward, then retreated, fairly making her scream in frustration before he began his amorous assault anew. Penelope had no notion how long he tormented her, for it seemed that time halted during his sweet seduction. She lost track of all but the sorcery of his touch and the answering tide that rose within herself.

And then, just when she thought she could endure no more, he was suddenly relentless, driving her on to an unknown summit. Her heart pounded, her breath caught, she shivered with the heat he conjured and then suddenly, Penelope cried out in pleasure, certain she had been cast into the stars.

While she struggled to catch her breath, Garrett kissed the inside of her thigh then rose from the bed. She heard him washing but did not want to move in case the spell was broken. She had never felt such pleasure before.

She had to tell him the truth.

But first, she wanted more.

~

A SEDUCTRESS AND A SIREN, a woman whose passion matched and invited his own, but one he had no right to claim. Garrett had not wanted a woman so much in a long time, but he dared not possess Penelope fully.

If she was not his wife in truth, then she was not his to take.

Her maidenhead was certainly not his to claim.

But there was something irresistible about introducing her to such sensual pleasures. He felt possessive as he had not with her sister, and Garrett guessed it was because this woman trusted him so completely. Her abandon was complete. Philomena had always held back some increment of herself, as if awaiting a more enticing offer.

Philomena had liked to be blindfolded, but he had always suspected it was because she imagined herself with another. Penelope, though, seemed to find a liberation with the loss of her sight. She had opened to him like a flower, and Garrett had never been so enticed by a woman before.

He rose from the bed to get a cloth, knowing he should send her back to her room but not wanting to be parted from her just yet. As he soaked the cloth, he watched her with satisfaction.

She lay on his bed, flushed from head to toe, lips swollen from his kisses, her release having made her warm and soft. Her trust had been humbling when she had let him blindfold her. Now it was redoubled as she awaited his command.

Garrett did not take such trust lightly.

Indeed, it reminded him of his honor and hers. He did not know why she had agreed to take Philomena's place, but he could not quibble all she had done since that choice had been made. She had served him and his family well, and he knew she deserved a better reward than to be ruined.

Even if she welcomed it.

Even if she was in league with the jewel thief. He had to believe that she was a mere pawn in the greater plan, perhaps compelled to assist by her family.

When he returned to the bed to wash her, her hands rose to the blindfold.

"Leave it for a moment," he commanded huskily. He ran his thumb across her mouth then bent to kiss her sweetly. "I would look upon you for a moment."

He thought she might argue. Instead, she flushed but ceded to him. As he washed her, he caressed her. She gasped, those lips parting with wonder, and he could not hold back a low growl of admiration. At that, she smiled, then languished upon the bed, displaying herself to him like a wanton. When he moved the rough cloth across her clitoris and she trembled, her lips parting with wonder, Garrett knew he had to watch her as she found her release.

He would please her one last time, then have the truth between them in the morning. They could discuss it at lunch, undoubtedly over an excellent soup, and resolve what was to be done.

It was a fine plan but one that did not account for the pearls. How many secrets did this woman hide from him? How could the awareness of her deceit not diminish his fascination? He felt like a spider caught in a web, but one with no desire to escape.

For the moment, he would enjoy.

Garrett stretched out beside her, watching the way she smiled in anticipation of his touch.

"Do you mean to bind me now?" she asked in a whisper.

He kissed her slowly. "Is that what you want?" he murmured in her ear.

Her smile turned playful. "Is it not also of import what you want?"

"I want you," he said, for it was true. "And I want your wishes to come true."

She hesitated for a moment, then nodded. Her smile was surprisingly wicked and her nipples were taut. "I'd like to have nothing to do but enjoy."

He lingered over their kisses, giving her time to change her mind, but she was surprisingly intrepid once she had chosen. Instead of binding her, he tangled her fingers with his, holding her hands captive as he stretched out his arm above her head. She was displayed to him, so glorious that his mouth went dry, then she arched her back and wriggled a little against his grip.

"Oh," she said, then smiled. "I truly am captive to

your whim, sir." Her contentment with that situation was more than clear and Garrett could only smile in satisfaction.

Though he longed to bury himself within her, this time, he touched her with his fingertips. He stretched out beside her, his length pressed against hers, holding her fast as he slid his other hand down the length of her and watched her expression. Her cheeks were flushed and her lips parted, her arousal more than clear. He eased his fingers between her thighs and she spread her legs, inviting him onward, arching her back so that she looked ecstatic. He slid a fingertip across her hard clitoris, savoring the welcome dampness he found there, and she gasped aloud, inviting his kiss. He claimed her mouth again, liking how fiercely she kissed him back, loving how she gripped his fingers. He caressed her boldly, then eased a finger inside her.

She was tight and hot, so slick that he had to close his eyes for strength. Penelope, for certain. He must have halted for she caught her breath and he knew he had to reassure her. "So many years, my lady," he murmured. "You have become as tight as a maiden again."

"I have?" she asked, her surprise clear.

"You have," he said and eased a second finger inside her. His thumb settled over her clitoris and he moved it back and forth, watching as he tormented her with pleasure. This time, her excitement grew more quickly and the sight of her was glorious. His own heart thundered, his body demanding satisfaction, but he could not indulge. He took her to the summit with all haste, knowing he would not be able to hold back otherwise. When she cried out and arched before him, her body trembling, he felt triumphant.

Then she collapsed beside him and leaned against his chest. "Oh, my lord," she said, her voice husky.

"Garrett," he murmured into her ear. "Call me by name, my lady."

"Garrett!" His heart leapt at the sweet sound of his name upon her lips. "Kiss me as if it's the last time you ever will."

He knew then that she intended to confess to him and tenderness swelled his heart. He had no words for this woman who had given so much of her life for the happiness of others and he kissed her soundly. If this was the only reward she requested, he was more than content to grant it to her.

"But you have not had your pleasure," she said when he finally broke his kiss.

"I have had it in pleasing you," he confessed, which was part of the truth.

She stretched up to kiss him then, her lips so hungry that he almost forgot his resolve.

Long moments later, Garrett moved away from her. He released her hands, kissing her once again before removing the blindfold. She flicked a gaze at him, then blushed, before she slipped from the other side of the bed. She was suddenly shy with the weight of his gaze upon her, as Philomena had never been. He watched her, affection swelling within him, but said nothing when she pulled on her chemise again. Her hair was a glorious dark tangle, an ebony river that hung to her waist and invited his touch. She seemed more vulnerable and Garrett remained in the bed with an effort.

He wanted to reach for her. He wanted to defend her against whatever foes she had.

He wanted to bring her back to the bed and begin their lovemaking anew.

If she stayed, he would take her before dawn. It was inevitable.

She seemed to sense as much for she hesitated beside the bed. "I thank you, sir," she said softly, her formal tone returned with her sight. Her eyes glowed though, lighting an answering glow in his own heart. He was tempted anew, but she smiled and moved quickly to the connecting door, again guessing his thoughts.

Garrett leaned back against the pillows, fists clenched, and exhaled mightily. Her scent was on his linens and he could nigh feel her smooth skin beneath his hands. He could yet taste her kiss and knew he would be restless all the night long, wanting what he dared not take.

In that moment, the lady screamed.

CHAPTER 9

*P*enelope entered the darkness of her chamber, floating on the cloud of pleasure that Garrett had summoned—until she stubbed her toe on a footstool that was not where it belonged. The room was in shadows, for the fire had long before burned down to embers, and there was a definite chill in the air. She located a lamp by touch and the tinder that was always in the drawer, then lit the lamp.

Only to cry out in horror at the disheveled state of her room.

It was chaotic.

Drawers had been pulled out and their contents dumped onto the floor. The bedding had been pulled back and the mattress was askew. Every trinket box had been opened: they lay on their sides or had been cast on the floor. Her wardrobe had been opened, and dresses were strewn across the room. Hat boxes and shoe boxes lay open, their contents disheveled, and every reticule in her possession was turned inside out. The winter wind lifted the curtains on one window, which was open to the night.

At her cry, Garrett strode into her chamber with

purpose, his expression grim as he surveyed the mess. "We must determine what is missing," he said.

It was only then that Penelope realized they must have been robbed.

The pearls! Someone had intended to retrieve them from her.

She sat down hard. When she had been jostled, someone had put them in her reticule. The villain must have followed her home to retrieve them. She darted a glance at the open window.

Garrett touched her elbow. "Your robe, my lady. The air is cold." He had plucked that garment from the tangle of clothing on the floor and held it for her. When she had slipped it on, he gripped her shoulders briefly, as if to give her strength. Then he opened the door to the corridor and shouted. "Wrigley! We have been robbed." Penelope looked at the destruction as Garrett rang the bell for Williams.

He moved to study the latch on the window, his scowl deepening. "It has been forced." He flicked a look her way. "Do you see anything missing?"

"I have my wedding ring," she said, holding up her left hand, before she recalled that it was not hers at all. She pointed. "And there is my grandmother's jet."

Garrett bent and picked the necklace from the floor. He located both earrings, then brought them to her. Their gazes met and Penelope swallowed. "I have a confession to make, sir," she whispered.

"I believe you do," he said softly before Wrigley and Williams appeared. Garrett turned then and gave orders for the perimeter of the house to be checked, instructing Wrigley to rouse the footmen, the driver and the stable hands to help. He also ordered that the head housemaid, Teresa, should come to assist Williams and Wrigley was dispatched to place the jet jewelry in the safe. Teresa arrived with such speed that she might have been awaiting the order, breathless, at the top of the servants' stair.

Williams' dismay was more than clear and she had immediately fallen to her knees in the middle of the room, repacking hats with shaking hands. "Who has done this thing?" she whispered.

"You must determine whether any item is missing, and with all haste," Garrett said to her, his voice crisp.

Penelope surveyed him with concern. It was as if he knew what he would find. Did he know about the pearls? She could not fathom how that might be so, and she dared not confide in him with so many others present.

"Might I have a word with you, sir?" she asked but he granted her a dark glance.

"I must ensure the security of the house, my lady," he said in that same brisk tone. "But I will return to you as soon as possible. Wrigley!" he said as the butler reappeared, the older man clearly flustered. "My lady wife will need a cup of hot tea."

"Of course, sir." Wrigley vanished again, and Garrett surveyed the disheveled chamber one last time. His gaze lit upon Penelope, now occupied in returning her reticules to rights, and he was impassive once again.

Dread filled her heart at his solemnity. It was a poor time to remember her sister's warning about his temper.

Williams, meanwhile, had recovered her usual capable manner, likely because of the task before her. "These are all the fine dresses," she said, restoring order quickly. "And all the evening slippers."

"I leave you to verify it all," Garrett said, then returned to his chamber. Moments later, Penelope heard his decisive tread upon the stairs. She silently willed him to return with all haste, for she could no longer bear to have any secrets between them.

But by the time he did return, it was too late for confessions.

~

ONCE OUT OF his wife's presence, Garrett's mind filled with questions that were long overdue. He had learned to be suspicious as a spy and had known more than one enemy agent adept at distraction. It was too powerful a coincidence that Penelope had surrendered to his touch at the same time as her chamber was ransacked.

Had she deliberately distracted him? He had to admit that he had been readily fooled.

Why had she been in the library? It was the first time he had ever encountered her there at night and that made the decision worthy of closer scrutiny. It was clear that she meant to intercept him upon his return. The question was why.

And how had she obtained the pearls?

It was possible that she had found the pearls in her reticule and wished to consult with him about them. He had to give her that benefit of the doubt. But then, why had she not spoken of them at all?

And why had she accepted his caress on this night of all nights?

Why had she attended the masquerade at all?

The fact that she had deceived him about her identity for years was not a good indication of her character.

Once dressed, he descended to the library. To his dismay, the bottom drawer of his desk was slightly ajar.

He had locked that drawer!

Garrett crossed the room with purpose, noting that the vessel on the mantle had been moved. Heart in his throat, he opened the drawer only to find the reticule cast at the bottom of it.

Empty.

The pearls were gone.

But how could that be? He had secured them there himself, and no one else had known of their location. Penelope could not have confided a detail she did not know in anyone. He had locked them away after she went to his chamber. He had watched her climb the stairs.

Then he realized that one of the windows was slightly ajar. The lock, like that of the window upstairs, had been forced but this window had been pulled closed again. He opened the window and looked into the night. There was a lane immediately outside, one that ran between Arlingview House and the neighboring residence. His neighbours were yet in the country, and their windows were dark, the draperies drawn. The draperies in his own library had been open.

And the marchioness' chamber was immediately above the library. Had the intruder ransacked her room, found nothing, then stood in the shadows outside the window and watched Garrett secure the pearls? The very idea made the hair prick on the back of Garrett's neck.

The fiend had been *watching* him.

If Penelope's ardor had been a deliberate distraction, he had been fooled by the oldest deceit known to any trickster.

Either she was a thief or the accomplice of one.

GARRETT DID NOT RETURN to hear her confession and Penelope thought she heard the carriage leave. It was almost dawn by the time the three women had returned all to rights and Penelope knew she was not the only one exhausted. She dismissed the maids and managed to sleep for a few hours, then rose to dress for church.

She was determined to confess all to Garrett, taking advantage of the privacy of the carriage to admit all she had done.

But she descended to learn that her husband had left early and had not yet returned.

She silently prayed that he had not visited the gaming hells.

She made an excuse and went into the library, only to find her reticule still in the armchair by the fireplace. Returning the pearls would see all set to rights with Garrett! She fell upon the purse with relief, only to discover that it was empty.

The pearls were gone.

She looked around herself, wondering. It seemed unlikely that one of the staff would suddenly stoop to thievery. She trusted them all. The marquis himself was the only new arrival.

Had he taken the pearls?

If so, he might have returned them to Lady Caroline, for he would have recognized them. That made sense but seemed most unsatisfactory. He had known she was awake. Why would he not have told her of this happy resolution?

Surely, he could not be the thief?

Once she would have discarded the very suggestion, but the tales of his gambling and merrymaking were impossible to forget in that moment. He had never taken funds from the estate and perhaps he routinely won when he gambled as Mr. Blakewell insisted.

Perhaps his luck had changed and he had a sudden need for funds.

Perhaps he was every bit the rogue he was reputed to be.

Penelope attended church alone, her doubts filling

her with dread, and prayed with more ardor than was her habit.

~

"I WONDERED when you would realize she was not the woman you married," the duke said once they were alone in a private room at his club. His father could always be found at his club on a Sunday, for that place had been his refuge on that day of the week for all of his adult life. Garrett had sought him out when he had no further avenues of his own devising to explore, and had confessed what he had realized of Penelope's identity.

He poured the coffee his father had ordered, glad of it after his lack of sleep the night before. He had scoured all the establishments of low repute of his acquaintance, in search of a whisper about Caroline's pearls, but had learned nothing at all. The sunlight seemed overly bright on this Sunday morning, but his father's words were more startling.

He looked up to find that man beaming at him with a satisfaction he did not share. "When did you know?"

"Your mother had suspicions as soon as Philomena returned from her illness in the country. Marjory said she was different. I suggested it was grief, but Marjory was convinced that Philomena would never grieve for anyone." He sipped his coffee appreciatively. "She never liked her, you know."

"I did not know." Not only was his wife not his wife, but his father and mother had known and never told him. And they had not liked his bride, though his father had encouraged Garrett to ask for her. Garrett took a sip of very hot coffee and scalded his tongue.

"Why did you not tell me?" he asked and earned a stern glare from his father.

"We were at war," that man said firmly. "You had matters of greater import to attend."

"Greater than the identity of my wife?"

The duke waved off this protest. "It could have been worse. This wife acted with sobriety and practicality. She guarded your assets with vigilance and raised your sons with care." He fixed a look upon Garrett. "Be assured that the other one would never have done so well."

"You might have mentioned it," Garrett said, disgruntled.

"I thought you would notice. Did you not bed the woman when you did return home?"

Garrett shook his head. "We argued after Matthew's birth, most bitterly. It was clear that we were destined to live apart thereafter." He would not recall that argument and he certainly would never repeat it to anyone. He would do anything to ensure that his sons never knew of it. "In part, that was why I found your suggestion appealing."

"But not the sole reason. You have always sought a higher purpose in life." His father smiled as he selected a biscuit. "You could never have been the man you pretend to be. I am shocked, in truth, that people were so prepared to believe so ill of you."

"I spent a great deal of coin to convince them."

"Which reminds me that you have not surrendered your expenses of late. Give me a summary and I will see you reimbursed promptly."

Garrett nodded, still feeling that the world had shifted beneath his feet.

"If nothing else, your disguise will be of use in this matter," his father continued. "Who better to prowl the depths of society in search of rumors of the gem than that immoral wastrel, the Marquis of Arlingview?" He chuckled to himself at that.

"Indeed," Garrett agreed, resigning himself to a greater duration of the ruse.

"That vain and flighty chit," his father mused. "That was what Marjory called Philomena. Ah, the diatribes I heard about her sins. Your mother feared she would break your heart."

"Ours was never a love match."

"No, but your mother knew you well. You would hope for infatuation to evolve into a more abiding affection, much as my match with Marjory did. Your mother did not believe Philomena capable of sharing her affections with only one man and you, my boy, were never one to be content with half-measures. A battle was inevitable. Your mother hoped there would be no divorce, for she feared the scandal, but once the boys were born, it was of less concern."

It was a bit troubling that his mother had foreseen his future so clearly. Garrett wished he had taken her long-ago counsel not to choose Philomena, but then he would never have known Penelope.

Who might be a thief.

When had his judgement of people become so flawed as this?

The duke set his cup aside. "Of course, your mother also liked the Philomena who came to visit her after the death of her sister. Marjory never changed her opinion upon any matter, so I thought for a while that she sought an excuse for the change, rather than cede that she had erred."

Garrett smiled into his coffee at that.

"But then I saw it, as well. It was when your mother was failing and Philomena offered to assist with the family charities." The duke gave Garrett a look. "The woman you married would never have made such an offer."

"Nor lived with such practicality in my absence," Garrett agreed.

"Indeed. You would have returned home to find your house full of jewels and dresses, your larder bare and your accounts overdrawn."

"I had returned to find that on several occasions."

"No doubt there would be a man in your chamber, as well. That chit would never deny herself anything, given the choice."

Garrett did not comment upon that. "I did wonder at the change in her."

His father nodded his head. "The boys were the ones to benefit. Suddenly, Philomena would not rest until they had the most suitable education. She cast out Mr. Kemp, you know, with such gusto that the boys still laugh about it. She won their hearts then and there. I have never seen a mother so intent upon choosing the proper tutor, both encouraging her sons and giving them proper guidance as well." He sighed. "I confess I cannot easily believe this one to be a thief, even so. A liar, to be certain, but perhaps one cajoled into that situation."

"How so?" Garrett himself wished he could find a solution that exonerated Penelope.

His father shook his head, frowning as he thought. "There was a bond between those twin girls. They were so opposite in nature yet so very close."

"Two halves of a whole?" Garrett suggested.

"I would not put it so strongly. Your mother noted their bond before you were wed to Philomena. She jested that you might wed one but gain them both. I believe she expected that Penelope would never wed and might come to live with you, perhaps to teach your children." He shrugged. "Perhaps a similar end was contrived in a different way."

"But what of the pearls?" Garrett had to ask, reminding his father of the reason for his visit. "How could she have had them in her possession? And who took them from my library?"

"That is troubling." The duke put his coffee aside. "Clearly, there is an accomplice, which makes me believe your conjecture about her mother might be right. Was her father not a goldsmith?"

"And Arabella's husband follows his trade." Garrett considered his words, but knew his father had to know the truth. "Perhaps they are often needful of funds. Penelope mentioned that they often ask for her assistance."

"Does she indulge them?"

"She said she gives as little as she can."

His father nodded. "There is the good sense I associate with her."

"I overheard the mother threaten her," Garrett admitted, meeting his father's gaze. "She said she would tell."

"Tell what?"

Garrett shrugged. "And when I visited the shop, Neilson knew of the stolen gems, though he tried to hide as much."

"Interesting. Do you think someone tried to sell them to him?"

Again, Garrett did not know the answer. "Or he knows more of their theft."

His father nodded. "Perhaps she is caught between her pledge to her dead sister and the demands of her family. I would wish this situation upon no one, but she should have come to you, or to me."

Garrett nodded.

"The fact remains that we must tempt the fiend to steal again in order to learn the truth."

"Surely that cannot be risked?"

"I would not tempt them to steal from an unsuspecting lady, but from one of their own."

"I do not understand."

The duke smiled, but there was a calculating gleam in his eye. "We cannot be governed by sentiment. We must rout the villains. I believe we should all attend the theater this week with Christopher and Caroline."

"But to what point? Caroline's pearls are gone."

"What of the emerald parure you bought Philomena upon the birth of James?" His father indulged in another biscuit, his eyes gleaming when he met Garrett's gaze again. "I think it might be the perfect bait. If the lady is involved, she will undoubtedly tell her accomplice of your request that she wear them."

Garrett was appalled. "But if she is not, she could be assaulted or injured."

The duke waved away this objection. "By the accomplice who relies upon her aid? I think not. We shall go Friday as Christopher may not linger long in town. He never does. His fields and furrows call him as effectively as any siren of the seas. You must insist that your lady indulge in a new gown to wear with the gems." He bit into his biscuit. "I am quite sure she is past due for a new one. And dressmakers are tremendous gossips. The appearance of the parure must be anticipated by all."

Garrett set down his cup, disliking the idea of deceiving Penelope, though that made little enough sense given her choices. "I will be vigilant and never leave her side," he said but his father shook his head.

"To what point? The thief must be given an opportunity. Leave the box for a moment or two. We all will do as much at intermission, but keep your wife in view."

Garrett exhaled, not liking this scheme in the least.

"Rest easy, my boy," his father said kindly. "She might confide in you, in which case we can create a trap together for the villain. There is little a woman likes better than to have a protector who will fight for her cause." He shook his biscuit at his son. "You might end up happily wedded yet."

Garrett strove to share his father's optimism. "Should we include Haynesdale in our scheme?"

"Of course. The man is observant beyond all others. I will invite him for dinner this very day, and Christopher as well, though I doubt he will attend and abandon Caroline. You must stay, lest the temptress undermine your resolve again." He shook his head with affection. "Always a noble nature and an urge to aid a damsel in distress. Your mother, you know, feared that you were so adamant about wedding Philomena because you had committed an indiscretion and that there was a child."

"Never!" Garrett knew his vehemence was fed by his difficulty in resisting Penelope.

"I know." His father finished his biscuit. "I guessed that you had been snared by a scheming mother and pretty but ambitious young woman, one disinclined to be refused in any matter. For a maiden, her arts were considerable. Are you certain she was innocent when you wed?"

Garrett blinked. "I believed as much at the time."

"Then let us not despoil her memory further." The duke reached for his ink and paper. "What is done is done, and you have two fine sons to show for it if nothing else. Let us strive to improve the future. When will James and Matthew be home from school next? I should dearly like to see them both again soon."

There was a roar from another room in the club as two men took exception to each other's comments. Father and son glanced up, then Garrett went to the door. He looked out to find the Earl of Queenston badgering another member.

"I say the courtesan dressed as Artemis last night

owes me a boon," he insisted. "And I demand that you tell me where to find her."

The other man shook his head. "And I say again that I do not know her. I never saw her before."

"I will hunt her down and have my due," the earl snarled. "She is a cheating whore and a liar…" Doubtless he had more to say of the lady in question, but Garrett was not inclined to let the earl's tirade continue.

~

THE SOLE ADVANTAGE of spending Sunday in solitude was that Penelope finished her book. It was dismal to dine alone so she indulged only in tea. She untangled her needlework but cast it aside with impatience as the hour grew late and no carriage returned to the door. She paced her chamber, restless for Garrett to return, but he did not. The clock was striking midnight when she finally retired and still there was no hint of his presence.

She heard him singing drunkenly at two in the street below her window and held her breath, but he did not try the connecting door. Where had he been?

What if his reputation as a rogue was deserved? She might have opened the door and asked him, if he had been sober. As it was, she could only stare at the ceiling and wonder.

Was she a fool to hope that the man she had originally met was the true one? Of course, she was. The marquis' reputation was firmly established. Even Mr. Blakewell had confirmed it.

The difficulty was that the man who had seduced her after the masquerade had been the man of her own dreams. Penelope grimaced. If only that could be his truth.

If only she knew what had happened to the pearls.

CHAPTER 10

*P*enelope awakened to another rainy day and an ominous silence in the house. She descended to the breakfast room, dispirited by her own company, and was startled to find Garrett already at his place. He flicked a glance her way, setting aside his newspaper, and she could not fail to note that he let the footman pull back her chair.

His eye was darkened, ripening to a hundred shades of blue, black and purple.

She knew she stared.

He had been beaten for not paying his debts. This would be the warning and if he did not render the balance due, he would be beaten within an inch of his life.

Penelope sat down hard, feeling faint. "Are the pearls returned to Lady Caroline?"

He blinked. "No. They have vanished."

Penelope looked down at her bowl, her innards in turmoil.

Garrett nodded amiably to the footman as the soup was served, then inhaled appreciatively of its scent. "A fine duck broth today," he said as if all was right in his world. "With asparagus yet." A plate of fresh scones was placed at his end of the table, a suggestion Penelope had made to the cook to ensure that the meal might be sufficient for him.

"Mrs. West noted that the spring produce was arriving early this year."

He nodded approval and began to eat, his gaze sliding to his newspaper. They might have been a couple married for years and bored of each other's companionship, though Penelope certainly felt no such ennui. Everything within her fluttered.

"Does the soup not find favor with you, my lady? I understood you were fond of all varieties."

"I find myself without an appetite today."

"Indeed?"

"What happened to your eye, sir?"

He started to lift a brow, then winced. "A small difference of opinion had to be resolved. I am certain you will hear of it by and by."

"I would hear of it now, if you please." She was as taut with fear as he was at ease.

He waited until the footman had left and the door was closed. "The Earl of Queenston disparaged a lady and her reputation last evening."

Penelope looked down at her soup. It was not about a debt, then. He had a mistress and defended that lady. How could she have expected otherwise, even for a moment?

It was somewhat better, but not much, for it meant his attentions to her were not unusual. He might have gone from her to his mistress and that was a most disappointing realization.

She was a fool to ever hope for the exclusive attention of the marquis.

"I see," she said and lifted a spoonful of soup.

"I doubt that you do. He said that the goddess Artemis was not only a whore, but one that failed to deliver on her promises."

Penelope gasped in outrage and her spoon clattered to the bowl.

Garrett was watching her closely and he smiled just a little at her reaction. "I see we share the same view of the lady's honor."

Penelope felt a curious mix of reactions, both delight that he had defended her and horror that he had been injured. "You should not have done it."

"I could scarce let the matter pass," he said mildly.

"But you were hurt!"

He put down his spoon to consider her. "I believe in this circumstance, my lady, it is considered polite to assume that the opponent was more injured than the champion."

She gripped her napkin in her lap. "Was he?"

The marquis smiled with a satisfaction that could not be denied. "He was, as a matter of fact."

Penelope took a breath to fortify herself for she did not share his satisfaction with this outcome. "You must have been at your club or a gaming hell."

"And if I was?"

"I must entreat you, sir, to abandon this impetuous pursuit of pleasure at any price." There was unusual heat in her tone and Garrett glanced up, his expression inscrutable. "You could be badly injured or worse, and the boys would be without your guidance and support. Even if you do not have a care for your own welfare, you must think of them."

He considered her. "In the unlikely case of my absence, they will have you."

She shook her head, impatient with it all. "I must speak bluntly to you, sir. This can continue no longer. I cannot bear it." She placed her napkin on the table and rose, her soup barely tasted.

He was watching her, his gaze assessing. "I had

thought to join you this afternoon, if that arrangement suits you well. Do you have any engagements?"

"I would return a book to Cavendish & Cavendish, then had thought to review the menus with Mrs. West."

He nodded. "If my accompaniment suits you, we might speak in the carriage in privacy." He lifted his gaze to hers and his eyes were very blue. "I believe you will need to visit your dressmaker today as well."

Penelope doubted that, given what she was going to tell him. "That would be perfect, sir. If you will excuse me, I will fetch my cloak and book immediately."

He rose then and held her chair, returning to his own to finish his soup.

Penelope would confess it all and have it done. She doubted she would defend herself coherently, for she had not composed her speech, but Garrett would know the truth.

She would be glad to surrender the truth but could not look forward to returning to Clapham in the least.

GARRETT WAS INTRIGUED. Penelope was resolute and he wondered what she would confess to him. He disliked that there were so many possibilities. He waited for her beside the carriage and she did not meet his gaze when she appeared. She wore a pink dress today, another fine choice for her coloring, though there was no tint in her cheeks in this moment.

If nothing else, she did not delay or flinch from whatever she had resolved to do. As soon as they were underway, she turned to him.

"I am not Philomena," she said. She removed her glove and the wedding ring from her left hand, offering it to him. "I am Penelope. We exchanged places when Philomena was ill three years ago. Though it was her suggestion, I am equally to blame for the outcome. I not only agreed to her plan, but I continued the charade for three years." She raised her gaze to his. "I apologize, sir, for deceiving you and all those in your household."

Garrett took the ring, uncertain what else to do. "You could have told me sooner."

"I could have, but I seldom was alone with you. You were away from home so much and seemed to avoid me when we might have had a private conversation." She pursed her lips. He supposed it was wrong that he found her consternation adorable, or that her confession lightened his heart as much as it did. She still might be a thief. "I thought, perhaps, there would be a moment at your mother's funeral."

"But I did not linger."

"And then, I thought perhaps last Christmas."

"But I did not return home."

She flicked an intent look at him. "And truth be told, Philomena warned me of your temper. She said you could not abide to be deceived so there were moments when I might have confessed, but failed to have the courage."

"I cannot be alone in disliking that."

"And yet I have deceived you for years." She lifted her chin, gripping her hands tightly together in her lap. "It shall stop on this very day. I will be Penelope again."

"My father will miss your efforts with his charities."

"He will find someone else, I am certain."

"What will you do?"

Her lips tightened. "I will return to Clapham, of course."

Garrett could not imagine that was an objective to be desired.

"There is no other possibility," she continued a little sadly, then fixed him with a look. "But you must see, sir, why I am concerned for the boys. They will have only you and your father. While your father dotes upon them, he is no longer young. You must abandon your dissolute habits for their sake."

"You seem particularly concerned."

"How could I not be? The pearls have vanished, sir, the pearls inherited by your brother's own wife. I cannot believe that you could sink to such levels of depravity as to sell them, but then, your debts must be horrendous to drive you to such a choice."

Garrett blinked. "You think I stole the pearls?"

"They were in my reticule. I came to the library to consult with you about them. I did not wish to believe that you had placed them there, even though you had ensured that I left the house with them before the search was made. And now they are gone from the reticule. I had hoped that you had returned them to Lady Caroline, but you say they are yet gone. How could you do such a heinous deed?"

"I did not."

She eyed him, her expression wary. "Then where did they go?"

"I thought you took them, or your accomplice."

Penelope was so aghast that he trusted her. "Me? My accomplice? What nonsense is this?"

Garrett chose to confide in her. "These are not the first gems to be stolen. When I went to Clapham, Mr. Neilson knew of the other stolen gems, though he denied as much most vigorously."

She rubbed her brow. "I do not know which statement is more remarkable, that more gems are missing or that you went to Clapham by choice."

Garrett smiled and claimed her hand, placing it on his thigh with his own atop it. "I suspected that you were not Philomena. It occurred to me at luncheon that Mr. Neilson, as your father's apprentice, might know more of your nature than I do."

"Odious man," she said and shuddered.

Garrett's attention sharpened. "How so?"

She shook her head. "Cupid reminded me of him, always trying to catch me in a corner."

He would not compel her to return to that!

Garrett dropped his gaze and kept his voice level. "Once there, I realized that as a goldsmith, he might have heard of the other gems."

"The thief might try to sell them."

"So I asked, under the guise of seeking a birthday gift for my wife, saying I had something special in mind. I described the stolen gems. He was visibly shocked, but said he had never seen such pieces."

"He is not an artful liar."

"While you are?"

He was teasing but she flushed crimson, pulling her hand free of his grip.

"And shortly before that, I heard your mother threatening to tell, though I did not know what she intended to reveal."

Penelope shook her head. "*Maman* is not always very clever about details." She lifted her gaze to his. "She does not realize that revealing my fraud to you will result in less bounty coming to her rather than more."

"She should content herself with leftover tart," he suggested and was rewarded by her smile.

"She should!" Then she laughed and raised a hand to her mouth as if to silence the sound. She sobered all too soon for Garrett's taste. "But it will not matter now." She squared her shoulders and faced him again. "Before I depart, I must impress upon you, sir, the import of paying your debts. You must control your wild urges, sir. I entreat you to make a single concession and pay your debts with money from your fortune in this one instance, then never gamble again."

It was a remarkable thing to have anyone show concern for Garrett's welfare. He could not recall when last such a thing had occurred. Penelope was evidently sincere and her appeal warmed his heart.

"It is only money, my lady."

"No," she said, shaking her head. "It is so much more than that. My own father was beaten severely several times as a result of his failure to pay his debts. We were threatened with debtor's prison twice. You must steer clear of such obstacles. You must!" This time, she gripped his hand. "Pledge it to me before I leave your house."

"Why does it matter, my lady?"

She blinked back tears and averted her gaze. "Because I could not bear it," she whispered and Garrett's doubts of her nature were undermined.

But it might be another feint. It was certainly a timely confession. He was susceptible to this lady, after all, and she seemed keenly aware of his vulnerability. Caroline's pearls had been in her possession, and they had vanished. She had been on the mezzanine when he had first glimpsed her at Rutherford House, therefore near the guest bedrooms upstairs. The gems had been taken by a woman in a black dress, and he could not forget her triumphant expression as she surveyed the ballroom. He could not dismiss the possibility that she knew more about the thefts than he might have preferred.

His father's plan must be followed, independent of her confession.

But he could still make a small confession to Penelope.

❧

PENELOPE FEARED that Garrett would refuse her advice. Instead, he captured her hand and sat back in the carriage, his brow furrowed in thought. She tried to pull her hand away but his grip was secure upon it.

It felt rather nice to have her hand enfolded in the warmth of his own.

"The trouble with honesty, my lady, is that once the confessions begin, it is difficult to know where to halt," he said finally. They rode in silence for several moments before he turned to meet her gaze, his own steady and resolute. She sensed that he had made a decision and she wondered what he would say. "I am not a wastrel. Like you, I have allowed others to believe that I am someone I am not."

Penelope exhaled with relief. "I am so relieved."

He smiled at her and kissed her knuckles once again. Even through her gloves, she felt the imprint of his touch and heat surged within her.

"And so there is no debt, and thus, no peril of my being abused by a moneylender. You may be at ease in that matter." He looked down at her hand. "I am, however, involved in an attempt to capture this thief."

That was a noble enterprise and one Penelope found admirable.

He spoke with such care that she wondered what he was not telling her. "And in this matter, I would greatly appreciate your assistance."

"But what could I do to aid in such an endeavor?"

"I think this a moment when routine would be best," Garrett said and Penelope sensed that he held back some detail. He lifted his gaze to hers. "Would you consider remaining at Arlingview House and continuing to pose as my wife for another fortnight? Perhaps until your birthday?"

Penelope smiled. "I cannot think of a scheme I would like better," she said with enthusiasm.

Instead of appearing to be reassured, Garrett's gaze slid away from hers and he looked out the window. "Good," he said crisply. "I will not, of course, compel you to suffer my attentions."

He could not believe that her pleasure had been feigned!

Before she could think of how to reassure him, Garrett seemed to recall something. He reached into the pocket of his waistcoat and removed her wedding ring, offering it to her again.

"After all, we are not wed in truth, my lady," he said softly, his eyes dark. "And I will not claim what remains in trust for your true husband."

Disappointment welled within Penelope, though she knew his choice was honorable and right. She removed her glove and held out her hand, watching as he slid the gold band onto her finger. She raised her gaze to his, finding his expression inscrutable again, and dared to make a tiny wish for her own future.

When he turned away, a matter of business concluded, she had to speak.

"I wonder, sir, if I might be so bold as to ask whether you know of any gentleman who might be a fitting suitor for me?" Penelope watched his eyes widen and knew that color flared in her cheeks. "I would not remain unwed, if I had the chance," she said hastily. "And though nothing could be done with haste, I am unlikely to encounter any men of suitable nature once I return to Clapham. If you had any inclination to make an introduction in coming months, I would be most obliged."

"You wish me to find you a husband?" he echoed.

"You are more likely to meet or know a suitable candidate than I."

He frowned and looked out the window, then

looked back at her again. "I see," was all he said and she had the sense that he was astounded.

She supposed it was an unusual request, but one made of desperation.

The prospect of living again in the house in Clapham offered more than sufficient encouragement.

~

PENELOPE WANTED him to find her a husband.

Garrett knew her appeal was not unreasonable, given the situation, and he struggled to contain his instinctive dislike of it. The woman possessed an extraordinary ability to set his world at odds, to be sure.

He cleared his throat, recalling himself to the business at hand. "My father has a most admirable notion," he said. "He suggests that we all attend the theatre on Friday, since Christopher and Caroline are in town."

"But Caroline has just lost her pearls. Will she not be too upset for such an outing?"

"She is in need of a distraction as a result," Garrett replied. Penelope looked down at her hands, clearly disagreeing with this conclusion, and he knew she was right. But his father's plan had to be followed. "It is my most devout desire that you wear the parure that I bought to celebrate James' birth."

She looked up in shock. "The emeralds?"

"The very ones." He watched her surprise change to confusion, then doubt. He averted his gaze before she could be fearful, for he knew his resolve would vanish then.

"Of course, I will wear them if you wish it," she said finally.

"And you will need a new dress," he continued. "I insist upon it. We will go this very day to the dressmaker to ensure that she has sufficient time."

"But I do not need a dress…"

He waved off this objection. "I will not hear a protest, Philomena." He spoke more loudly now, in case the footmen or driver could hear them. "Time was you loved nothing better than to buy a new dress, save to attend a ball in splendor." He smiled at her, hating the sight of her uncertainty. "I would see you garbed in splendor once again."

Her lips parted, then she closed them again, her expression turning resolute. She sat straighter and pulled her hand from his grasp, clearly understanding his implication. "Of course, sir," she said, her voice hard. "Your every request is as my command."

And Garrett felt as if he had been slapped.

~

WHAT A FOOL PENELOPE WAS. She had believed Garrett to be a gentleman. How dare he imply that she was the thief, or knew more of the missing pearls than she did? How dare he insist that she wear the parure to prove her innocence? She would be as bait to the thief and Garrett knew it well.

Yet he did not care.

It seemed he was a scoundrel of an entirely different variety than she had believed.

Penelope had known that she would not be able to remain at Arlingview House without a price of some kind, but she had assumed it would be fulfilling the duties of mistress of the house.

It was rare for her to be angry, but she was furious to be so maligned—and after she had confided the truth in him, as well.

She was sufficiently furious to do precisely as he asked—and not one bit more. Penelope would prove him mistaken about her, then she would leave his house and never see him again.

Though she suspected she would be the one to feel that punishment more keenly.

Wretched man!

~

At Carruthers & Carruthers, Garrett chose a book absently, watching Penelope chat with the shopgirl. The third volume of the novel she was reading had been set aside for her, so she was quick about her business. They were in the carriage again when he noticed that there was a piece of paper concealed in the volume she had collected.

Was this how she communicated with her accomplice? He supposed the matter could be arranged with a coin to the shopgirl.

It would also explain her vexation with him.

They rode in silence, a decided gap between them, then arrived at the dressmaker's shop. Garrett handed her out of the carriage, noting that she left the book on the seat. He made to close the door before hesitating for a moment. "My lady, what is the date today?"

"It is the third of February." She spoke crisply, a sure sign that she was annoyed.

Garrett grimaced, as if surprised. "I have an errand which must be attended this day, one I had almost forgotten. I will be only a few moments. Please consider a silk in green or gold, and I will join you shortly to make the final choice." He bowed over her hand. "Do forgive me, Philomena."

Her lips were tight when she surveyed him. "You need not return at all if you have pressing business."

Garrett smiled at her, noting how her eyes snapped.

"But I will. I promised my opinion and so you shall have it." He kissed her hand then returned to the carriage. He watched her enter the shop, then rapped on the roof. "Once around the block will suffice, Watkins," he said, then removed the piece of paper from the book.

An excerpt from the Ladies' Essential Guide to the Art of Seduction

Garrett frowned at these unlikely words, then his eyes widened as he read on.

Upon the merit of the chase...

What the Devil? He felt his astonishment rise as he read the enclosed advice, then could make no sense of it.

Penelope sought advice on how to seduce him? The notion was both wicked and enticing. Had this been her intended means of distracting him from the thief's antics? If so, she had succeeded admirably.

Garrett read the counsel again, both titillated and confused.

But she had just asked him to find her a husband. Did she intend to seduce another man entirely? That thought was entirely unwelcome, which was utterly unfair.

Truly, the more he learned about his wife's sister, the more puzzled—and intrigued—Garrett became. How could he instinctively trust a woman who was such an enigma? Or was that an indication of her skill with deceit?

CHAPTER 11

They returned to the house in time for tea, but the marquis excused himself, claiming a prior commitment. Once the menus were reviewed with Mrs. West, Penelope found herself at loose ends. There was little to be gained in stewing over the excursion to the theatre or Garrett's evident distrust. Instead, she opened the novel she had collected from Carruthers & Carruthers. Once again, there was a handwritten note secured within it, but this one had a title, as if it had been copied from a book.

An excerpt from the Ladies' Essential Guide to the Art of Seduction

Upon the merit of the chase...

It is an established fact that men appreciate a victory more if triumph is not readily won. A woman who surrenders her favors quickly will often be forgotten with a speed that astonishes. In contrast, a woman who teases and tempts, withholding her attention at intervals and the prize of her surrender, will strengthen the ardor of her suitor. By the time this fortunate man has earned her capitulation, he will be more apt to linger and savor his success.

There is an art to ensuring the chase satisfies both parties, an advance and retreat reminiscent of a duel between those of almost equal skill. Thrust and parry, advance and retreat, the longer the contest endures, the more satisfying the win. So it is in matters of love—an easy conquest is readily discarded, but one that requires all the effort of the triumphant fighter is a success to be cherished. Do not surrender readily to the touch of any man, no matter how deep your desire for him, lest you, too, be assumed to be readily won and thus not worth the earning.

What a remarkable passage.

Was it intended for her? Penelope had the strange sense that someone had witnessed her departure from the ballroom with Garrett, and had not only recognized her but knew her identity. The hair prickled on the back of her neck for she felt revealed. Worse, that person disapproved of her choice to accompany Harlequin to the garden.

But that could not be.

Still, it was unsettling to receive this counsel in this moment. If nothing else, it was a reminder that she should not capitulate to Garrett's touch, no matter how she was tempted.

She was not Philomena. She was not his wife, and he knew it. The man had said himself that her favors were not his to claim.

She would treat him as an indifferent stranger might. That was the only safe course.

If she had not been so vexed with him for insisting that she wear the emeralds, Penelope might have struggled to follow that course. When the man bent his attention upon her, every sane thought abandoned her.

When he kissed her, she could only melt in his embrace. When he touched her…

But he had vowed he would not do as much again.

She should be glad of his resolve, but Penelope felt herself to be in a tangle of emotion. Garrett stirred her as no other man had ever done, but he was her sister's husband. She had confessed the truth to him, and he had shared a truth with her, but still he did not trust her. He defended her honor, yet swore he would not touch her again. As grateful as she was for the chance to remain at Arlingview House until her birthday, Penelope wanted more.

Perhaps she truly became more like her sister, no longer satisfied with half-measures or the crumbs from the marquis' table. She should know that such wishes were not destined to come true.

Perhaps this counsel, even if supplied by coincidence, was an apt reminder for her so long as she remained in Garrett's home.

~

PENELOPE DID NOT SEE Garrett again on Monday, though she heard his return home early Tuesday morning. He was absent from luncheon on Tuesday, which could only leave her wondering whether his confession was true at all. The man certainly kept the habits of a wastrel. She dismissed him from her thoughts with some effort and departed for the meeting of the duke's charity for war veterans.

The marquis returned home close to dawn on Wednesday, singing a scandalous ditty with such gusto that his arrival could not be overlooked. It was clear from this that his assertion to her was a falsehood. He did not come up the stairs, though, for Penelope listened at the door. It seemed he was in the library. She descended to luncheon with some trepidation of what she might discover, but the library door was securely closed.

There was a letter from Mr. Blakewell but she left it in the salver until she had eaten her soup. It was leek and potato, one of her favorites, but she barely tasted it. Bracing herself for the worst, she opened the letter, only to gasp aloud.

> *Dear Lady Arlingview—*
>
> *I hope that you do not find this missive overly forthright on my part, but after your concern of last Friday, I feel compelled to advise you of a significant—and perhaps dire— change in the marquis' habits. His choices seem to have taken a turn for the worse, which may have implications for more than his fortune. I have heard this very morning that he fought a duel some hours ago...*

A duel? The man had fought a duel?

It was too much to be ignored. Penelope impulsively rose from the table and crossed to the library, rapping upon the door and opening it before her courage faded. The marquis was sitting in the leather chair before the fire, attired in only his breeches and boots. The sight of his bare chest reminded Penelope of the feel of his arms around her, yet she could not tear her gaze away. His valet, Wharton, was bandaging his upper arm and there was blood in the bowl of water at the valet's feet.

Penelope gripped the back of the chair in closest proximity. It was true!

"Good day, my lady," the marquis said with a cool smile. "I regret that I am indisposed and was unable to join you for luncheon." His blackened eye had changed hue since she had seen him last. Though parts of the bruise were still purple, the eye was less swollen. There were tinges of green and yellow around his eye, which only made him look less reputable than she hoped him to be.

"A duel," she said.

He did not appear to be besotted and she could not smell brandy. Did men agree to fight duels when they were sober and in their right thinking? If so, she could not imagine why that might be.

"A duel," he agreed mildly, checking the bandage. He thanked his valet, who gathered the cloths and bowl of water, bowing before he departed. Penelope waited until the door closed behind him.

"How badly are you injured?" she asked in a whisper.

He sat back in his chair to survey her, that infuriating smile playing upon his lips. Goodness, but he was a handsome creature. The weight of his gaze made her heart flutter with predictable ease. "Do you fear for my welfare, Penelope?" he asked softly.

"Do not say that!" she hissed and he chuckled.

"Whyever not? We are alone with no secrets between us." He lifted a brow. "Or are there secrets you have not yet confessed?'

Her heart rose to her throat, but he could not know.

"And what of you?" she demanded in a whisper. "You say you are not a rakehell, but come home at dawn. Your eye is only beginning to heal when I hear that you fought a duel. How could you be so cavalier with your own welfare?"

Her outrage seemed only to amuse him. "How did you know?"

She shook the letter. "Mr. Blakewell wrote to me of the matter. I hoped he was mistaken."

"But he was not." Garrett surveyed her and, to Penelope's surprise, the man appeared to be amused. "I confess it is a novelty to have anyone be concerned for my welfare. It is doubly a surprise to find that individual to be one with so little connection to me."

"How can you say as much?" Indignation took her across the floor at that. "I live in your house. I tend to your obligations. I endeavor to care for your sons."

"Ah, so it is a matter of responsibility, not that you hold me in any affection at all." His tone was teasing, but the words silenced Penelope completely.

Surely he had not discerned her last secret?

He was watching her, his eyes bright, but she evaded his gaze. He was trying to don his shirt, but winced as he stretched behind himself for the second sleeve, which granted her the perfect excuse. Penelope put down the letter and held his shirt for him, though the move put her in close proximity to him. Her mouth went dry when he looked up at her, his gaze dark.

He was the hunter again, yet she did not wish to flee.

She swallowed and felt her flush rise.

"I thank you," Garrett said in a low murmur, sitting back in his chair. His lips tightened as if he was in pain.

"You are hurt," she said, her tone accusing.

"A scratch, no more and no less. It will heal within the week."

"And your opponent?" Penelope sat on the ottoman before him.

Garrett laughed. "Very good, my lady. You ask the noble question this time."

Penelope found herself blushing.

Garrett sighed. "The Earl of Queenston may have a limp from this day forward, but he will not make that assertion again." He appeared to be supremely unconcerned and leaned forward to reach for a cup set on the table beside him. The contents steamed and Penelope realized it was strong tea.

She found him smiling at her when she looked up. "You are surprised?"

"I thought you might have brandy, sir."

"Sir," he echoed after he sipped, them put the cup back in its saucer. "Have you forgotten my name again? You have not uttered it since our visit to the dressmaker."

"Of course, I have not forgotten," she said, feeling her color rise. "I thought it inappropriate. And I have not been in your company since then."

"You are now," he said, an obvious invitation.

Penelope took a breath. "Garrett." His name felt like heaven on her tongue, audacious and intimate, and their gazes clung for a long moment.

With an effort, she looked down at her hands. "Why did you fight him again? Surely not over the same difference of opinion?"

"The very one," Garrett said, fixing her with a look. "And yet again, I could not allow the insult to pass. It appears to be a malady of mine, with regards to this particular lady. I regret that her identity may be guessed as a result."

"But you could have been killed!"

"The Earl of Queenston is a notoriously bad shot, and I am a very good one, but yes, the possibility did exist." He studied her and sipped his tea. "I thought it might please you that I defended your honor."

"Again," she felt compelled to note.

"Again." He inclined his head, waiting for her reply.

"It does," she had to admit. "Who would not be glad of a champion?" She waited for Garrett to smile. "But it also concerns me that you would take such a risk for the sake of appearances. I will be revealed as a liar soon enough."

His gaze darkened. "And yet the Earl of Queenston is not a suitor I would send to your door."

"I thank you for that." Her voice was almost a whisper and they stared at each other, their gazes clinging as a heat grew between them.

How Penelope wished in that moment that matters might have been different, that there had never been a deception, that he was not her sister's husband, that she might find such a man for herself—no, she wished that this man might care for her. Even though she knew that to be unreasonable, still she could not wholly discard the notion. The fire crackled and Penelope did not wish to look away. She would have preferred that this moment continue forever, though she knew it could not.

Then Garrett rose to his feet and she hated that he winced with the effort. He went to a bookshelf, obviously knowing precisely what he sought. The library was so well stocked that Penelope had never investigated all the titles—indeed, she felt that she trespassed in his domain when she ventured to borrow even one. He pulled a book from the shelf and smiled at it, then offered it to her when he returned to her side.

It was an early edition of *Marmion* by Sir Walter Scott.

"Oh! I had no notion this book was here," Penelope said with pleasure.

"You have read it?"

"Many times. It is a highly satisfying story."

"Which part is your favorite?" Garrett asked, his expression watchful.

Penelope's cheeks heated. "I could not say."

Garrett laughed as he settled into his chair again. "When you look like that, Penelope, I must know the truth. I promise not to share your confession with another."

It was enough that he would know, but she reminded herself that he would not care. "When Lochivar steals his beloved away from her own wedding, of course."

He smiled, but his expression was not mocking. It was almost tender.

"Doubtless, you think me a foolish romantic," she said quickly.

"There is nothing foolish about romance, my lady," Garrett said with resolve. "But an abiding love is assuredly rare." He frowned as he considered the book. "I bought this volume as a peace offering, when it was newly published. I had not read it, but it was well reviewed, and though Philomena was not a great reader, I thought we might enjoy it together." He paused and Penelope had a sudden inkling of why he had hoped Philomena might show a love of reading. She held her tongue, though. "Instead, there was that argument, and I never offered the book. It has been here all this time."

"The argument," she said when he did not continue. "She never told me of it."

He nodded. "That is probably best. It was a great row with many unkind things said." He tapped his hand on the arm of the chair, watching it idly. "I had never been so furious in my life."

"She warned me of your temper."

"And fairly so. I was livid with her." He lifted his gaze to hers. "Yet she was unrepentant."

"What had she done?" Penelope asked in a whisper, but Garrett shook his head.

"It is all in the past, and I would not disparage her memory with my view of the matter. It is over and nothing can change that." He seemed saddened by this and Penelope feared then that Philomena had broken her husband's heart. She recalled those last days and the decision that had brought her sister to death's door, and wondered whether it had been the first time Philomena had made that choice.

She hated that she did not know.

Penelope offered the book to Garrett so he could replace it on the shelf, but he shook his head.

"I would give it to you," he said. "For it seems an apt choice in the circumstance."

"How so?" she asked, confused.

"*Oh, what a tangled web we weave, when first we practice to deceive*," he said, quoting from the volume in question. He did not even seem to blink as he watched her. "I have kept secrets from you, my lady, just as you kept secrets from me."

It was true enough.

Penelope looked down at the book and stroked the leather cover with one hand. "I thank you for the book," she said, her voice husky. "I will treasure it."

"And I will be glad it is in the possession of one who appreciates it," Garret said, then rose to his feet. He looked tired in that moment, and she feared the strain of his injuries. "If you will excuse me, I must change my linen. Be assured, my lady, that I regret nothing more than the loss of my temper that day. If I could recall the words said in anger, I would have done as much a thousand times." She looked up at him as he bowed to her, then he left the library.

What exactly had that argument been about?

Who had been the father of the child Philomena lost at the end?

And what had her sister done? Penelope had always had the definite sense that more than nature took its course at Arlingview Manor. She should have asked then but she had been arguing with her sister about the future.

But Philomena was dead, taking her secrets to the grave, and there was no one left to ask. Penelope suspected that Garrett did not even know all of what Philomena had done.

Oh! Sara Underwood, Philomena's lady's maid, might know. Philomena had trusted that woman completely, and Underwood had ensured the success of Penelope's ruse. Underwood had left service a year later to tend her ailing mother, but Penelope sent her a gift each Christmas and had her address.

She hastened to write a letter to Underwood before her afternoon appointments, hoping the former lady's maid would reply soon.

As PLANNED, the family went to the theatre on Friday night at the duke's behest. The performance was to be Shakespeare's *Much Ado About Nothing* and Garrett hoped mightily that it might prove to be a portentous choice. He had wrestled with the decision to have Penelope wear the emeralds, but the plan was made and his father was adamant. His sole argument against the plan was that his instincts warned against it, but his father would hear none of that. The jewel thief had to be caught and in that, Garrett agreed. Indeed, the duke had jested that the lady clearly had a protector already, teasing Garrett about his blackened eye.

At least, Lord Queenston had the wits to keep his distance for the rest of the week.

On the evening in question, Penelope was radiant in the green silk dress. The hue was perfect both to highlight the emeralds and to draw attention to the clear green of her eyes. When she appeared to descend the stairs, Garrett stood at the base, admiring her and not caring who knew. His perusal made her color rise predictably but that only made her more alluring. Her slippers matched the darkest shade of green in the dress, her gloves were palest ivory, her hair was coiled up to provide a perch for the emerald tiara. He caught a glimpse of her sheer stockings as she approached him and her smile made his heart leap.

"Your vest is of the same embroidered silk," she said with real pleasure and he felt a cur that he was part of any scheme that might imperil her.

He had to ensure her safety above all.

He kissed her hand. "There should be no doubt that we are together." He wrapped her in her cloak of white velvet, then led her to the door. His father's carriage had arrived and happy greetings were exchanged. Garrett found himself beside Christopher, his father seated opposite and beaming with satisfaction to have a lady on each side.

There was a crush at the theatre, and the duke soon disappeared into the crowd as he greeted old friends. Garrett and Christopher ushered the ladies to their box, and Garrett felt his agitation rise. There were so many people. He was reminded of the ball at Rutherford House and began to fear that the villain might succeed again.

He felt that Penelope was horribly exposed when his father insisted that she and Caroline sit with him at the front of the box. Penelope sat very straight, her hands folded tightly together in her lap, and he feared that she understood her own risk. She had guessed that he did not fully confide in her and he wished this evening might be over so he could share the details with her.

What if his father's theory was wrong?

The lights dimmed and the curtain opened, a patter of applause greeting the first appearance of the actors, and the merry war between Benedict and Beatrice resumed.

Garrett, however, watched the audience and those moving, searching for any actions that might be suspicious.

He spied Esmeralda Ballantyne in a box with a more

commanding view than the duke's. She appeared to be alone, which was unexpected. She blew him a kiss, then beckoned to him, and he wondered what she wished to share.

He left the box quietly just before intermission, assured that his father and Christopher would remain with the ladies.

~

Where had Garrett gone?

Penelope turned from the performance to realize he had vanished from the box. Christopher seemed to realize as much in the same moment, for he also vanished, presumably in pursuit of his brother.

Perhaps they went for refreshments, hoping to avoid the line at intermission.

"Who is that woman?" Caroline asked with a touch to Penelope's arm. "I've never seen anyone so very beautiful."

Penelope followed her gaze to another box, just as Garrett appeared there. He looked both elegant and virile in evening attire and she simply appreciated the view for a moment before noting the lady who greeted him so prettily. She had to be the woman Caroline meant, for she was remarkably lovely. Her coloring was not so different from Penelope's own, but she was more lushly curved—and evidently more inclined to display her natural blessings.

Her dark blue velvet dress had a low decolletage and her skin was flawlessly creamy. Her lips were ruddy and she laughed heartily at some comment Garrett made.

She had been dressed as Leda and the swan at the masquerade! Penelope recognized her smile and her laugh.

A pang shot through Penelope at Garrett's smile of satisfaction. Obviously he was pleased to be in the lady's company. Christopher appeared then, apparently demanding an introduction, for Garrett gestured to him and the woman in turn. He leaned toward the woman to speak to her earnestly as Christopher listened. She took Garrett's arm in an overly familiar way.

"That is Esmeralda Ballantyne," the duke provided, rising to his feet. "The famous courtesan." He lifted his quizzing glass and trained it upon the lady in question. "And she is a beauty, to be sure. Excuse me, ladies. I have need of an introduction of my own." With that, the older man left the box, tweaking the ends of his moustache to perfection.

Caroline and Penelope exchanged a glance. "A courtesan?" Penelope said, noting how Esmeralda held Garrett's arm in a familiar way.

"Oh, yes!" Caroline said. "We've heard the most scandalous rumors of her seductions and intrigues. Christopher was quite resolved to meet her."

"And so he has," Penelope said lightly.

Christopher looked back toward the box then, as if fully aware that his wife was watching, and even from a distance, the mischievous delight in his expression was more than clear.

Caroline laughed. "I owe him a boon, the wretch, and he knows it."

"How so?"

"Oh, I told him that a respectable married man from the country would never manage to even meet such a notorious woman, and he made me a wager that he could do it." She gasped and Penelope looked again, just in time to see Esmeralda press a kiss to Christopher's cheek. He clutched his heart and rolled his eyes, and she could barely hear the courtesan's throaty laughter.

"He did not confide until later that the deed was as good as done, since Garrett knows her."

Penelope's heart sank. "Indeed?"

"Oh, Esmeralda has been named as Garrett's mistress for years," Caroline said with confidence, then she gasped, raising a hand to her lips as she stared at Penelope in horror. "Oh, I do apologize. I was sure you knew."

"Of course, I knew," Penelope lied. She forced a smile. "My husband is a most notorious rake, after all."

Caroline's eyes widened and she leaned closer. "But I thought that was a ruse," she whispered, her gaze searching Penelope's own.

"A ruse?"

"Oh, I should hold my tongue," Caroline said, blushing furiously. "I have already revealed too much and Christopher will be vexed with me. What do you think of the play?"

What else did Caroline know that Penelope did not?

She was determined to find out, and that before the gentlemen returned.

CHAPTER 12

"I know where Lady Caroline's pearls are," Esmeralda whispered to Garrett when she kissed his cheek in greeting. "Do not show any sign of surprise. It would be better if you appear to be besotted with me."

"I thought that was always your preference," he said quietly and her brows rose.

"But on this night, I am watched and if it is guessed that I have revealed any detail, matters will not go well for me."

"Watched by whom?" Garrett asked, his gaze bright.

"I know the thief. I knew him years ago in Paris, much to my own detriment, and he sought me out here."

"Where is he?"

"Here, tonight, in search of your wife's emeralds." Esmeralda fixed a look upon him. "How could you treat her thus?"

"She had the pearls…"

"Because he put them in her reticule," the courtesan said with impatience. "I saw him bump into your wife when you were leading her to the terrace. I wager he did as much since his disguise was as a tall woman in black." She inhaled. "A most unattractive lady in black, but evidently he hoped to divert attention from himself while he escaped."

Garrett realized that the thief had followed Penelope back to Arlingview House and ransacked her room in search of the pearls. He must have lingered in the alley to consider his course and seen Garrett lock them away through the windows of the library. Then, of course, he had stolen them outright.

"But what of the earlier thefts?" he asked.

"Rubies shaped as fruit and a pearl bracelet?" Esmeralda asked. "He visited every goldsmith in London in an attempt to sell them and is bitter about the low price he received. He complained that he even went as far as Clapham without success."

Penelope had no accomplice. She was innocent.

Esmeralda continued. "Of course, even a jeweller of no repute would fear that such distinctive pieces might be recognized. I have told him to go to Paris to sell the pearls but would see him foiled." She fixed him with a look. "He has lingered, tempted by the tale of the emerald parure."

Garrett's heart skipped. "He is here?"

"You will never find him." Esmeralda spoke with disdain. "The man is like a rat in his ability to vanish."

"But where are the pearls now?"

Esmeralda shook her head, then laughed as if he had made a jest. "You cannot simply take them. He watches too closely. They must be replaced with a copy, if one can be made in time."

"Christopher already has one," Garrett said just as his brother appeared. He made introductions, then added. "Miss Ballantyne knows the location of the pearls."

Christopher's eyes lit. "Have you a scheme to regain them?"

"They must be exchanged with the copy first," Esmeralda said.

"I can collect it tomorrow," Christopher said. "Shall I call upon you?"

"No." Esmeralda shook her head. "He must have no inkling that I plot against him."

"Oh, this is exciting," Christopher said. "We might all be spies!" Garrett had time to glare at him before the duke appeared.

"Mademoiselle!" the older man said with gusto, twirling his moustache. "I have long sought the honor of making your acquaintance." He bowed low over Esmeralda's hand, pressing a kiss to its back. "You are even more lovely than your reputation implies. Might you be interested in a glass of wine?"

"Not at the moment, your grace, but do not let me interfere with your pleasure." She smiled at Garrett and her hint that she wished to be alone with him was taken by his father and brother. Those two departed as Esmeralda leaned closer. "Do you not intend a small dinner party to celebrate your brother's arrival in town?"

Garrett blinked that she knew of this, then balked at her suggestion. "Tomorrow evening, they come to dine, but you cannot be added to the party. Esmeralda, you know that I cannot expect my wife to entertain a courtesan."

Esmeralda laughed. "Your respectable wife will not have to endure such a scandalous situation," she said, her eyes dancing. "I will send a friend to collect the copy. You may expect Mrs. Oliver."

"Mrs. Oliver?"

"A widow recently returned to town, not an aristocrat but with some connections." Esmeralda's smile hinted that she knew more than this about the lady in question.

"But how can you be certain of her availability?"

Again, Esmeralda laughed. "I know her very well," she said, which explained nothing at all. "When you escort my friend to her residence, the exchange can be made in the carriage, without witnesses."

"And the pearls?"

"I will retrieve them for your brother, if it is the last deed I do." Esmeralda spoke with uncommon resolve and Garrett believed her.

"Dinner at Arlingview House tomorrow night then," Garrett said. "I will ensure that all is arranged."

"Tell no one of the details," Esmeralda advised. "The cur has ears everywhere."

Garrett nodded reluctant agreement. "Describe him to me."

She shook her head. "There is no point. He is cunning with disguise. He is tall and slender, and often pretends to be a woman. Beyond that, he could change any detail."

Garrett looked back to his father's box in time to see his father and brother appear there. Penelope was not alone. He could seize the opportunity to seek the thief.

The villain was here, after all.

"THE PLAY IS ARTFULLY PERFORMED," Penelope said to Caroline. "But like so many of Shakespeare's comedies, it is about secrets and disguises."

Caroline averted her gaze. "Oh, they are leaving her box. I do hope they bring wine."

Penelope leaned closer. "Tell me, please, Caroline. Why do you think that Garrett only pretends to be a rakehell?"

The other woman looked uncomfortable. "I should not say."

"Please!"

"Because he was a spy during the war. He pretended to be a wastrel to have the ability to go wherever he desired and watch whoever he must," Caroline said, glancing over her shoulder. The men were no longer looking their way, the duke having joined that party. "That part must be true. Christopher is ever so proud of him." She appealed to Penelope. "I was sure you knew. I was sure you were one person to whom I could safely mention it."

A spy? Penelope had to admit that such an endeavor would explain Garrett's many absences, as well as his return to Arlingview House since the end of the war. It was a romantic notion of great appeal, but with only Caroline's note of a rumor, it was hardly a certainty. Indeed, being a rake would explain his absences equally well.

But he had told her he was not a rake.

What was the truth?

"A wastrel must have a mistress, if not two or three," Caroline continued with a confidence Penelope did not share. "Never mind a spy! Perhaps that too is a ruse." She sighed. "How terribly exciting to be married to such a man! You are fortunate indeed, Philomena."

Penelope was far less certain of that. Even as she watched, the courtesan leaned closer to Garrett so that her breast was against his upper arm. He smiled down at her, evidently quite content with his situation and the view, and Esmeralda stretched up to whisper in his ear. She had his undivided attention, to the point that Christopher sighed dramatically and turned away. The duke patted him on the shoulder and they left as one. Garrett and Esmeralda did not even notice their departure, so enthralled were they with each other.

"Father has a taste for wine," Christopher said, appearing at the back of the box. "Come with me, Caroline, and I will try to introduce you to someone notorious."

Caroline laughed with delight. "Will you excuse me, Philomena? I simply must hear whatever he means to tell me about Miss Ballantyne."

"And pay him that boon," Penelope managed to jest.

"Indeed." Her brows rose. "I will see him repaid for welcoming the attentions of a notorious courtesan, even for a moment." And then she was gone in a swirl of silk, leaving Penelope wondering what it would be like to be utterly in love with one's husband, and have complete confidence in his fidelity.

She sought a glimpse of Garrett again, but both he and Esmeralda had left her box. Penelope used her opera glasses to survey the crowd and spied Esmeralda laughing at the comments of another man, perhaps Lord Standish. She spotted the duke, expounding some notion with a gentleman with a cane whose face Penelope could not see. Was that Garrett with Lady Augusta Rutherford? That woman had two ostrich feathers in her hair and they bobbed as she spoke with great animation. Her companion *was* Garrett. Though he had his back turned to Penelope, but she would have known him anywhere. She leaned a little to the right to better observe him, then caught her breath when she felt a blade dig in her back.

"Remain quiet and give me the emeralds," commanded a man with a raspy voice. Was he French or pretending to be? She started to glance over her shoulder, but the knife point dug a little deeper into her back. Penelope gasped as she felt a warm trickle of blood. "Do not turn around," he instructed. "You will give no sign of my presence. Smile. Use your glasses. And give the emeralds to me with all haste. I will show no hesitation in cutting you, *madame*."

The villain was crouched behind her and Penelope

doubted that anyone could see him. He might have been visible to anyone in either of the neighboring boxes, but all of those patrons had left their boxes in search of refreshment. Penelope was quite alone after Caroline's departure.

She lifted her glasses again, as if nothing was amiss, and wondered what she could do to defend herself. Her hand shook just a little as she pretended to look through the glasses.

"I cannot unfasten the necklace with one hand," she murmured, keeping her tone calm and reasonable as she gave every appearance of continuing to survey the crowd.

"Then put down the glasses. Or drop them and bend to retrieve them," the villain instructed. "Do not try to be clever, madame, and do not delay."

She would have to trick him somehow. There was a fortune in emeralds around her neck and she would not surrender them readily.

"I think you err in this strategy," she said mildly.

"My choices are not for you to judge," he snarled. "Quickly!"

"First you must tell me," she said, ensuring she sounded more indifferent than she was. "How did the pearls come to be in my reticule?"

"I put them there, of course. I had been spotted leaving the guest bedroom and knew they would be looking for a tall woman in a black dress."

"So you implicated me."

"And followed you to your home. I almost lost the pearls, but I am more clever than you. The emeralds. Now!"

Penelope looked one last time for Garrett and saw him turn toward her. He glanced up and she let alarm show in her expression before she composed her features again. He straightened a little, then she gasped and dropped the opera glasses, certain he would reach her shortly.

She chose to trust him, despite appearances. He had defended her before and she chose to believe that he would do as much again.

If nothing else, he would defend the emeralds.

Penelope reached for the opera glasses. When her fingers brushed against them, she pushed them hard to the other side of the box. "How clumsy of me," she said, then dove after them.

The move ensured that the blade was no longer against her skin. She spun and kicked at her assailant before he realized her feat. She could not see his face for he wore a black domino mask, but his hair was dark —unless he also wore a wig—and his clothing was both dark and nondescript.

He swore and seized her ankle, drawing her inexorably closer. She was on the floor of the box and no one could see her, yet she could not rise because of his grip. "Quickly!" he ordered.

Penelope reached for the clasp of the emerald necklace, pretending it was more difficult to unfasten than it was.

"You are too slow!"

"I am shaking in fear, sir," she said, ensuring that her voice trembled. The clasp opened in that moment and she gripped the two ends so the necklace so it appeared to still be fastened around her neck. "Have mercy."

"I have none. Give it to me!" The thief's lips tightened in fury and he slashed the blade across her calf, making Penelope gasp aloud in mingled surprise and pain. At his move, she dropped one end of the necklace and felt one end of the jewelled band slither toward her decolletage. On impulse, she released the other and let the gems slide between her breasts.

"Thief!" Garrett cried from welcome proximity. "A

thief is assaulting my wife!" He named the number of their box and there were footsteps in the corridor.

Her attacker swore and Penelope feared for a moment that he would snatch at her bodice to claim the gems. She scurried backward to put distance between them but found the rail of the box behind her.

"Who is the fiend?" cried someone in the throng below and a beacon of light shone across the box.

The thief swore again and bolted, leaving Penelope seated on the floor with her hand clasped over her bosom to keep the necklace from falling free. Her heart was racing and she was shaking in terror, the sight of the blood on her ruined stocking doing little to aid her composure.

"That way!" Christopher cried from some close point. "Stop him!"

A shadow fell across the entry and Penelope looked up with fear.

It was Garrett and the sight of him was enough to summon her tears of relief.

"My lady!" he murmured with such dismay that her tears fell free. He was on his knees before her in a heartbeat, gently dabbing at the wound on her calf with his handkerchief. "Is this the sum of it?" he asked, his words uncommonly hoarse as his gaze rose to hers. His eyes were vividly blue and his jaw was tight. She could not imagine his concern was feigned.

But then, the emerald necklace would appear to be gone to him.

His concern was solely for the gems.

~

MOST WOMEN GARRETT had known in his time would have wept or raged after such an attack, but Penelope only shed a few tears before regaining her composure.

She was not quite sitting on the floor of the box, her dress bunched around her knees, her stocking stained with blood. One slipper had fallen off and the emerald tiara was askew, her throat bare without the necklace. Her hand shook, though, as she reached to steady herself. He was impressed by her composure, then awed that she was his wife, at least for the moment.

He could not permit that situation to change.

He had almost lost her by failing to trust his own instincts. He would not make that error again.

"Are you injured beyond this?" he asked and to his relief, she shook her head.

She lifted her gaze to his. "I still have it all," she confessed in a whisper. She reached into her bodice and removed the necklace, presenting it to him as if it was the only prize of import.

Surely she could not imagine the safety of the jewels was his sole concern?

"I would surrender it all and more to ensure your welfare, my lady," Garrett said with heat. "I should never have agreed to this scheme and can only entreat your forgiveness." When her eyes widened, as if she was amazed, he lifted her to her feet and pulled her into his arms. She surrendered immediately, not only leaning her cheek against his chest but slipping her arm beneath his jacket and around his waist. He gathered her closer, grateful that matters had not gone even more awry. Once the necklace was fastened around her throat again, he cupped her nape in one hand and captured her mouth beneath his in a possessive kiss. He poured all of his relief into his embrace and he was awed when she kissed him back.

There was a rousing round of applause when she was visible to the crowd below again, and she was visibly startled by the attention.

"Forget them," Garrett counseled with a smile and

when her own tentative smile made her eyes light, he kissed her again.

"Gone," Christopher said, emerging suddenly into the box. "He vanished as if by magic."

Garrett broke their kiss but did not release Penelope. She was flushed now and he could still feel her slight tremble. She had been badly frightened, to be sure, and it was his own fault.

He should never have agreed to his father's scheme.

He looked up to meet the concern in Christopher's eyes, seeing Caroline behind him. She appeared to be dismayed but when she would have stepped past her husband to assist, Christopher touched her arm and she halted.

"He must have had a plan," Garrett said, then looked down at Penelope. "Did you recognize him?"

She shook her head. "He was masked." She frowned. "He had a French accent, but it might have been feigned. I think he was tall."

"I think our evening is at an end," Garrett said, wanting only to get Penelope home to safety. He turned to fetch her cloak and saw the blood on his own hand. It was only then that he saw the fresh blood on the back of her gown.

"He had a knife," she whispered. "But he only pricked me with it."

The amount of blood indicated that it was more than a prick, but Garrett was in no mood to dispute the matter with her. He wrapped her in her cloak with purposeful gestures, handed her reticule to her, then swept her into his arms to carry her out of the theatre.

"I will summon the carriage," Christopher said, helping Caroline with her cloak. The pair hastened past Garrett, reaching the exit ahead of him. The duke was already waiting for them outside, the carriage summoned. A crowd had gathered on the stairs and in the lobby but parted before Garrett, whispering avidly behind their fans.

"You will be the talk of the town, my lady," Garrett said, trying to make her smile.

"They have had more of a show than anticipated, to be sure." She glanced up at him. "You could put me down, sir."

"There is little chance of that," he murmured, tightening his grip around her. "I intend to keep you very close for the foreseeable future."

"That might prove inconvenient, sir."

"Not for me," he said then smiled down at her. "Indeed, I am looking forward to it."

Their gazes held and a welcome heat rose between them, one that fed his optimism for the future. He lifted Penelope into his father's carriage.

"We will remain," the duke said. "Caroline must see the rest of the play."

"And I will see what can be learned," Christopher added in an undertone. "Someone must have seen something."

"We can ask Haynesdale," the duke added and they stepped back.

When Garrett got into the carriage, Penelope looked so pale that he could not resist his urge to slip his arm around her and pull her closer. She did not fight his move, but leaned against him, one hand over his heart, seemingly glad of reassurance.

He had nearly lost her by failing to trust his own instincts. The realization had his arm tightening around her. "I should never have allowed it," he said roughly, then pulled back to look into her face. "I am so glad you are quick-witted," he said as the carriage lurched forward. In truth, he never wanted to let her go.

He realized in that moment that he loved Penelope, that her courage and her loyalty was what he had been seeking for the entire duration of his marriage. He realized then that she had one last secret, and knowing it meant that he was hers completely.

He could only hope to convince her of his own merit, and after this night's deeds, he would not blame her for thinking him unworthy.

"I am glad the thief did not succeed," she said and he heard that she was regaining her composure. "But what did you mean that you should not have allowed it?"

Garrett bowed his head, knowing he had to confess it all. "A trap was set for the thief after the loss of Caroline's pearls. I asked you to wear the emeralds to draw the thief's attention."

She watched him and he knew she was not surprised. "You intended for them to be stolen."

"It was hoped that an attempt would be made to do so, but I was to ensure its failure." He was determined to have the truth between them. "You guessed as much."

"I knew you did not trust me. I ceded to your plan that the situation might change."

It had. "It was believed that your family were behind the thefts. Thus, the assumption was that you would not be injured by your allies, making you the ideal one to tempt the thief." Garrett shook his head. "I should never have agreed and put you in peril. My instincts were to trust you, but I failed you in this."

"But you did not believe I was in peril." She spoke gently, granting him a forgiveness he did not deserve. "After all, Mr. Neilson knew something of the stolen gems."

"Evidently, the thief visited every goldsmith in the city, even venturing so far as Clapham, in an effort to sell them."

Penelope nodded, her thoughts hidden to him. "I can well understand your doubts," she said softly.

"What about this night? What will happen to the emeralds?"

"We will have Wrigley lock the parure in the safe as soon as we arrive home."

She frowned and shook her head. "No. We should set another trap."

"What is this?"

"The thief already knows where we live. Doubtless he will follow and seek another opportunity to claim them. They must be in my chamber and he must be seized when he tries to steal them."

Garrett's blood ran cold. "Penelope! No. I will not hear of you being at risk again."

She smiled at him, more serene than the suggestion merited. "But I will not be. I will retreat to another room, and you will await the villain in mine."

Garrett frowned as he considered her suggestion, then shook his head. "No. There is too much risk. If he is watching, he will see that the emeralds will be locked in the safe."

She looked up at him, an admiring glint in her eyes. "You appear to be most fierce, sir."

"I will take a reckoning from his hide if he is fool enough to attempt it. You will not be imperiled again, Penelope, not while I can defend you." Before she could argue with him, Garrett claimed her lips in a heartfelt kiss, needing to show how much he regretted his mistake.

They only parted when the carriage halted before the house, and both were breathless. Garrett carried Penelope into the house, despite her protests, and into the library. There he commanded that all the lamps be lit and the drapes left open. Wrigley brought the box for the parure and the emeralds were returned to it. Then Wrigley and two footmen took it to the safe, at Garrett's command, while he dispatched three more footmen to stand watch outside the house. Once the gems were secure, he carried Penelope to her own chamber, hating the prospect of leaving her alone.

"You could come to me this night," he said softly. Her gaze flicked to him and then away, and she shook her head.

"I thank you, sir, but I think not." She was prim, which surprised him, for her kiss had been sweet. But she would not meet his gaze and he feared that his doubt had hurt her feelings. It was not an unjust reaction and Garrett was resolved to win her trust and affection anew.

He knew it would not happen quickly.

He also knew he would not sleep that night, for he would be vigilant in Penelope's defense.

CHAPTER 13

*P*enelope did not sleep.

It was not for fear of the thief's return. She stared at the ceiling and considered all that Caroline had said. Had Garrett been a spy? She must ask him, though she had no notion whether he would confess the truth to her. Was Miss Ballantyne his mistress? She could not imagine that he was a man to forgo sensual satisfaction and the courtesan was beautiful. Her manner to Garrett had certainly been welcoming, and hinted at intimacy.

Penelope had heard the carriage leave long after she had retired and could only wonder where Garrett had gone.

Perhaps she should not have taken the advice of that last missive. Perhaps she should have gone to his chamber and welcomed whatever might happen in his bed. She was unlikely to ever wed, thus no one would ever know of her transgression.

But she would never be certain that Garrett desired her, instead of an opportunity to seemingly be with her sister again. It was infinitely wiser to forgo a fleeting pleasure.

Even if she was very tempted to know his touch.

In a week, she would be back in Clapham again. There was a sorry notion. Perhaps she should return there on Friday, forgoing the celebration of her birthday at Arlingview House. It would not be very celebratory, after all, and her mother and sister would arrive for luncheon on Friday, on schedule. It might be better to save the expense of another carriage, even if it meant returning to Clapham one day sooner.

Penelope sighed and rolled over, knowing there would be no sleep for her this night.

GARRETT WAS EXHAUSTED the next morning, as a result of watching over Penelope all night, though there would be no rest for him as yet. He had dispatched the carriage the night before, sending a footman who wore his jacket for a ride around the town. His hope had been that his apparent absence might tempt the thief to approach the house, and he had awaited the villain, with no success.

He made only the briefest appearance at luncheon, taking heart that Penelope also seemed to be less than her usual self. Perhaps she missed him.

He could only hope as much.

"I neglected to mention last night that I invited another guest to dinner tonight," he said to her. "I hope it does not set your table off."

"Who have you invited?"

"A Mrs. Oliver."

Penelope put down her spoon. "Mrs. *Oliver?*"

Did she recognize the name?

How could that be?

Who was Mrs. Oliver, other than the confidante of Esmeralda?

"Yes, she is lately returned to town and a friend of a

friend. I thought she might be a good addition to the party." His explanation sounded impossibly feeble, but he had given Esmeralda his promise to confess no more.

Penelope appeared to be startled, but she hid her reaction so quickly that Garrett guessed the difficulty was the arrangement of the table settings. "Of course," she said, her words tight, and returned her attention to her soup.

"I mean to return the emeralds to the bank today," he said and she flicked him the barest glance. "If you will excuse me?"

"Of course." There was a formality to her words, but Garrett had a plan to win the lady's favor once more.

First, this evening had to be behind them.

~

MRS. OLIVER.

How and why Garrett would invite that horrible woman to dinner was a puzzle Penelope could not solve. She hoped it might be a different Mrs. Oliver than the one she had met at Carruthers & Carruthers, but was proven to be wrong when the clock chimed eight.

The very same woman emerged from a hack, crooked and hunched, leaning on a cane and dressed in the most awful dress. Her hat was broad-brimmed and swathed in veils of indeterminate hue, and she declined to remove it when she entered the house. She scratched at the back of her wig with a vigor that did little to encourage the possibility that she was clean, and studied the house interior with the sharp gaze of a tax assessor. She tapped her cane on the rug in the foyer when she stepped upon it, then peered at it.

"Aubusson?" she asked Wrigley who could not disguise his affront.

"I believe so, my lady." The butler surveyed her. "Might I take your fur?" His expression revealed his lack of enthusiasm for that prospect, but Mrs. Oliver clutched the garment more closely.

"I might be cold," she said. "These old houses are draughty, after all. Good neighborhood, though." She rubbed her finger and thumb together. "Costly."

Wrigley inhaled sharply then took Caroline's wrap, the duke's carriage having arrived immediately after the hack.

Mrs. Oliver turned her attention upon Penelope, then cackled with satisfaction. "I know you!" she declared before they might be introduced. She marched toward Penelope with purpose and Penelope was aware of Garrett's curiosity.

"I believe our paths crossed at Carruthers & Carruthers' lending library," Penelope said. "Though we were not introduced. Did you obtain the book you desired?"

The older lady harrumphed, evidently no longer interested in that volume.

Penelope caught a glimpse of Caroline's alarm, then Garrett introduced everyone.

"I hope there is a decent joint for dinner," Mrs. Oliver said with gusto. "I have not eaten good beef in a fortnight." She marched into the drawing room, leaving Penelope blinking and Caroline striving to hide a smile. The duke appeared to be chortling to himself and Christopher was so solemn that he had to be hiding his thoughts. Garrett urged them all to follow Mrs. Oliver into the drawing room and Wrigley appeared with glasses of champagne.

"The devil's wine," Mrs. Oliver said with approval, then hesitated before accepting a glass. "Is it that cheap swill from Portugal? Or do you rebottle your own French wine from the cask?

"This vintage is from Épernay," Wrigley supplied, exuding disapproval though his expression remained impassive.

"Ha! Good." Mrs. Oliver seized a glass and made half its contents vanish before Wrigley finished serving the others. She waved the glass at him in search of a refill with a vigor that was alarming. "Fair enough, but I would have a good sherry next."

And so it continued through the entire meal. Penelope could not fathom why Garrett had invited the woman at all. She drank enormous volumes. She gobbled every delicacy set upon the table. She commented upon the weight of the cutlery and the quality of the dishes, upon the silk in the drapes and Caroline's dress. She was so vulgar that most of the party was reduced to silence—save the duke, who seemed to enjoy goading her on to greater excesses.

Garrett, to his credit, appeared to be startled by his guest and rightly so, to Penelope's thinking. What had been in his mind?

When the ladies retired to the drawing room, Penelope could only hope that the men would follow shortly. Mrs. Oliver belched as she rose from the table, laughing when a morsel of bread fell from her open mouth. She then plucked it off the cloth and gobbled it up before leaving the room. In the drawing room, she dropped into a chair near the fire so heavily that Penelope feared the piece of furniture might break. Mrs. Oliver laughed wickedly, the sound somehow familiar to Penelope, then proceeded to fall asleep.

Penelope turned to survey her.

That laugh. She had heard that laugh before.

And to fall asleep so suddenly. It was almost as if Mrs. Oliver wished to avoid conversation.

Or scrutiny.

Caroline met Penelope's gaze as she accepted a cup of tea. "Who is she?" she whispered.

Penelope shrugged, her gaze trailing to her unlikely guest. Mrs. Oliver began to snore loudly, prompting Caroline's giggle, but it was better than her conversation.

Penelope chose the closest chair to her guest and looked at her, curious about that laugh. The courtesan, Esmeralda Ballantyne, possessed a similarly throaty laugh, one that sounded both provocative and a little bit wicked. It was low, seductive even, and had seemed an unlikely sound for Mrs. Oliver to emit. A cackle would be more fitting, or a snort. Penelope stole glances at the lady in question, noting that her eyes slanted similarly to those of Miss Ballantyne. Perhaps she was an older relation.

Perhaps Garrett had invited her because his mistress had asked him to do so.

But why?

And why should his household be compelled to endure a woman, simply to please his mistress? It seemed most unlike him to be so callous. Penelope could not fathom the situation, but she had no opportunity to ask. The men joined the ladies promptly, much to her relief, but it seemed the brothers had a plan to depart again.

"I have told Christopher about that new play," Garrett said.

Penelope was surprised. To leave again after dinner was the choice of a man more interested in the distractions of the city than his own household. "You cannot mean to go out now."

"Whyever not?" he asked, his manner jovial even as he evaded her gaze. The man contrived something, to be sure, but Penelope had no notion what it might be.

"The allure of London summons us," his brother said with obvious anticipation. "I am the one to lead him astray and beg that you humor me."

Caroline's lips parted. "You intend to leave, as well?"

"What better chance will I ever have of being introduced to the city's pleasures?" Christopher said. "Garrett will be the best guide possible." He seemed to take note of his wife's disapproval. "Only one night, my dear. Indulge me, if you please."

"I will escort Caroline home," the duke offered gallantly and the two younger women exchanged a glance. It seemed they had no choice in the matter, for it had been arranged.

"Do not bankrupt us, then," Caroline said lightly.

Christopher laughed. "I might win us a fortune."

"I doubt as much," Penelope said. "I believe the house wins with reliability."

"There is a lady of wisdom," Garrett said with a smile.

"We will not be much later than one," Christopher said as he kissed Caroline's cheek.

"Or three," Garrett corrected.

"Father, are you prepared to leave?" Caroline asked the duke, who offered his arm to her.

"Of course, my dear."

Penelope cleared her throat and subtly indicated the snoring Mrs. Oliver. "Perhaps your guest might like an escort home."

"An excellent notion," Garrett said, then gently nudged the older lady's elbow. Mrs. Oliver snorted and coughed, then cleared her throat as she sat up unsteadily. She looked around herself as if she was uncertain of her location. "Mrs. Oliver," he said. "Might my brother and I have the honor of seeing you home?"

"If there is no more brandy to be had, I might as well depart," she said, apparently disgruntled.

Penelope and Caroline's gazes met in silent agreement. Penelope knew the older woman had consumed the better part of half a bottle of brandy herself.

She had some difficulties rising to her feet, but Garrett took one elbow and Christopher the other. Between them, they hefted Mrs. Oliver out of her chair. Christopher seemed to be on the verge of laughter but Garrett was solemnly attentive.

She wondered whether she would ever know the truth of his choice.

Caroline laughed lightly as she watched the brothers' departure from the doorway. "Goodness!" she said. "She might tip the carriage." She turned to Philomena with sparkling eyes. "You must tell me who she is and why you invited her."

"I have no notion," Penelope admitted. "Garrett invited her."

Caroline appeared to be as perplexed as Philomena. She looked out the window again. "How very curious."

"Indeed," Penelope agreed. She saw then that the novel she had borrowed from the lending library had been moved. Had someone else been reading it? Or perhaps Caroline had taken a look at it. She picked it up, intending to replace it on the table where she always kept her borrowed books, and saw the tip of a piece of paper sticking out from between the pages. Caroline was busily donning her wrap and talking to the duke, so Philomena risked a peek.

It was another excerpt from *The Ladies' Essential Guide to the Art of Seduction*.

Her heart skipped but she closed the book quickly when Caroline turned. "Now, there is a hint!" Caroline said with a laugh. "Philomena would rather be reading. Come along, Father, and we will leave her to it."

"Of course, of course," that man said, giving Penelope a kiss on the cheek. "A lovely meal, my dear. Thank you for a most entertaining evening." His eyes twinkled and he twirled his moustache, then he strode for his waiting carriage. Caroline kissed Penelope's cheeks then hurried after him, chatting about the evening as she went.

When the door closed behind them, Penelope wilted. Wrigley was already setting matters to rights and knew his task better than she did. She took her book and retired to her chamber.

~

SOMETHING WAS AMISS.

Garrett had seen the change in Penelope's expression and knew she had realized some detail of importance. His instincts warned him not to leave her alone and this time, he would heed them.

His brother had already revealed the copy of the pearls. "I have them, Mrs. Oliver," he said.

"We must ensure that the copy is exact," Mrs. Oliver said briskly. Her voice had changed to a more familiar one and Garrett stared as she reached beneath the layers of clothing. Her gloved hand finally reappeared, clutching the necklace.

"You were wearing it?" Christopher demanded.

"What better way to ensure I knew its location at all times?" she asked, surrendering it to Garrett.

He held the two necklaces toward the light, marvelling at the exactitude of the copies. "It is an excellent replica," he said.

"The jeweller is said to be the best," Christopher agreed.

"Keep track of which is in which hand, lest they be exchanged inadvertently," Mrs. Oliver advised.

Christopher shook his head. "There is a mark on the replica, here beneath the clasp."

"It looks like a maker's mark."

"Except it is a very small jester. See?" Christopher offered his quizzing glass so Garrett could examine it.

"So tiny! What remarkable work."

Mrs. Oliver stretched out her gloved hand. "Give it here, and deliver me to Covent Garden, if you please. The stage door."

"Why does your voice sound familiar?" Christopher asked, and Mrs. Oliver laughed.

She laughed like Esmeralda Ballantyne.

She lifted her veils away, smiling at Garrett. "I believe we have met, my lord," she said and he saw the truth.

"Esmeralda!"

She raised a finger to silence him. "Tell no one. Take me to Covent Garden, please."

"Are you certain your identity will be hidden?" Garrett asked.

"There is no better place for it," she said, her tone grim.

"I would not have you take any risks," Christopher said but Esmeralda shook her head. She returned to the voice of Mrs. Oliver.

"My risks have all been taken already," she said with a cackle and Garrett wondered whether that was the truth. "Halt at the coffeehouses in Covent Garden first. You can say I asked to be taken there. It is easy to disappear in the throng. Plus no one there will tell of what they saw or did not see."

Garrett rapped on the roof of the cab. "Halt here," he said to the driver. "I must return home with haste." Christopher nodded and Mrs. Oliver watched as he alighted. "Take them to Covent Garden," he told the driver, who nodded and cracked his whip.

Then Garrett strode back down the street toward his

home. He was little more than a block away but felt an urgency that lent speed to his steps. His task was done, and he would be with Penelope again, with all haste.

Tonight, he would tell her all.

HAYNESDALE ORDERED the hack to stop a block from Garrett's townhouse. Though he would never admit as much to the lady in question, he had taken Esmeralda Ballantyne's criticism to heart. He had been walking as much as possible in order to rebuild the strength in his injured leg and could already feel the difference. Just as she had suggested, the improvement also had a beneficial effect upon his mood.

On this particular evening, though, the strategy undermined his other objectives. He had no sooner alighted from the cab than he saw a hack in front of Arlingview's home. Two men escorted a plump woman to the carriage and fairly hefted her into it. That had to be Garrett and his brother Christopher, and the woman had to be Mrs. Oliver.

Haynesdale shouted but the brothers did not hear him. They climbed into the cab and it set off at a brisk clip when he was still near the end of the block. The hack that had brought him this far was easing into the street but he lunged after it, shouting at the driver to halt.

"But this is where you asked to be taken, sir," the driver said.

"I have changed my mind."

"To my understanding, it is women who are cursed with that affliction."

Haynesdale nearly growled in irritation. "I would follow that cab."

"And you would be left far behind, given the speed you make with that cane."

Impertinence! "I would have you drive me in pursuit," he clarified.

"Then you will have to climb in, sir."

Haynesdale did precisely that and the driver clicked his tongue to his horse. The nag moved more slowly than the most ancient mule at Haynesdale's country estate.

"We must go more quickly," he said.

"It has been a long day for Parsnip," the driver said with supreme indifference. "She is tired, as you can see."

"I will pay you double if you do not lose sight of that carriage."

The driver whistled and the horse perked up its ears, trotting at such a crisp pace that Haynesdale knew the feint had been well-practiced.

It would be coin well-spent, though, if he finally cornered the elusive Mrs. Oliver.

That woman owed him more than one explanation.

An excerpt from the Ladies' Essential Guide to the Art of Seduction

Upon a timely gamble...

There comes a moment in many relations when it seems that love cannot triumph over a surfeit of trust and that all is destined to go awry. In such instance, the astute lady may rely upon the advantage known to shrewd champions of games of chance, that of knowing that not all risks are equal. It is very seldom that all proceeds according to plan or that all details are known at all times—the experienced practitioner of the hunt learns to rely upon her instinctive or intuitive understanding of which course to follow. It is possible to take a chance upon an encounter and not lose all. In fact, the very act of trusting one's partner, and surrendering to temptation as a result, can often lead to a union of hearts and minds, and even a very happy resolution.

I leave it to you, dear reader, to surmise when is the best moment to leap.

PENELOPE SAT at her dressing table, reading the note. This one had a definite resonance, as if it had been left for her by someone who fully understood matters between herself and Garrett. They had resolved many mysteries and made confessions to each other. Was it even possible to know all of another person's secrets? Was it advisable?

She eyed her own reflection. If Garrett came to her again, would she only be denying herself by turning him aside? In a week, their ways would part forever. Surely one night was worth the surrender of her principles. Given her chances of making a match, it was unlikely that anyone would ever know of her indiscretion, if there was one, and she did not wish to live out her life in ignorance. The pleasure he had offered her once had been nigh overwhelming.

Penelope wanted to know more.

That might make her a harlot but as she weighed the risk against the reward, Penelope could not find it in her heart to care.

She would welcome him.

She opened the connecting door to his chamber then paused at the sound of a scratching at the window behind her. Cool air slid around her ankles, evidence that a window was open, but the one behind her did not appear to be so. Penelope cautiously moved toward the sound, then flicked back the draperies quickly, only to find a branch tapping against the outside of the window. She sighed with relief, then gasped at the imprint of a knife in her back once more.

"I will have the jet," that same voice said. "And no tricks this time."

The thief had entered through a window in Garrett's chamber—and she, by unlocking the connecting door, had let him into her own room.

She was alone and she feared what this man would do if she did not surrender her grandmother's jet necklace and earrings. She could not reach the bell to summon Williams and the servants were likely below stairs, cleaning up after the dinner.

Penelope was on her own.

"*Maintenant*," the thief said, jabbing with his knife to emphasize his point and Penelope reached for the clasp.

CHAPTER 14

Garrett entered the house from the back door, listening as he did so. It was very quiet upstairs, but he doubted that Penelope was already asleep. He caught a glimpse of Wrigley and nodded to that man, then took the stairs two at a time.

Silently.

There was a cold draft in the upstairs hall, though all was quiet. He moved quietly to pass a hand across the gap beneath the door to Penelope's chamber. The cold air was not coming from there. He found the source beneath his own door and drew a knife from his boot as he eased open the door.

He could not sense another presence.

The window was open, the latch broken, the curtain moving slightly in the night breeze. He slipped into the room and let his eyes adjust to the darkness. He could smell the skin of someone who smoked and he scanned the shadows in search of the villain.

"*Maintenant*," came a man's command from Penelope's chamber.

"They were my grandmother's," she said, her voice breathless.

She had been wearing her grandmother's jet at dinner. Garrett prowled toward the connecting door, alert for a trap. The man might have an accomplice.

"And not worth so much for all of that," the thief snarled. "But I will have something from you, for foiling my plan."

"I foiled no plan. You have the pearls."

"But not the emeralds," he replied. "Where are they?"

Penelope did not reply, then gasped, which was no good sound to Garrett's thinking. He eased to the very door.

"Returned to the bank," Penelope said, her words breathless. "I cannot get them for you."

"How unfortunate for you," the thief said softly.

Garrett reached the door and peeked around the trim. Penelope stood before her dressing table, her features pale, a tall man holding a knife at her back. She had removed her jet necklace and he seized it from her, jamming it into a pocket.

"The earrings, or I will rip them free."

Her lips tightened and she removed the first earring slowly, surrendering it to him with obvious reluctance. "It is a paltry claim for you," she said. "Particularly when you desired a fortune in emeralds."

"I should cut you again for your interference." Then the thief chuckled. "*He* could get them," he said darkly and the hair pricked on the back of Garrett's neck. The villain slid the knife across Penelope's skin and she audibly caught her breath. "What would he do to save you from injury?"

"A great deal," Garrett roared and lunged at the thief. He caught the man's elbow and spun him around, punching him hard in the face. The thief staggered backward to regain his balance and crashed into her dressing table. The knife fell and Garrett kicked it away, brandishing his own. The thief tried to snatch for Penelope but she darted for the other side of the room.

He leapt and snatched at her skirts, catching a fistful of cloth. Penelope tried to haul it out of his hand but the thief swung her around so that she was before him. He locked his gloved hands around her throat. "One step and I end her days," the thief said.

Garrett halted.

"Put down the knife," the thief instructed and Garrett did as he was told. "And kick it away." Garrett grimaced and followed instruction. "How unfortunate for you that the emeralds are at the bank," he said and Penelope's eyes widened as his grip tightened. "Your wife might have survived this night otherwise."

"But they are not at the bank," Garrett said, his tone reasonable. "They are in the safe downstairs."

"She said they were gone."

"I told her that, because she was fearful." Garrett shrugged. "I intended to return them Monday."

"Can you get them now?"

"Of course," Garrett said. "But you will have to release my wife first."

"*Non*," the thief said, shaking his head. "I will hold her until I have the gems."

Garrett raised his hands and stepped back. "I will not get them unless she is free."

"I will kill her if you don't comply."

"No," Garrett said with assurance, meeting Penelope's gaze for the barest moment. "I will never permit that."

The man's eyes flashed. He lifted Penelope higher and began to squeeze. She cried out, then her skirts moved as she drove her heel high against him. The thief staggered and Garrett was upon him. He tore Penelope free of the man's grip, and pummeled him in the face and the stomach. The thief fell to the ground and rolled in place, moaning in agony. Garrett bent and searched his pockets, removing Penelope's jet earrings and necklace. He turned to offer them to her and she cried out. When he looked back, the thief was running for the window. He tore it open and leapt into the night.

Garrett followed and looked into the alley, barely discerning his figure as he fled. "Good," he said with satisfaction, then turned to find Penelope behind him. There were marks on her throat and he immediately caught her close.

"You let him escape on purpose," she said softly.

"He must flee with the false pearls for this nightmare to end."

She opened one hand to look down at her grandmother's jet and her hand was shaking. "I thank you for this."

"Are you injured?" he demanded and she shook her head. Then, she took a shaking breath and retreated from his outstretched hand.

"You returned," she said, her gaze searching. "Why?"

"I had a feeling and I trusted it fully," he said, sweeping her into his arms. "There was too much at risk to do otherwise." He held her tightly and held her gaze. "Tell me if you are hurt, Penelope."

She shook her head. "Surprised and a little bruised, no more than that."

"That is still too much," he said fiercely.

She smiled at him. "There is no one to hear you, sir. You need not pretend."

"But I do not pretend, Penelope, and I will convince you of that this very night, if you will let me."

She eyed him, then glanced toward a book of all things, then nodded.

Relief surged through him. "I am sorry that I was sworn to secrecy," he said.

"By your mistress," she said, her eyes flashing.

"By Esmeralda, it is true, but she is not my mistress."

"But at the theatre..."

"She wanted to tell me that she knew the location of Caroline's pearls. She had a plan to exchange the copy for the genuine ones, so that the thief was deceived and said she would send a friend to collect them."

"Mrs. Oliver." Penelope, to his relief, was fighting a smile. "That is no friend but the lady herself."

"I had no notion until we escorted her home," he said.

"Were you a spy?" she demanded. "For I would think a spy might have discerned that truth sooner."

"I should have," he admitted. "But I have been distracted by a certain lady and her charms."

Penelope blushed. "You will not blame your omission upon me."

"No, but I will beg your forgiveness in any way I can."

She seemed unable to hold his gaze. "I would like to come to you tonight," she confessed and Garrett could not believe his good fortune. He kissed her soundly, glad to feel her soften against him, and was encouraged that all could yet be brought to rights.

Then footsteps sounded in the hall and Wrigley was knocking on the door.

PENELOPE FELT audacious and yet she knew her choice was absolutely right. She loved this man and she wanted one night with him. This was the moment to take a chance and hope for the best.

Garrett never left her side while arrangements were made and never relinquished his grip upon her hand. That could only be a good portent.

And when the servants retired, he caught her up again and carried her to his room. His chamber was filled with romantic shadows and the flickering light from the fire blazing on the hearth. The heavy drapes were drawn against the night and the room was a warm haven. He carried her to the bed, then kissed her once again, leaving her both dizzy and shivering. He was more intent than he had been before, more fixed upon her, and she found his attention both thrilling and nigh overwhelming.

There would never be another man for her. Penelope knew it well. There would never be another man who stirred her very soul with such ease as this one.

He set her on the bed, her skirts around her hips, and stood beside it. He caught her face in his hands and kissed her slowly, ravaging her with his touch and setting her very blood aflame. When her heart was racing, he broke their kiss, then smiled as he removed the pins from her hair. He was methodical, seeming to draw out the exercise, his gaze dark with desire as he looked down at her. "I like your hair loose," he said, spearing his fingers through its length and spreading it over her shoulders. "I like how it gleams darkly, how soft and thick it is, how it tempts my touch." He caught her nape in his hand and his mouth locked over hers again. He feasted upon her with his kiss and Penelope was melting with need for him.

He stepped back then and removed one of her satin slippers, sliding his thumb possessively across the arch. It tickled but not quite, his grip sending heat through her veins. He flattened his hand and slid it up her calf, his fingers curving around her until he bent and kissed the inside of her knee. Her garter was deftly unfastened and even as his hands eased the stocking down to her ankle, he ran a line of kisses down her skin. He pressed careful kisses to the cuts from the night before, a shadow darkening his brow when he examined them. Then he slid his hand over her again, the heat of it prompting shivers of anticipation to race over her flesh. She caught her breath as his fingertips danced up her thighs, teasing her with his sure touch.

Then he retreated again, and removed the other slipper and stocking with the same deliberation. He leaned over her when he kissed her, urging her to lie back on the great mattress. He braced himself above her, almost but not quite touching her, the heat from his proximity making her nipples tighten. His kiss turned a little rougher, a little more demanding, and Penelope was only too glad to respond in kind. She trusted him completely. She felt his hand close over her breast, still beneath the bodice of her dress, and she arched her back to rub against him, wanting all he could give to her.

"You like that," he murmured, his words a husky whisper in her ear.

"I do," she admitted, hearing that her own voice was breathless. She felt his chuckle fan across her neck, then he was pushing down the front of her dress, exposing her nipple to his view. He admired it, his breath fanning across her skin, then he closed a finger and thumb around it and pinched it lightly. Penelope gasped in satisfaction and he chuckled again, flicking a wicked glance at her before he bent to capture the taut peak in his mouth.

He teased and tormented her as he had once before, and Penelope loved it all the more this time. She was writhing in her pleasure when he turned his attention to the other nipple, and breathless when he lifted his head. His hair was tousled and his expression so satisfied that she could only smile.

"I love you," she said, without intending to do as much. Immediately she feared that she had said too much, but his smile was quick and hungry. He kissed her fiercely then, with a possessiveness that nearly made her heart stop.

"Good," he whispered into her ear, the feel of his lips making her shiver, the sound of his pleasure making her heart soar.

Then he rolled her to her stomach so abruptly that she laughed. She felt his fingers busy with the laces at the back of her dress and in a moment, his palms were flat against her knees. He slid them up the length of her in a long caress, removing her dress and chemise in one smooth move. He cast both aside, then caught her fingers in his one hand and stretched her out before him. His hand was on her buttocks, then the small of her back, his lips on the back of her neck and then below her ear.

"Temptress," he whispered, then pulled her closer so that she rolled to her back again.

"But it is not an empty temptation," she said softly, watching him smile.

"Then I must make it worthwhile." His hand remained on her waist, the other holding her hands above her head. He was stretched out beside her but fully garbed and Penelope felt both wicked and wanton. It was not an entirely unsatisfactory feeling, especially given Garrett's expression. "You are magnificent," he informed her and she felt her cheeks heat.

Then his mouth was on hers again, his kiss slow and sultry. His hand slipped between her thighs, and knowing what to expect, she parted her legs in invitation. He eased one leg over hers, pinning her down in a way that she found most delicious, then braced his knee against her other thigh. He lifted his head and arched a brow, but she nodded eagerly. "I like when I can only enjoy," she said and he chuckled.

"As I like to ensure that you do, my lady."

Before she could reply, his fingers landed upon her. She heard him catch his breath and knew he had not realized how aroused she was. She felt wet and hot, burning for his touch, and when he caressed her boldly, she arched against him and moaned with satisfaction. His eyes glittered and his touch became more demanding, the feel of his finger and thumb closing around her clitoris making Penelope gasp with need. She watched him smile as he tormented her with pleasure and knew he was fully aware of the sensation he aroused within her. His fingers were inside her again, his thumb moving across her with a surety that she was sure she would not survive. He urged her higher and higher, summoning the tumult within her. Just when she thought she could bear no more, he claimed her with a kiss and prompted her release. He swallowed her cry of satisfaction, lowering his weight atop her and crushing her into the mattress as she shook with the tumult.

When she finally opened her eyes, she was warm to her toes, her heart was racing and her breath was quick. He was smiling at her, so utterly pleased with himself that Penelope could only smile in return.

He kissed the tip of her nose, the affectionate gesture making her chest squeeze tightly. "Satisfied?" he asked in a low growl and she could not resist the urge to tease him.

"Appeased," she said, loving how his smile flashed. "But perhaps your satisfaction will make the difference."

He sobered then, his face close to hers, his gaze searching. "Are you sure?"

"I am," she whispered, loving the gleam that lit his eyes. He inhaled sharply and she thought he might refuse her in the last moment, liking this sign of his honor. "I want to know," she confessed. "I want you to show me."

With that, his expression was alight. "Penelope," he whispered, but she ran a hand over his shoulder, loving the solid feel of him.

"You wear too many garments for my satisfaction, sir," she said lightly.

He smiled again, then rolled from the bed, almost bounding to his feet. There was no seduction in his disrobing: he simply removed his clothes with efficient haste. His vest was cast aside, then his shirt and cravat, just as before—but this time, Penelope watched him avidly, not hiding her interest. He smiled at her as he tugged off his boots, facing her as he removed his breeches and kicked them aside.

She tried to hide her surprise at the size of him and knew she failed when he chuckled. "It is your fault, Penelope," he growled. "You tempt me beyond all others."

He let her look upon him, by crossing the room nude to tend the fire. She tried to keep from staring at him, but it was a futile effort. He was every bit as beautifully wrought as she recalled from the day she'd watched him swim.

When he turned back to face her, he caught her at it and smiled. "No blindfold tonight," he said flatly as he closed the distance between them, his manner so purposeful that her heart skipped. "It is you and I together, and no one will dream of another."

There was such resolve in his tone that she understood not only that her sister had been unfaithful but that he knew it.

"And you will call me by name," she said, having no desire that he should believe her to be another.

Garrett smiled then spoke with rough authority. "My Penelope, there is not another like you. Never imagine otherwise." His kiss was commanding and she reveled in his hunger for her, realizing only now that she had power in this union as well. When he broke his kiss, she braced herself on her elbows and liked how his eyes darkened as he surveyed her. It was a potent thing to know that he found her alluring, and it made her feel more beautiful.

He lowered his hands to the bed and prowled across it until he was braced over her, those eyes gleaming. His lashes dropped as he looked over her, his satisfaction undisguised, then he met her gaze again. "No secrets on this night," he said and her heart fluttered. "Nor ever again."

"Never again," she agreed and they smiled at each other for a moment.

Then Garrett kissed her and Penelope opened her mouth to him, holding nothing back as she surrendered all she had to give. If she was to make love only once in her life, this would be the most splendid coupling ever.

And she would never forget it.

~

IRRESISTIBLE WOMAN. Penelope was sweet and willing, so passionate that Garrett knew he would not last long. Perhaps there could be a second time before morning, if she was not too sore, but he would not wager upon it.

And she loved him. That marvel was all he desired and yet more. What a gift to have this woman hold him in affection, to give herself to him, to trust him with her maidenhead. He felt a cur for not having trusted her, but from this moment forward, he would never doubt her again. He would give her everything she desired, the very breath from his lungs and the blood of his body, if only she would remain by his side. He would earn her trust again, even if it took every moment of his life.

She was wet and warm, so welcoming that even touching her took him near to his release. He caressed her again, conjuring her arousal, then when her eyes were sparkling and her lips were parted, he moved between her thighs. She lifted her knees on either side of his hips, opening herself to him with a trust that made his heart thunder. He eased to her portal, then kissed her sweetly as he moved inside. She was tight, so tight that he knew there would be at least a twinge.

"It may hurt a little," he murmured in her ear, only wanting to reassure her.

She nodded, gasped, then caught her breath, her grip tight on his shoulders. Garrett was inside, easing deeper, burying himself in her sweet heat. It seemed that they fit together perfectly and he moved as slowly as he could until he was fully buried within her.

Then he dared to meet her gaze. Her uncertainty was clear, but he kissed one corner of her mouth and then the other. He moved just a little, letting her become accustomed to him, then rolled his hips so that he rubbed against her clitoris. She gasped and flushed, and he smiled down at her as he made the same move again. He watched as her own smile dawned, her eyes beginning to glow with pleasure. Her hands slid across his shoulders and he bent to claim her mouth again, savoring a slow potent kiss as he began to move within her.

Surely he would die of such sweet sensation.

If that was the price of this night, Garrett did not care.

An infinity later, Penelope released a shuddering breath when he was completely within her again, then wonder of wonders, she rolled her hips beneath him. He lifted his head to find her smiling at him, and he slid his arms beneath her, gathering her more closely against his chest. He moved with greater vigor and she moved against him, their gazes locked as the passion rose between them. He felt her nails on his shoulders and the shimmer of heat that rose from her, even as his own desire rose impossibly higher.

He rolled them over suddenly so that she was atop him. Penelope gasped in surprise, then with his gesture of encouragement, she sat atop him, her knees on either side of his hips. He let her set the pace, then, and she did it beautifully, moving quickly and then slowly, as if she would ensnare him with her spell. Her hair flowed over her shoulders, her nipples were taut and her lips were parted. She was a vision of beauty, a seductress who held him captive, and he loved the look of triumph that dawned in her expression as she drove him wild. When the heat was torrid between them and he was sure he would die of need, she suddenly dropped down, her breasts colliding with his chest. He rubbed against the lady, feeling a primal satisfaction when she began to tremble once again. She framed his face in her hands and kissed him hungrily, and he seized her waist. The tumult rose hard and hot, undeniable in its demand. Garrett had only to thrust deeply twice more before release claimed him and he shouted with satisfaction as he made Penelope his own.

They fell back against the bed entangled with each other, as he strove to catch his breath. His heart was thundering and there was only Penelope with her sweet warmth atop him. He pushed his hand into her hair and lifted her lips for his kiss, only to find her eyes sparkling.

"I might be satisfied now," she whispered, her tone mischievous.

"I think not." Garrett smiled and touched her with a fingertip, watching her gasp, then pressing upon her clitoris so that she gained her release again. She cried out and trembled, then collapsed atop him. He could feel her heart pounding against his own and he gathered her close, pressing a kiss to her temple.

"You are wicked," she said, with no hint of recrimination.

"I try," he said and she laughed. He watched her then touched her cheek with a fingertip, sliding his hand into her hair and drawing her close for a highly satisfying kiss.

This was the kind of partnership he had always desired, and Garrett would do whatever was necessary to defend both it and Penelope.

In the morning, he would seek out lawyers to set all to rights so that they could marry. He did not care what it cost, for he and Penelope belonged together forever.

~

NOT ONLY WAS their mating a marvel, but Garrett would not allow Penelope to retreat to her own chamber. Nor, evidently, would he permit her to wear a nightgown. Penelope laughed at him, more than content to surrender whatever he desired of her.

The night had exceeded all expectations.

In the end, she found herself in the highly satisfactory situation of being nude in his bed. Garrett was behind her, his heat ensuring that the bed was warm. His arm was around her waist, holding her close. His leg was entangled with hers. His breath was in her ear and his other arm beneath her head to pillow it. His heartbeat was against her back, the fire had burned down to embers in the grate, and there was nowhere else Penelope wanted to be.

She would worry about the future in the morning. For this night, she would savor.

CHAPTER 15

Esmeralda changed with haste backstage with the assistance of Ophelia Pearl, the actress who was both Esmeralda's friend and ally. Ophelia had dressed as Esmeralda and appeared in Esmeralda's box at the theatre so the courtesan would not appear to be absent at all. Now she donned the hat of Mrs. Oliver and left the backstage area.

Esmeralda emerged as her own self once more.

She wore an evening dress of velvet in a hue of emerald so dark that it was almost black. A small train trailed behind her, which allowed her the opportunity to pick it up when the street was mired and display her ankles to any who cared to look. Her gloves were long and black, and she wore a black lace fichu. Its ruffles pressed against the underside of her chin and it fell over her shoulders in ruffled tiers, hiding her bare throat and shoulders from view—save for a small gap over the bodice. The black lace ended a finger's breadth above the top of the dress bodice, revealing an increment of creamy skin, one that drew the gaze of every male in her vicinity.

No one would forget that dress, whether she wore it or Ophelia.

As Esmeralda returned to her box, Ophelia headed for the popular coffee shops outside the theatre. Esmeralda's heart was racing but she ensured that her progress was leisurely and that many people saw her. She enjoyed the remainder of the performance then turned away several interested gentlemen as she made her way to the street.

There was quite a crush of people seeking hacks and she was in no hurry to return to the man who sought to destroy all she held dear. When finally she reached her own doorstep, it was past two. Latimer opened the door for her, evidently having been watching for her, and she smiled.

"Thank you, Latimer."

"You're late," Jacques snarled. He lounged in the door to the dining room, smoking a vile cigar. His eyes were as small and mean as ever and his expression hinted that his mood was foul.

"I could not obtain a hack. Everyone left the theatre in the same moment, it seemed." She surrendered her wrap to Latimer and went into the dining room. She sank into a chair and waited for the storm.

"You have a black eye," she said to Jacques. "Who took exception to your charm?"

"It does not matter," he said. "They're gone." He slammed the door. He marched toward her, his fury clear. "They're gone and you took them and if you think you can trick me, you can think again. I will tear Sylvie to shreds and I will make you watch and..."

While he was speaking, Esmeralda began to unfasten her lace fichu. A line of jet buttons ran down the front of it and she released each one, gradually revealing her throat. "I could think of no safer place," she said softly when Jacques ran out of threats, then opened the last button.

He fell silent and stared at the pearls around her neck.

Esmeralda smiled. "There is, after all, a jewel thief in town. I did not dare to leave them at home unguarded."

"Give them to me," Jacques demanded and she complied. He checked them intently and her heart lunged to her throat that he would realize that they were false. "Did anyone see them?"

"Of course not." Esmeralda scoffed. "I have no desire to go to prison."

"You should never have done it."

"If I had left them here, they might have been stolen," she said, letting her voice rise. "You should have remained here yourself."

"I had an errand," he said grimly.

"You have them back now, so all is well." She poured herself a brandy, knowing it was the last thing she needed. She often had a brandy when she returned home in the evening, though, and did not want him to think that anything was amiss.

The man was more suspicious than anyone she had ever known.

"Don't become overly fond of them," he snarled. "I will sell them tomorrow."

"Then you will go to prison," Esmeralda said, casting herself into a chair. "And good riddance."

"What do you mean?"

Esmeralda laughed. "Do you imagine that any jeweller in this country would fail to recognize the famed pearls of Lady Caroline Wright?"

"Not so loudly," he hissed. "I do not trust that Latimer."

Esmeralda lowered her tone slightly. "They were her mother's before her and worn to every event of merit for forty years. Nigh half of England could tell you they are the Finch pearls."

"I will take the setting apart," Jacques said.

"And sacrifice most of their value," Esmeralda replied. "They are matched. Their high price is a reflection of not just the perfection of the gems but their artful arrangement." She shook her head and sipped. "Truly, you could not have chosen a more distinctive piece to steal. Oh, perhaps you should consider the crown jewels next time."

He sat down hard and glared at her. He seized her brandy and finished it.

"How many jewellers and goldsmiths did you visit with the rubies?"

"All of them," he ceded sourly.

"And did you get their value in the end?'

"You know I did not." He eyed her. "I suppose you have a suggestion. You always thought yourself the clever one."

"You must sell them in Paris."

"You could sell them in Paris for me. I will send you there and stay in your house and keep your staff captive until you return."

Esmeralda laughed. "Now, there is a scheme." She put out her hand. "Give them to me. I will be gone by daybreak and you will never see me or Sylvie again."

"But your servants."

Esmeralda shrugged as if she did not care.

And he was fooled. Jacques leapt to his feet and paced the room. Esmeralda feigned indifference as she also pretended to drink. "You are right," he said finally. "I will leave by the dawn." He lunged toward her and seized her throat, a familiar madness in his eyes. "And if you betray me, I will take a reckoning from your hide." He smiled. "No, I will take it from Sylvie's."

Esmeralda's heart leapt but she held his gaze, despising him with every fibre of her being. She lifted his hand away from her throat. "You always ensured you did not leave a bruise where it would show," she reminded him. "And in my trade, *all* skin shows."

His eyes flashed a warning, then he struck her across the face. The glass fell from her hand, the brandy spilling across the carpet, and Esmeralda saw stars. He hit her again, harder and on the other side. "There," he hissed in her ear when she gripped the arms of the chair to remain upright. "That will ensure your discretion."

"I would never dream of interfering with your plans," she said, forcing a cool smile.

"Then you have learned something after all." Jacques crossed the room with purpose and bellowed for Latimer.

All Esmeralda could feel was gratitude that he would leave.

And she would ensure his downfall, bruises or nay.

THE MORNING SUNLIGHT AWAKENED PENELOPE. A beam slanted through the window and fell upon her face, bathing her in radiant gold and warmth. She smiled as she opened her eyes, knowing that she was in Garrett's bed. The drapes on the bed had been pulled back and those on the window as well, the entire room filled with sunlight. She was still naked and she was alone.

She sat up, holding the linens before herself. There was no fire set on the hearth and no sign of Garrett. His boots were gone and his linen had not been collected by his valet.

It must be very early.

She thought as much then heard the great clock in the hall chime seven times.

She might have been a harlot, brought home for the gentleman's pleasure, and his morning absence planned to give her a chance to depart. As wondrous as their night together had been, Penelope knew there was truth in that unwelcome thought. Her choice meant her ruin: even if the tangle of deceit was unravelled, she could never present herself to another suitor as an innocent.

Garrett had chosen to possess her, which meant she might be the next of his mistresses. Perhaps she would not even be the last of them. She recalled the advice of the note about men accepting what was readily offered to them without compunction and knew her decision of the night before had changed everything.

She gathered her discarded clothes and returned to her own chamber, closing the connecting door behind herself. Then she arranged her clothes as if she had undressed herself, put on a nightgown and rumpled the bed. She rang for Williams, then sat brushing her own hair, her thoughts churning.

No matter what, she could not regret the night before.

CONFOUNDED LAWYERS. Every argument Garrett made in favor of a special license made him sound like a bigamist. He had been referred from one clerk to another and his temper thinned as the hours passed. It was nigh eleven when the third clerk fixed Garrett with a disapproving look. He was an older man and moved with precision. Garrett began to fear that his errand was ill-fated.

"You are wed, my lord, yet you would wed again, in haste even." The clerk removed his spectacles and peered at Garrett. "Surely you realize that this is highly irregular, even for a marquis."

"Are the choices of marquises particularly erratic?"

"One comes to realize in my occupation that many of the aristocracy believe that the laws of the land do not apply to them," the man said primly. He set a finger upon Garrett's affidavit, his gaze unswerving as he clearly included Garrett in that assembly. "And your reputation precedes you, sir."

"My wife is dead and buried," Garrett insisted. "It has been three years and I would wed again. That cannot be uncommon."

The clerk put on his spectacles and studied the affidavit again. "You would wed her sister," he noted with disapproval.

"There is nothing illegal in that."

"Of course not, my lord, though you must admit it is…unusual."

Garrett glared at him. "They were twins."

The clerk's brows rose, but he sorted through documents again. "I have no evidence of your wife's death save your own affidavit, which cannot be considered objective under the circumstances. And if I were to consult the parish records in…Shropshire, would I find that your proposed bride is legally deceased?"

"Yes. It is because my wife was believed to be her twin sister at the time. Philomena died at my country manor and this was her own scheme, to ensure her sister's future. The stone in the churchyard has her sister's name upon it, which is incorrect."

"This would be the sister you intend to wed?"

"They exchanged places, at my wife's behest."

The clerk's eyebrows nearly disappeared beneath his wig. "And you did not guess?" His opinion of that was more than clear.

"I was abroad. I seldom saw her."

"But now you would wed her?"

"Exactly." Garrett saw that the man was disinclined

to be of assistance. "Her place in my household and my life must be protected."

The clerk's lips tightened in understanding. "As a mistress would not be," he said under his breath.

Garrett nodded. "And it must be contrived in haste, for she is a woman of principle."

"This despite the fact that she apparently pretended to be her sister for three years." The clerk fixed Garrett with a look that had a measure of sympathy in it. "You think she will leave you."

"I cannot imagine that she will do otherwise."

The clerk nodded and began to rise to his feet. Clearly, he had to consult with yet another superior. "This may take more time than you prefer, my lord. I do not suppose your father, the duke, might also swear to the truth of your claim?"

"He would indeed."

The clerk nodded. "That might make sufficient difference, my lord," he warned. "It would be ideal to have the sworn word of someone less intimately connected with the situation, someone perceived to be impartial."

"I understand," Garrett ceded. "But who?"

The clerk could only shrug.

THERE WAS a letter from Sara Underwood in the morning post. It had come from a different address, as evidently Underwood had moved since Christmas. In the missive, she noted that she would welcome the prospect of a visit.

Penelope needed no further encouragement.

Fortunately, she had already dressed for the day, and needed only her hat, coat and gloves before departing. She requested a hackney cab, insisting to Wrigley that she would not wish to interfere with any plans of her husband. In truth, she did not wish anyone to know where she had gone.

The neighborhood proved to be an impoverished one, more so than she had hoped. The driver was reluctant to leave her in front of the rooming house, and despite Penelope's assurances, he lingered until the door was opened to her.

To her relief, she was welcomed.

The foyer was small and the stairs were narrow. The carpet was dirty and the lighting was dim, thanks to the grime on the window panes. Penelope's heart ached that a loyal servant had been reduced to such straits, and then she was ushered into a front parlor to await Sara Underwood.

"I will bring you some tea," the landlady said and closed the door behind herself.

Sara Underwood, once Philomena's lady's maid, was almost unrecognizable when she arrived. She had always been a slender woman but now was thin beyond belief. Her hair had been streaked with silver when Penelope had last seen her, but now was snowy white. Her face seemed more lined and her cheeks sunken, and Penelope guessed her weight loss had been quick.

"My lady!" she exclaimed, seizing Penelope's offered hand. "It is a marvel to see you."

Penelope quickly learned that Underwood's mother had passed away before Christmas, and that her illness had consumed all of the funds of both mother and daughter. Underwood had been compelled to move to a cheaper room, though she despaired of finding another post.

"I am too aged, my lady," she said. "No one will welcome me."

Penelope's heart twisted, for she guessed the other woman's hope but could not make a promise. "But you had the annuity and I sent you money each Christmas…"

"I sold the annuity and I gave all the coin to the church, after the physician was paid. My mother wanted a service and a place in the churchyard." She gripped Penelope's hand again. "I am so grateful that you came."

"You knew I would, after all you did for me." Penelope bowed her head. "After all you did for my sister."

Sara smiled. "She was an easy woman to admire and a difficult one to love," she said softly. "And truly, she loved herself more than anything or anyone else." She frowned. "Until James was born. I remember the expression upon her face when first she held him."

"And rightly so. He was perfect."

"It softened something within her, to have a son," Sara said. "She did not change, not my lady, but she worried about him as well as herself. When Matthew came, it was only worse." She nodded at Penelope. "That was why, you know, my lady. She had to see that they not only survived but received their due."

"But why would they not have done so? They were both healthy children."

The older woman frowned and her voice dropped low. "Because of what she had done, of course. Because she feared her deeds would change their prospects."

The landlady brought the tea then, bustling into the small space noisily to set down the tray. The dishes were chipped but there was both milk and sugar, as well as a small plate of biscuits. They were such a sad offering that Penelope wished she had thought to bring some baking from the house.

"You look disappointed, my lady," Sara teased.

"I should have brought you something."

"It is no matter. I am delighted to see you."

When the landlady was finally gone, Penelope

leaned closer to Sara. She had to know, and there was no one else to ask. "Sara, you must tell me, please. Are both boys the marquis' own sons?"

Something lit the other woman's gaze. "Does he fear otherwise?"

Penelope shook her head. "But I have always wondered, after the end."

"It is not an unfair question," Sara said. "My lady loved the gentlemen. But she had given her word to her husband, indeed, they had sworn to each other that they would both be true to their marriage until they had two healthy sons. I know she kept her pledge."

Penelope felt a tension ease within her.

"Perhaps their match might have been happier if they had not succeeded so very quickly, if there had been daughters to impede their progress to that goal." Sara smiled sadly. "But once the deed was done, they parted with all speed. It was as if they could no longer bear the sight of each other."

"He told me that they fought."

"Oh, they did and for certain, my lady." Sara dropped her voice to a whisper. "He caught her with her lover, and he was not pleased."

"I cannot think any man would be," Penelope said and the other woman studied her.

"You have become fond of him."

"I think I always was," Penelope admitted. "But the truth has come out and I will leave Arlingview House this week to return to Clapham."

"I am sorry, my lady."

"I am, as well, for it means that I cannot offer you a post in either house."

Sara nodded and looked down at her tea, her disappointment tangible. "How are the boys?" she asked after a moment, yearning in her voice.

"Well. They are both at school, of course, and grown so tall."

Sara smiled at that then sighed. "She loved you, my lady," she whispered. "She loved you, more than even she knew. For a long time, I thought she loved only herself, and then the boys, but I saw the bond between you at the end. You were the only one she could trust completely, more even than she trusted herself."

"I have tried to do well by her faith in me," Penelope replied softly and they sat in silence for a long moment.

Then Sara cleared her throat. "Do you recall her insistence that she supervise as you learned to mimic her?" Her tone was lighter, as if recalling a merry frolic.

Penelope could only respond in kind. "How could I forget?"

"And the chastising, from one so sick, upon which shoes and gloves should be worn with which dress." Sara chuckled to herself. "She was always so particular."

Their smiles faded quickly.

"I would not have managed that first fortnight without you," Penelope confessed.

"You would have been fine and she knew it." Her voice softened. "Do not forget her, my lady, I entreat you. I never will."

They sat together and drank all of the tea, talking of the past as the room slowly became darker. A chill rose from the floor and Penelope gave Sara the little money she had.

When Penelope stepped out into the street, it was mid-afternoon and the air had turned chilly.

Before the rooming house was the fine carriage of the Marquis of Arlingview, that man himself standing beside it. Garrett wore his dark great coat and top hat, his boots gleaming. His arms were folded across his chest, his gaze locked upon her and his expression grim.

He was waiting.

For her.

And she knew from his posture and his expression that he had divined her last secret.

In a way, it would be a relief to have all the truth laid bare.

~

THE DUKE OF HAYNESDALE knew he was calling earlier than was appropriate, but he dared not delay. Something was afoot. He had lost sight of Mrs. Oliver the night before and was mightily concerned with her actions. The marquis was nowhere to be found. Haynesdale had to appeal to someone who knew all the rumors in London, and there was only one person he could name who might be able to answer his query.

Miss Esmeralda Ballantyne.

His knock was answered promptly and he could find no fault with the house, despite her trade. It seemed utterly respectable. His coat was taken by an admirably attentive butler and he could smell fresh baking. He was shown into a bright morning room, where Esmeralda Ballantyne was pouring tea. Steam rose from the cup as she stood and offered it to him.

"Good morning, your grace. Would you care for tea?"

He would, most certainly, having forgone his own breakfast in his haste.

She was dressed modestly, which surprised him, but no less alluring for all of that. Her dress was of an aqua silk with long sleeves and a high neck, and so suitably demure that he would have approved of the choice for his own sister. All the same, Miss Ballantyne's figure was such that there was no doubting her femininity and he imagined no measure of cloth could ever make her appear to be dowdy.

He accepted and sat down opposite her, taking a fortifying and welcome sip. It was sufficiently hot to scald his throat, just the way he liked it, hot and sweet, good China tea made well. "I thank you," he said, aware that she was watching him, her eyes seeming even more vividly emerald in the morning light. He thought her face looked rounder than he recalled and he had the sense that she wore paint, even this early in the morning, but perhaps she had not slept well. Her eyes seemed puffy, and he wondered whether she had been weeping.

Her polite smile gave no hint of her feelings.

She offered him a scone, which he was delighted to discover was still warm. Then she sat back and watched him, sipping of her own tea before setting the cup aside.

"I sense I have been anticipated," he said and that smile broadened ever so slightly.

"It would not be due to any habit, for certain, or any declaration of intent," she replied then lifted a dark brow in silent query.

Haynesdale frowned. "I believe I have asked you previously if you know of a Mrs. Oliver."

"And I believe I have told you that I was certain our paths had not crossed."

"I wondered if that might have changed since our discussion on the subject."

She picked up her tea again, and he noted that her gaze was averted at what might have been a telling moment. "Have you any reason to suggest as much?"

"I heard that you might have encountered her last night."

Her expression was one of surprise. "From whom?"

"Does it matter?"

"I do prefer to know who is watching my movements. It is prudent in my trade."

"I cannot say. Regrettably."

She nodded and sipped her tea. They sat in silence for several moments. He could hear a few carts on the street outside and conversation carried from the rear of the house, perhaps from the kitchen for it was a woman's tones. The sun shone, the woman before him enjoyed her tea as if she had all the time in the world, and he felt his presence was awkward.

He frowned again. "I seek her on a matter of great urgency," he said, beginning again. "For the sake of another, not for myself. And I had hoped, since you are aware of so many in the city, that you might have heard even the slightest rumor of her location."

"I have not," she replied crisply. Once again, she set down her cup but this time she rose to her feet. "You said that you felt you might have been anticipated, and in truth, you were." She had moved to the tray of mail on a desk and lifted the bottom missive. "It also seems that this Mrs. Oliver shares your assumptions of my knowledge of those in the city." She offered the letter and he was astonished to see that it was addressed to him.

But at this address.

He met Miss Ballantyne's gaze and she shrugged. "It came by the first post this morning. I assumed that you knew of it and would arrive shortly to collect it." She sat again in a rustle of silk that Haynesdale found enticingly feminine but this time, she took a scone onto a small plate and sat back to eat it. Her gaze never swerved from him, nor did she seem to blink. She might have been a watchful cat.

The sole sensible thing to do was to open the missive, so Haynesdale did. It was dated the night before.

·   ·   ·

YOUR GRACE—

I understand that you have been seeking me, though I know not why. If and when there is cause for us to meet, you may rest assured that I will see the matter arranged.

In the meantime, I have tidings of the thief you seek. By the time you receive this, he will have left London, with the objective of selling a certain pearl necklace in Paris, where it is less likely to be recognized. His plan is to ride for Dover by dawn and cross to Calais on the first tide. His name is Jacques Desjardins and his foul reputation is well known in France. Be warned that he is deceitful beyond all measure

I wish you luck in apprehending the fiend.

Your (unlikely) ally—

Mrs. Delilah Oliver

HAYNESDALE LOOKED at the ormolu clock that ticked on the mantle and rose to his feet. The thief was hours ahead of him!

"Does she send tidings of merit?" Miss Ballantyne asked mildly.

"Is she trustworthy?"

She smiled. "How would I know such a detail about a stranger, sir?"

"I regret I must depart with all haste," he said, seizing upon his cane. "I thank you for this missive and for the fine cup of tea."

"There is a measure of urgency in your manner."

"I must ride for Dover immediately."

"Then finish your tea and your scone, your grace," she said firmly. "It may be some time before you find sustenance again."

She was right. He drained the cup, welcoming its heat and might have devoured the scone in a single bite.

In the meantime, Miss Ballantyne had risen to her feet. She spoke to her butler, who vanished in the very moment that Haynesdale desired his coat. Before he could fume, that man returned with a small basket and surrendered it to Miss Ballantyne. She packed the rest of the scones within it as the butler retrieved his coat, and presented the basket to Haynesdale. "It is poor for the constitution to eat in haste," she said with a little smile that awakened a heat within him. "I wish you safe travels, wherever you ride, your grace."

"Thank you, Miss Ballantyne," he said and bowed. He lingered for a moment, feeling that he should say more but not knowing what it would be, then spun on his heel and departed. His carriage was yet at the door and he was glad that he had chosen to disregard any possibility of gossip resulting from his visit. His horses were fresh and they were always fast.

He spoke to his driver and got into the carriage, looking back to see Miss Ballantyne at the front window. To his surprise, she appeared to be distraught, though he could not imagine why she should regret his departure.

He must have been mistaken.

"Drive on!" he roared and they were off.

CHAPTER 16

*P*enelope, being Penelope, did not falter when she found Garrett awaiting her. She paused only a moment, then lifted her chin and walked toward him with purpose.

Garrett had been distraught when he returned home to find her gone—he had arrived in time for luncheon—but Wrigley, fortunately, had been attentive. They had not spoken this morning because he had not wanted to awaken her, and in that moment, he feared the import of his choice when she had vanished.

As she walked toward him, he knew he had never seen a more beautiful woman in his life. She paused before him as regally as a queen and he took her hand, pressing a kiss to its back.

"I did not think to find you here, sir," she said and he heard vulnerability in her voice. He wanted nothing more than to gather her up and carry her away.

"I could scarce abandon you," he said, and meant every word in every possible way.

She flicked a glance toward him then climbed into the carriage, retreating to the far side when he followed her. The door was closed, the whip cracked and the carriage rocked slightly as they moved away.

226

"Are you cold?" he asked when she shivered.

"A little. The room was chilly."

He seized the blanket from the opposite seat and tucked it over her.

"Why are you in this neighborhood?" he asked.

"I had to visit my accomplice," she said. "It was the only way to learn the truth."

Once again, she was an enigma to him. "Your accomplice?" Garrett echoed.

"Sara Underwood," she replied. "I could never have successfully pretended to be Philomena without the assistance of her lady's maid…"

Sara Underwood! Of course!

"Halt!" Garrett said crisply then rapped his cane upon the roof of the carriage. He ordered Watkins to return to the house, and found it impossible to disguise his satisfaction. Sara Underwood! He had located the ideal objective witness, thanks to the lady beside him.

"I could kiss you senseless," he said and Penelope stared at him in astonishment. He kissed her gloved knuckles instead, then leapt from the carriage before it had fully stopped.

Sara Underwood was surprised to see him but came to the door to speak to him. She was visibly relieved when he explained his mission. He gave the former lady's maid a card for his solicitor and entreated her assistance. She promised to visit the next day and give her statement, and he thanked her heartily.

"You must know, Underwood, that you would be welcomed at Arlingview House if ever you are in need of a post."

"But my lady just said that she could not make such an assurance, my lord. She said she will be leaving the house by the end of the week." The former maid was clearly as troubled by this as Garrett.

"I hope not, Underwood. With your assistance, I will be able to offer for Miss Penelope's hand in marriage."

"Oh!"

"And should I have the good fortune to win her agreement, you will be most welcome at Arlingview House."

Underwood smiled with pleasure. "I do not think you require good fortune, my lord."

"I thank you most heartily for that encouragement." Garrett bowed, then returned to the carriage, climbing into it with delight. He captured Penelope's hand in his and the carriage was soon underway again.

"You look most pleased with yourself."

"I should be pleased with you," he said. "I have been seeking an impartial witness to swear that Philomena lies in the churchyard in her sister's place."

"But why?"

"I cannot obtain a special license to marry the lady who holds my heart when the law considers me to be already wed." He watched her eyes light. "I had wished to surprise you, but then *Underwood!*" He stole a kiss. "You are fiendishly clever, my Penelope. Dare I hope that you will wed me in truth?"

She blushed delightfully and dropped her gaze. He guessed her doubts and meant to allay them with haste.

"Before you reply, let me explain one detail." He held fast to her hand. "I must confess that I had no intention of offering for Philomena's hand all those years ago. My mother had advised me against it from the outset and I came to share her view that we should not be happy together, despite your sister's many charms. I had already offered to escort her to Vauxhall Gardens and that was to be our last evening together, to my view."

Penelope did not appear to be surprised. "She guessed that your interest had faded."

"I wondered." He gripped her hand a little more securely, watching her closely. "Because that evening was wondrous. We talked as we never had before and I believed that Philomena showed me her heart, in the nick of time. The evening was too short, though we remained out quite late, and I returned home with complete confidence that I had found the bride of my dreams. I proposed solely because of that evening's companionship."

"Oh," Penelope said, her cheeks pink.

"I spent years seeking the lady who had been my companion that night, but I could never find a glimpse of her in Philomena. We had talked of books at length, but my wife did not care to read. The lady in question had seemed to be as enthralled with my companionship as I was with hers, but my wife consistently favored the company of other men. I could not fathom it." He frowned. "And then I found her with a lover and we argued mightily, our words proving that we were each as unhappy with the match as the other. I assumed that evening had been a stratagem to ensure that I proposed and no measure of the truth. We parted ways, though I warned her most stridently to never bring the child of another man to our household." He paused and nodded. "Then I became a spy, for I had little interest in remaining at home."

Penelope did not speak, and he thought her silence was telling.

"Until, against every expectation, some years later, I came to luncheon and felt again the way I had felt that night at Vauxhall Gardens. The lady I had once sought without success was evidently resident in my own house."

"You guessed that first luncheon," Penelope said quietly.

"I did," Garrett agreed. "Not only that my newly

prudent wife was in truth Penelope, but that the lady who had claimed my heart at Vauxhall Gardens had been Penelope as well."

"My last secret," she admitted with a shy smile. She looked out the window then back at him, her resolve clear. He knew then that there was more to the tale and that she feared he might not welcome it. "Philomena had realized that your interest was lost. She was always keenly observant of others and seemed to know their view of her before it was uttered aloud. She guessed that the evening at Vauxhall Gardens was to be her last with you and she was vexed, as always she was when she did not call the tune. She refused to dress to meet you. Our mother was furious at her defiance, for she still hoped for the match. They argued but Philomena was adamant that she would not go."

"And so your mother contrived that you should take her place."

Penelope nodded. "I did not like the deception. I never liked when we exchanged places, but neither of them would hear a protest once they had resolved upon a course of action." She cast him a smile that gave him hope. "And truly, I had always wanted to see Vauxhall Gardens. I suspected I might never have another opportunity." She fell silent for a moment, her gaze fixed upon his hand. "I did not expect you, though, sir," she admitted softly. "I thought you must be frivolous, and much like Philomena, but I was enchanted with your company that night. I treasure the memory of how we talked and danced, the fireworks and the music." She shook her head at the memory. "It was magical and there was not a whit of deceit about it."

Garrett kissed her hand, his heart full. "Then I proposed to Philomena, believing she had been my companion."

"She would have refused, but *Maman* would not

hear of it. There was another tempest with many threats made, and in the end, Philomena relented. It was pointed out to her that she was unlikely to secure the affections of another man of your fortune and position." She frowned. "She did not like that it was my company that had convinced you to propose, for certain," she admitted softly. "Philomena desired always to be first, and any man who chose me over her was certainly one who failed to appreciate her." She met Garrett's gaze. "I think that was why she was unfaithful to you. She was seeking that perfect courtier, the man who held her above all others, and she already knew you were not that man."

"I gave her everything I could."

"But not your adoration," Penelope said gently. "Many women would not have cared, but Philomena did."

Garrett nodded, recognizing the truth in that. "I could not lie about a matter of such import."

"No. Nor could she. She gave you two sons, as she had promised, but she was not one to surrender more of herself than was due." Penelope frowned. "You should know that I sought out Sara Underwood to ask about my sister's infidelity."

"You knew of it as well?"

Penelope met his gaze steadily. "This last truth will not be an easy one for you to hear."

Garrett knew his surprise showed.

Penelope continued so solemnly that he knew this tale was not an easy one for her to share either. "When Philomena summoned me to Arlingview Manor, she was not suffering from pneumonia as she told everyone." She frowned and her throat worked. Garrett realized that she felt she was betraying her sister's trust and that it was not easily done. He tightened his grip on her hand and she turned hers so that she could clasp his fingers. He sensed that she drew strength from him and he was more than content to offer it to her. She shook her head, then spoke with haste. "She was with child."

"She was not!" Garrett replied. "We had not been together since Matthew's conception…"

Penelope spared him a glance that silenced him.

Of course. Philomena had taken a lover.

And he had forbidden her to bring another man's child into his home. A horrible dread rose within him as Penelope continued.

"Philomena went to Arlingview Manor because no one knew her well there. She chose the destination deliberately, for she had visited a healer. I do not know what healer. I do not know what concoction she bought much less whether she erred in the dose or the healer did."

"God in heaven," Garrett whispered.

"She was dying when I arrived. The blood…" Penelope raised a hand, at a loss for words and he drew her closer. "She refused to have a reputable physician summoned, for he would have seen at once what was amiss. She swore me to secrecy and I did all I could, along with Underwood. I think they both knew there was nothing truly to be done. I think that was why she summoned me."

"To be with her at the end?"

"To take her place. She had the scheme concocted well in advance. By the time I learned of it, she and Underwood had considered all the details. I refused, of course. It was a mockery of marriage, a deceit and a lie, but then Philomena entreated me to do it for the sake of the boys. She feared you would wed again and put them aside. I could not believe that you would deny your own sons, but Philomena warned me of your fearsome temper."

Garrett shook his head, seeing his own unwitting part in the tragedy.

"They tutored me, the two of them, in her moves and choices, until she died. It was only a bit more than a day, but it felt like an eternity." She took a shaking breath.

"And I was not there." He heard the regret in his own voice.

"You did not receive word in time."

Garrett shook his head. "No, I did. I thought she lied that she was ill. I thought she meant to prove that she could summon me on a whim, to win our dispute, in a way, so I chose not to come home." He looked down at the hand he held clasped in his own. "When she apparently recovered, that only convinced me that I had been right. I am sorry that I was not with her at the last. I am more sorry that my words, uttered in anger, drove her to make such a choice. I would never have cast her out."

Penelope's grip tightened on his hand for a moment. "It was easier to do as she wished because you were not there," she said softly. "You inadvertently helped fulfil her last wish."

Garrett was not convinced. "Tell me how it was done," he urged.

"Underwood presented the lie that the illness was highly infectious and that she feared for her lady's sister. She swore she would die in her lady's service and the others were glad to stay away. She then said I had contracted the sickness. On the day Philomena died, she was dressed in my clothing and I in hers. I was the one to emerge in tears to tell the household that my beloved sister had died in the tending of me." She shook her head. "I did not imagine anyone would believe us, but they did. It was almost too simple."

They rode on as she looked out the window, blinking back her tears. Garrett held fast to her hand, hating that she had been alone, save for a lady's maid, in such a moment of loss.

"The difficulty was that I could not feign to be as merry and frivolous as Philomena. It was Underwood who concocted the tale that I was so bereft by the loss of my twin that I had resolved to follow my sister's example thereafter."

"The tale was believed by many," Garrett said.

"Was it? I wondered several times whether your father guessed the truth, but he never spoke of it. There was a look in his eyes at times, but it never lasted and perhaps I imagined it."

"He said my mother knew immediately."

She nodded, then turned to look at him, her gaze clear. "But she never spoke of it."

"She liked you better, by all accounts."

Penelope shook her head. "There should have been no comparison. I apologize to you for the deception and can only offer the excuse that once it had begun, it could not be readily undone."

"I can imagine as much."

She took a deep breath. "Philomena was not perfect by any reckoning, but she was my sister and I loved her dearly. She could light a room with her smile and fill hearts with joy with her presence. I miss her every day. Perhaps I loved her more because she was not perfect. Truly, if only perfect people were worthy of our love, then there would be far less affection in the world."

"Perhaps then there is hope for me in your affections," Garrett dared to say and Penelope raised her gaze to his, a glint of hope in her eyes. "I am far from perfect, my lady, and I have erred in failing to trust my instincts about you. I have deceived you just as much as you have misled me, perhaps more for I placed you in peril."

She reached up and touched the skin around his eye, which was still sufficiently tender that he flinched.

"That is of no import," he chided. "I cannot tell you how relieved I am to have such honesty between us, for I love you with all my heart."

She smiled. "You are as far from a rakehell as any man could be."

"Accept me and society will believe I have reformed for you." He leaned closer. "I would do anything to become worthy of your esteem, my lady. If you have any mercy in your heart, grant me a chance to win your heart anew."

Penelope smiled at him so sweetly that he could not summon a breath. "You have my heart, sir. Indeed, I believe you have possessed it since that evening at Vauxhall Gardens."

Jubilant, Garrett claimed both her hands and dropped to one knee on the floor of the carriage. "Wed me, Penelope," he entreated even as he strove to keep his balance.

"I will, sir, happily."

"Sir?" he echoed, teasing her, and was delighted when she laughed aloud.

"Garrett," she said, her eyes shining. "My own Garrett." And she bent down to kiss him, a most appropriate salute under the circumstances.

She would be his wife, and there would never again be secrets between them.

~

GARRETT'S FATHER welcomed the news that Penelope had accepted his son. More than that, the duke used his connections to ensure that Sara Underwood's testimony reached the right hands with speed so that a special license could be issued for their marriage. He also insisted that

Penelope should be his guest at Montford House until the wedding, arguing that Clapham was too far away from the church. Garrett knew he did not imagine Penelope's relief.

He went to his father's house for dinner each night, savoring the opportunity to be in her company. He took her shopping in the afternoons and to the lending library, and looked forward to meeting her for luncheon each day once they were wed.

Penelope's family, of course, could have challenged the match, so the marquis made another visit to Mr. Neilson in Clapham. A fairly blunt discussion resulted in an agreement and the continuance of the visits for luncheon every fortnight. Garrett was confident that the matter was resolved.

Penelope recounted the entire tale to Caroline and Christopher, and the two women's friendship deepened most admirably. It was Caroline's suggestion that the wedding should be on Penelope's birthday, the following Saturday.

Penelope was delighted by the possibility of the boys being in attendance, as was the duke. Garrett undertook the task of collecting the boys from school, wanting the opportunity to answer all of their questions before they reached the house. It made for a long day in the carriage, but he would have done even more to ensure Penelope's happiness.

The master seized the chance to explain to Garrett how well his sons were doing, and to compliment their abilities. James, it seemed, was particularly skilled with languages and a fencing foil, while Matthew loved mathematics and rode like the wind. It took some time to hear all their accolades, and he found them waiting for him in the foyer when he finally left the master's office.

"You never brought us home for *Maman's* birthday

before," James said when they were underway and Garrett recognized an opportunity for the truth to be shared.

"There is going to be another event that I thought you would like to attend," he said, watching them both. They sat opposite him, their expressions curious, and he decided upon simplicity. "There will also be a wedding."

"Who is getting married?" Matthew demanded but James began to smile.

"You owe me five shillings," he said to his younger brother.

"I do not! Papa! Who is getting married?"

"I am," Garrett confessed and James gave a hoot.

"I knew it!" he said, then nudged his brother. "I *told* you."

"*Maman* is not her sister," Matthew said crossly. "She is not Aunt Penelope. I told you before that you were wrong…"

Garrett could only stare at the pair of them.

"Then who is Papa going to wed?" James challenged and Matthew fell silent.

"He is right," Garrett acknowledged. Matthew looked so shaken that Garrett removed the five shillings from his own purse and gave them to James. "When did you know?"

"From the first," he confessed readily. "She released Mr. Kemp from his duties which *Maman* would never have done."

Garrett had no notion of the tutor being held in esteem by Philomena. "Why not?"

Matthew made a face. "He composed poems for her."

"Odes to her beauty." James placed a hand over his heart. "*Across the stricken hearth I flee, hoping only for a glimpse of thee.*" His expression turned pitying. "What is a stricken hearth?"

Garrett knew he should appear stern. "But *Maman* appreciated his prose?"

"She liked him following her about, to be sure." James raised a finger. "But then, she was ill and he wrote an entire poem to her. The first day, she came to look upon our lessons, he presented the ode to her. The look upon her face!" He chortled despite himself. "She was shocked, then she began to read it and became angry. She told him such a tribute was utterly inappropriate and that she could not tolerate such a breach of decorum in a tutor employed to teach two boys such as ourselves."

Matthew turned to his brother. "You are right. She never called us her sons."

James nodded wisely. "She told him that he should be ashamed of himself and she dismissed him. He was stunned, then tried to argue with her to keep his post."

"I will wager that did not proceed well," Garrett guessed, marveling that he had heard little of this tale.

"She summoned Maines to cast out Mr. Kemp's belongings," James said, referring to the butler at the country house.

"We never liked him," Matthew supplied.

"But *Maman* would not heed us when we complained. She was always choosing new slippers or going to tea somewhere."

"And this is how you guessed the truth," Garrett said.

"She let us come to London after that," James said with satisfaction.

"Maman always said we had to stay in the country, with Mr. Kemp," Matthew added, wrinkling his nose.

James nodded. "And she played chess with us."

"She never lets us win," Matthew complained. "I do miss that."

"And then she went to Grandfather, who arranged for us to go to school. He said it was past time and that he was glad she had changed her mind about our education. There was a look about him, though, as if he thought something else had changed."

"I never noticed that," Matthew said.

"Because you do not pay attention," James chided. "Grandmother could not disguise her satisfaction, which was another hint. They two had always been at odds, then suddenly, they were amiable in each other's company."

"That is true," Matthew acknowledged, then flicked a glance at Garrett. "When did you know, Papa?"

"Only when I returned earlier this month to Arlingview House."

"That is not very observant of you," James noted.

"It is not. I vow to be more vigilant in future." He chose to reveal it all. "The truth is that I was misled much sooner. I admired your aunt Penelope, but believed her to be your mother."

"You proposed to the wrong sister!" Matthew exclaimed.

"Perhaps and perhaps not. I might not have had the two of you if I had chosen rightly in the first place."

The boys exchanged a glance of satisfaction.

"But why did Aunt Penelope pretend to be *Maman* at all?" Matthew demanded.

Garrett shrugged. "Your mother was very concerned about your futures if you had no mother. It seems she feared I might wed again and you might be neglected."

"You would not so as much," James insisted loyally and Matthew nodded vigorous agreement.

"But your mother and I had argued mightily after

your birth and we were estranged. I doubt her opinion of me was as fine as yours is on this day. And so, she begged her sister to take her place to see you both protected." He paused, then knew he had to confess it all. "I blame myself, in truth. I did not return home when I received word that she was ill. That could only have made her dread what else I might do. If I had not been so proud and had come to her deathbed, I believe she would have shared her fears. I hope I might have reassured her."

"You might have wed Aunt Penelope years ago," James guessed.

"I might have done so." Garrett found himself smiling. "There is much to admire in that lady."

"I like her," James said with an approving nod. "I am glad that you will wed her, Papa."

"I, as well," Matthew said. "And I like that we are returning home for a birthday and a wedding."

"Not just that," Garrett said with a smile. "We have a Grand Tour to plan together. I thought we might depart in May for a summer abroad." The boys shouted with delight and the carriage rocked slightly with their enthusiasm, then they both began to simultaneously present their suggestions of itinerary.

THE WEDDING COULD NOT HAVE BEEN MORE perfect, in Penelope's view. She was surprised to receive a gift when she was dressing for the wedding, and opened the box to find that the emeralds of the parure had been reset. Now they nestled with diamonds and pearls in a necklace that was entirely her own. She wore a new dress of creamy silk and rode to the church with the duke, whose moustaches seemed particularly snowy and fine that day.

Her heart skipped when she saw Garrett awaiting her at the front of the church. He smiled at her when she reached his side, his eyes fairly glowing, and she was so happy that tears pricked behind her eyes. The boys stood proudly behind them, along with Christopher, Caroline, and Garrett's younger brother Anthony. Caroline wore her pearls with pride. Penelope's mother attended, of course, as well as Arabella, Mr. Neilson and their four children. Garrett had cancelled their luncheon on the day before since Penelope was not in residence at Arlingview House, and she was uncertain when those meals might commence again, if ever they did. Several of the servants from Arlingview House had also come to witness the service, including Wrigley, Williams and Sara Underwood, who sniffled happily throughout it all. She had already returned to Arlingview House and was much happier there.

It was only when their vows had been made that Garrett glanced over his shoulder toward the back of the church.

"Do you seek someone who is missing?" Penelope asked, turning to follow his gaze, and he smiled.

"I fear only the arrival of your Lochivar, come to sweep you away from me."

Penelope laughed, her response prompting his own smile. "You are my Lochivar, sir, and you must know it well."

"Indeed," Garrett murmured, pressing a kiss to the back of her hand, his gaze clinging to hers. "But a gentleman should never take a lady's favor for granted."

And Penelope knew neither of them would ever do as much.

~

IT WAS the third Wednesday in February when Esmeralda rose and dressed. She was relieved to see that the swelling in her cheeks was completely gone and she would be able to resume her activities. Per routine, the newspapers awaited her in the morning room and Latimer arrived immediately with hot tea. There were warm rolls on this morning from the bakery at the corner and strawberry jam. She opened the first paper and felt her eyes widen at an item lower on the page.

Dover—M. Jacques Desjardins was apprehended last week at the docks, awaiting the changing tide and the departure of his passage. M. Desjardins, well known in Paris for his thievery, was found to be in possession of a valuable pearl necklace believed to have been stolen from Lady Caroline Wright earlier this month. Upon closer scrutiny, however, the necklace proved to be a replica and not the genuine gems. M. Desjardins was released from the custody of the crown but banished from these shores. He was escorted to another ship and granted passage back to France, with the injunction that he not return to England for a year. Lady Caroline Wright's gems, in the meantime, were mysteriously returned to her by persons unknown before M. Desjardins reached Dover and are safely in her custody once again.

Esmeralda put down the newspaper with a trembling hand. Jacques was gone, which was a relief, but at best, he was banished for a year. She could not discount the possibility of him managing to return without detection and dared not lower her guard.

He would return to her, of that Esmeralda had no doubt.

She pushed to her feet and paced the width of her parlor, as restless as a caged animal. She had an almost undeniable urge to go to France herself, to find Sylvie and ensure her welfare, but she knew Jacques would anticipate that impulse. He would await her there.

If only the pearls had been her own. She would have let him flee with the genuine article, taking the risk that he might evade detection, the better to ensure that he was apprehended with the gems in his possession. But it had not been her right to take that risk. In the end, Lady Caroline had her gems back and all was well.

Save for herself and Sylvie.

What would Jacques do to her? It was too easy to guess. He would do to Sylvie precisely what he had done to her. Sylvie was old enough now.

And there was nothing she could do to defend the younger woman, not from such a distance.

Esmeralda folded her arms around herself, suddenly chilled. She added to her cup, her hand shaking so badly that she nearly spilled the tea, then wrapped her hands around the warm porcelain.

Sylvie. She would do anything for Sylvie. She had already done all that was possible for Sylvie and it had not been sufficient.

Despite her efforts, Jacques would win.

But Esmeralda would not weep. No. She would find a way to defeat him, if it was the last deed she did.

It was a glorious September day when the Marquis of Arlingview, his wife and two sons were met at Dover by the family carriage. Watkins grinned as he held the horses and two of the footmen from the house loaded the trunks and baggage onto a cart. Penelope was a little unsteady, having endured a miserable crossing, and held Garrett's arm as he greeted his staff. The boys were tanned and a little taller than they had been, both filled with enthusiasm after their adventures.

It had been a marvelous trip.

"We should make another visit next year," Matthew said and James heartily agreed.

Penelope only smiled, reminding Garrett of the Mona Lisa.

Garrett sent the boys to supervise the collection of their luggage and caught his wife close.

"I would wager you have another secret," he said to her and she laughed.

"Only because you have not guessed it as yet."

"You are not so interested in another such voyage?"

"Oh, I am, but next summer will be too soon," Penelope said as he handed her into the carriage.

"You cannot fear the expense."

"It is not the expense that concerns me," she said mildly, exhaling mightily once she was in her place. "It is good to be home," she said, her words so heartfelt that Garrett could only agree.

She seemed content to simply sit and not illuminate him further on her comment.

"Why will next summer be too soon?" he asked finally.

"I will be busy next spring, if all proceeds well."

He remained mystified.

"Do you think a daughter conceived in Rome would be different in nature to one conceived in Venice?" Penelope asked as she watched him. Garrett straightened in surprise. "It seems to be that the first would be practical and pragmatic, while the second must become an artist."

"Rome or Venice," he repeated, then counted the months on his fingers. "Late March or early April?"

Penelope smiled.

"And a daughter? How can you know?"

"I am quite certain of it," she said with conviction. "Philomena told me so."

Garrett regarded her warily.

"I dreamed of her!"

"Have you dreamed of her before?"

"Not often. But I dreamed of her in Paris. She always wanted to go there." He watched Penelope catch her breath. "She gave us her blessing and bade me be happy." She gripped his hand. "She told me to make you happy as best I could, but not, under any circumstances, to name our daughter after her. I fear dire repercussions if I ignore this edict."

Garrett almost smiled. "Did she offer an alternative suggestion?"

Penelope shook her head. "What was your mother's name?"

"Margaret Georgiana, but she was called Marjory."

"Georgiana," Penelope repeated softly. "I like that."

"As do I, but the choice, my lady, is yours." Garrett kissed her hand and then her cheek as she smiled at him. The boys returned. "Are you sufficiently well for the ride?" he asked.

"I want only to be home again," Penelope said with vigor and Garrett could only agree.

Home, with his beloved bride, his sons, and a daughter in the spring. Garrett held his bride close as his sons climbed back into the carriage and knew few men were as fortunate as he.

Could a man marry his dead wife's sister in the Regency? Technically, he could, although the marriage could be challenged as being within the prohibited degrees i.e. because the couple were too closely related, according to ecclesiastical law. If the marriage was challenged by an interested party, it could be voided or annulled, so long as either husband or wife were still living. This could cast the inheritance of any children into question.

All the same, men did marry the sisters of their dead wives without those matches being challenged. Examples include Richard Lovell Edgeworth, Matthew Boulton and Rear Admiral Charles Austen. Charles was Jane Austen's brother: he married Frances Palmer in 1807 and Frances' sister Harriet in 1820 after Frances had died.

Given the nature of Penelope's blood family, I think it unlikely that they would challenge Penelope's marriage to Garrett, as that would end their relationship with both the marquis and the duke, and any benefits resulting from that association. Theoretically, Christopher or Anthony could challenge the match in the hope of securing more favor for their own children, but Garrett has an heir and a spare by his first marriage whose claims are beyond dispute. I think we can be confident in Penelope and Garrett's HEA.

The 1835 Marriage Act made all such existing marriages legal and any subsequent marriages of this type void. It ultimately became legal for a man to marry his dead wife's sister in 1907, and for a woman to marry her dead husband's brother in 1921.

My thanks to author Rachel Knowles for her research and blog post on this very subject.

THE WIDOW'S WAGER

THE LADIES' ESSENTIAL GUIDE TO THE
ART OF SEDUCTION #3

She wed once for duty but will only wed again for love...

For as long as she can remember, Eliza North's heart has been in the possession of her older brother's friend, Nicholas Emerson. But Nicholas has always been oblivious to Eliza, and when he bought a commission and sailed to war, she wed sensibly instead. Returned to her brother's house a widow, she meets Lieutenant Emerson again and realizes neither of their feelings have changed. She accepts his request to chaperone his younger sister, Helena, hoping she might win his attention yet, with the assistance of the mysterious Mrs. Oliver and her guide for seduction.

Nicholas Emerson could never aspire to wed the daughter of a duke, especially one so pragmatic as Eliza has always been. That she married for the whimsy love makes him wonder how well he knew Eliza after all. She is still the only woman who captures his attention, but he knows his injuries mean he can never marry. Still, he cannot resist the chance to request Eliza's assistance with Helena's second season, and the chance to share her company.

Neither of them anticipate Helena's wild behavior or their necessary alliance to defend her reputation.

Entrusted with the manuscript of Mrs. Oliver's advice on the seductive arts, Eliza puts its counsel to use, much to Nicholas' delighted astonishment. How can he refuse the woman he loves, even knowing that he can never ensure her happiness? Caught between honor and love, Nicholas must accept his legacy from the war for this pair to have a future—is Eliza the woman who can heal his wounds forever?

The Widow's Wager
The Ladies' Essential Guide to the Art of Seduction #3
Coming March 2023!

ABOUT THE AUTHOR

Deborah Cooke sold her first book in 1992, a medieval romance called **Romance of the Rose** published under her pseudonym Claire Delacroix. Since then, she has published over ninety novels in a wide variety of sub-genres, including historical romance, contemporary romance, paranormal romance, fantasy romance, time-travel romance, women's fiction, paranormal young adult and fantasy with romantic elements. She has published under the names Claire Delacroix, Claire Cross and Deborah Cooke. **The Beauty**, part of her successful Bride Quest series of historical romances, was her first title to land on the *New York Times* List of Bestselling Books. Her books routinely appear on other bestseller lists and have won numerous awards. In 2009, she was the writer-in-residence at the Toronto Public Library, the first time the library has hosted a residency focused on the romance genre. Currently, she writes paranormal romances and contemporary romances under the name Deborah Cooke and historical romances as Claire Delacroix. Deborah lives in Canada with her husband and family, as well as far too many unfinished knitting projects.

Visit Deborah's websites to learn more about her books:
http://DeborahCooke.com
http://Delacroix.net

To learn more about Deborah's contemporary and paranormal romances, please visit

http://DeborahCooke.com

www.ingramcontent.com/pod-product-compliance
Lightning Source LLC
Chambersburg PA
CBHW030922210726

48290CB00007B/2035